# NOWHERE MAN

"Who gave you the right to torture me like this?" Nickie shouted.

"You did."

"So I committed what you call a crime. But I was never put on trial, never convicted!"

"You're not entitled to a trial."

"Anybody's entitled to a trial, damn you!"

"That is absolutely true. But you see you are *not* anybody. You are *nobody*. And you chose to be so of your own free will. Legally—officially—you simply don't exist!"

". . . BRUNNER WRITES ABOUT THE FUTURE AS IF HE AND THE READER WERE ALREADY LIVING IN IT!"
—*THE NEW YORK TIMES BOOK REVIEW*

# 1968: STAND ON ZANZIBAR
# 1972: THE SHEEP LOOK UP

—AND—

# 1975: THE SHOCKWAVE RIDER
### John Brunner's New Novel
### Now Hailed by Reviewers

"In a world where data is king, can men survive as more than bits of information? Brunner evokes an all-too-plausible future and the personal crises and growth of an individual who attempts to deal with these problems. In moving convincingly along both levels, Brunner has once again asserted his claim to a place at the top of serious speculative writing."      —*Library Journal*

"The future simply isn't coming in 2000 anymore. It's coming on Monday—maybe every Monday. As the first book to deal thoughtfully with the problem of future shock, Brunner's story deserves serious attention."
—Lester del Rey
*Analog*

"The best novel Brunner has written since *Stand on Zanzibar* . . . one of the best books of the year . . . very highly recommended."      —*Locus*

". . . this intelligent tale is irresistible."      —*Booklist*

# THE
# SHOCKWAVE
# RIDER

## JOHN
## BRUNNER

BALLANTINE BOOKS • NEW YORK

Library of Congress Catalog Card Number: 74-23861

ISBN 0-345-24853-8-150

This edition published by arrangement with
Harper & Row, Publishers, Inc.

Cover art by Murray Tinkelman

Manufactured in the United States of America

First Ballantine Books Edition: March, 1976

# CONTENTS

# ACKNOWLEDGMENT

People like me who are concerned to portray in fictional terms aspects of that foreign country, the future, whither we are all willy-nilly being deported, do not make our guesses in a vacuum. We are frequently —and in this case I am specifically—indebted to those who are analyzing the limitless possibilities of tomorrow with some more practical aim in view . . . as for instance the slim yet admirable hope that our children may inherit a world more influenced by imagination and foresight than our own.

The "scenario" (to employ a fashionable cliché) of *The Shockwave Rider* derives in large part from Alvin Toffler's stimulating study *Future Shock,* and in consequence I'm much obliged to him.

J.K.H.B.

# BOOK 1

## THE BASIC STRAINING MANUAL

# A THOUGHT FOR TODAY

Take 'em an inch and they'll give you a hell.

## DATA-RETRIVIAL MODE

The man in the bare steel chair was as naked as the room's white walls. They had shaved his head and body completely; only his eyelashes remained. Tiny adhesive pads held sensors in position at a dozen places on his scalp, on his temples close to the corners of his eyes, at each side of his mouth, on his throat, over his heart and over his solar plexus and at every major ganglion down to his ankles.

From each sensor a lead, fine as gossamer, ran to the sole object—apart from the steel chair and two other chairs, both softly padded—that might be said to furnish the room. That was a data-analysis console about two meters broad by a meter and a half high, with display screens and signal lights on its slanted top, convenient to one of the padded chairs.

Additionally, on adjustable rods cantilevered out from the back of the steel chair, there were microphones and a three-vee camera.

The shaven man was not alone. Also present were three other people: a young woman in a slick white coverall engaged in checking the location of the sensors; a gaunt black man wearing a fashionable dark red jerkin suit clipped to the breast of which was a card bearing his picture and the name Paul T. Freeman; and a heavy-set white man of about fifty, dressed in dark blue, whose similar card named him as Ralph C. Hartz.

After long contemplation of the scene, Hartz spoke.

"So that's the dodger who went further and faster for longer than any of the others."

"Haflinger's career," Freeman said mildly, "*is* somewhat impressive. You've picked up on his record?"

"Naturally. That's why I'm here. It may be an atavistic impulse, but I did feel inclined to see with my own eyes the man who posted such an amazing score of new personae. One might almost better ask what he hasn't done than what he has. Utopia designer, lifestyle counselor, Delphi gambler, computer-sabotage consultant, systems rationalizer, and God knows what else besides."

"Priest, too," Freeman said. "We're progressing into that area today. But what's remarkable is not the number of separate occupations he's pursued. It's the contrast between successive versions of himself."

"Surely you'd expect him to muddle his trail as radically as possible?"

"You miss the point. The fact that he eluded us for so long implies that he's learned to live with and to some extent control his overload reflexes, using the sort of regular commercial tranquilizer you or I would take to cushion the shock of moving to a new house, and in no great quantity, either."

"Hmm . . ." Hartz pondered. "You're right; that is amazing. Are you ready to start today's run? I don't have too much time to spend here at Tarnover, you know."

Not looking up, the girl in white plastic said, "Yes, sir, he's status go."

She headed for the door. Taking a seat at Freeman's gestured invitation, Hartz said doubtfully, "Don't you have to give him a shot or something? He looks pretty thoroughly sedated."

Settling comfortably in his own chair adjacent to the data console, Freeman said, "No, it's not a question of drugs. It's done with induced current in the motor centers. One of our specialties, you know. All I have to do is move this switch and he'll recover consciousness—though not, of course, the power of am-

4

bulation. Just enough to let him answer in adequate detail. By the way, before I turn him on, I should fill in what's happening. Yesterday I broke off when I tapped into what seemed to be an exceptionally heavily loaded image, so I'm going to regress him to the appropriate date and key in the same again, and we'll see what develops."

"What kind of image?"

"A girl of about ten running like hell through the dark."

## FOR PURPOSES OF IDENTIFICATION

At present I am being Arthur Edward Lazarus, profession minister, age forty-six, celibate: founder and proprietor of the Church of Infinite Insight, a converted (and what better way for a church to start than with a successful conversion?) drive-in movie theater near Toledo, Ohio, which stood derelict for years not so much because people gave up going to the movies —they still make them, there's always an audience for wide-screen porn of the type that gets pirate three-vee satellites sanded out of orbit in next to no time— as because it's on land disputed between the Billy-kings, a Protestant tribe, and the Grailers, Catholic. No one cares to have his property tribaled. However, normally they respect churches, and the territory of the nearest Moslem tribe, the Jihad Babies, lies ten miles to the west.

My code, of course, begins with 4GH, and has done so for the past six years.

*Memo to selves:* find out whether there's been any change in the status of a 4GH, and particularly whether something better has been introduced . . . a complication devoutly to be fished.

## MAHER-SHALAL-HASH-BAZ

She ran, blinded by sorrow, under a sky that boasted a thousand extra stars moving more swiftly than a minute hand. The air of the June night rasped her throat with dust, every muscle ached in her legs, her belly, even her arms, but she kept right on as hard as she could pelt. It was so hot, the tears that leaked from her eyes dried as they were shed.

Sometimes she went on more or less level roadway, not repaired for years but still quite sound; sometimes she crossed rough ground, the sites perhaps of factories whose owners had transferred their operations up to orbit, or of homes which had been tribaled in some long-ago riot.

In the blackness ahead loomed lights and illuminated signs bordering a highway. Three of the signs advertised a church and offered free Delphi counseling to registered members of its congregation.

Wildly glancing around, blinking her eyes to clear perception, she saw a monstrous multi-colored dome, as though a lampshade made from a puffer-fish were to be blown up larger than a whale.

Pacing her at a discreet distance, tracking a tracer concealed in the paper frock which was all she wore except sandals, a man in an electric car fought his yawns and hoped that on this particular Sunday the pursuit would not be too long or too dull.

## MINOR PROFIT IN THE BELLY OF THE GREAT FISH

As well as presiding at the church, Reverend Lazarus lived in it, his home being a trailer parked behind the cosmoramic altar—formerly the projection screen, twenty meters high. How else could a man with a minister's vocation afford so much privacy and so much space?

Surrounded by the nonstop hum of the compressor that kept his polychrome plastic dome inflated—three hundred meters by two hundred by ninety high—he sat alone at his desk in the nose compartment of the trailer, his tiny office, comping the take from the day's collections. He was worried. His deal with the coley group who provided music at his services was on a percentage basis, but he had to guarantee a thousand, and attendance was falling off as the church's novelty declined. Today only about seven hundred people had come here; there had not even been a jam as they drove back on to the highway.

Moreover, for the first time in the nine months since the church was launched, today's collections had yielded more scrip than cash. Cash didn't circulate much any more—at least not on this continent—except in the paid-avoidance areas, where people drew a federal grant for going without some of the twenty-first century's more expensive gadgetry, but activating a line to the federal credit computers on a Sunday, their regular down-time day, meant a heavy surcharge, beyond the means of most churches including his. So churchgoers generally remembered to bring coins or bills or one of the little booklets of scrip vouchers issued to them when they joined.

The trouble with all this scrip, though—as he knew from sad experience—was that when he presented it to his bank tomorrow at least half of it would be returned marked VOID: the bigger the sum pledged, the more likely. Some would have been handed in by people already so deep in pointless debt the computers had banned expenditure on nonessentials; any new church inevitably attracted a lot of shock victims. But some would have been canceled overnight as the result of a family row: "You credded *how* much? My God, what did I do to deserve a twitch like you? Get that scrip deeveed *this minute!*"

Still, some people had been ignorantly generous. There was a stack of over fifty copper dollars, worth three hundred to any electronics firm, asteroid ores being poor in high-conduction metals. It was illegal to sell currency for scrap, but everybody did it, saying they'd found old saucepans in the attic of a secondhand house, or a disused cable while digging over the back yard.

Riding high on the public Delphi boards right now

was a prediction that the next dollar issue would be plastic with a one- or two-year life. Well, *plus ça* small change *plus c'est* biodegradable. . . .

He tipped the coins into his smelter without counting them because only the weight of the eventual ingot mattered, and turned to the other task he was obliged to complete before he quit work for the day: analysis of the Delphi forms the congregation had filled out. There were many fewer than there had been back in April; then, he'd expected fourteen or fifteen hundred, whereas this week's input was barely half that. Even seven hundred and some opinions, though, was a far wider spread than most individuals could hope to invoke, particularly while in the grip of acute depression or some other life-style crisis.

By definition, his congregation *all* had life-style crises.

The forms bore a series of bald statements each summarizing a personal problem, followed by blank spaces where any paid-up member of the church was invited to offer a solution. Today there were nine items, a sad contrast with those palmy days in the spring when he'd had to continue on the second side of the form. Now the word must be out on the mouth-to-mouth circuit: "Last time they only gave us nine things to delph, so next Sunday we're going to . . ."

*What's the opposite of a snowball? A thawball?*

Despite the failure of his old high hopes, though, he determined to go through the proper motions. He owed it to himself, to those who regularly attended his services, and above all to those whose heart-cries of agony had been eavesdropped on today.

Item A on the list he disregarded. He had invented it as a juicy lure. There was nothing like a scandal of the kind that might eventually make the media to grab people's attention. The bait was the vague hope that one day soon they might notice a news report and be able to tell each other, "Say, that bit where the poker got shot for messing with his daughter—remember we comped that one at church?"

A link with yesterday, tenuous, but to be prized.

Wryly he re-read what he had dreamed up: *I am a girl, fourteen. All the time my father is drunk and wants to plug into me but he creds so much for liquor I don't get none to pay my piece when I go out and they repossessed my . . .*

The responses were drearily predictable. The girl should apply to the courts and have herself declared of age, she should tell her mother at once, she should denounce her father anonymously, she should get a doc-block put on his credit, bale out of home and go live in a teener dorm—and so forth.

"Lord!" he said to the air. "If I programmed a computer to feed my confessional booth, people would get better advice than that!"

Nothing about this project was working out in the least as he had hoped.

Moreover, the next item enshrined a genuine tragedy. But how could one help a woman still young, in her thirties, a trained electronics engineer, who went to orbit on a six-month contract and discovered too late that she was subject to osteochalcolysis—loss of calcium and other minerals from her skeleton in zero-gee conditions—and had to abort the job and now was in danger of breaking bones if she so much as tripped? Without chance of appeal her guild had awarded her contract-breaker status. She couldn't sue for reinstatement unless she worked to pay the lawyer, she couldn't work unless the guild allowed it, she . . . Round and round and round.

*There's a lot of brave new misery in our brave new world!*

Sighing, he shook the forms together and piled them under the scanner lens of his desk computer for consolidation and a verdict. For so few it wasn't worth renting time on the public net. To the purr of the air compressor was added the hush-hush of the paper-sorter's plastic fingers.

The computer was secondhand and nearly obsolete, but it still worked most of the time. So, provided it didn't have a b-d overnight, when the shy kids and the worried parents and the healthy but inexplicably unhappy middlers and the lost despairing old 'uns came back for their ration of spiritual reassurance, each would depart clutching a paper straw, a certificate redolent of old-fashioned absolute authority: its heading printed in imitation gold leaf declaring that it was an authentic and legal Delphi assessment based on contributions from not fewer than _____* hundred consultees (*_Insert number; document invalid if total fails to exceed 99_) and delivered under oath/deposition in presence of adult witnesses/notary's seal ** (**_Delete as applicable_) on _____ (month) _____ (day) 20_____ (year).

A shoddy little makeshift, memorial to the collapse of his plans about converting the congregation into his own tame CIMA pool and giving himself the place to stand from which he could move the Earth. He knew now he had picked the wrong pitch, but there was still a faint ache when he thought back to his arrival in Ohio.

At least, though, what he had done might have saved a few people from drugs, or suicide, or murder. If it achieved nothing else, a Delphi certificate did convey the subconscious impression: _I matter after all, because it says right here that hundreds of people have worried about my troubles!_

And he had made a couple of coups on the public boards by taking the unintentional advice of the collective.

The day's work was over. But, moving into the trailer's living zone, he found he did not feel at all sleepy. He considered calling up somebody to play a game at fencing, then remembered that the last of the regular local opponents he'd contacted on arrival had just moved out, and at 2300 it was too late to try and trace another player by calling the Ohio State Fencing Committee.

So the fencing screen stayed rolled in its tube along with the light-pencil and the scorer. He resigned himself to an hour of straight three-vee.

In an excess of impulsive generosity, one of the

The Basic Straining Manual

first people to join his church had given him an abominably expensive present, a monitor that could be programed with his tastes and would automatically select a channel with a suitable broadcast on it. He slumped into a chair and switched on. Promptly it lit the screen, and he found himself invited to advise the opposition party in Jamaica what to do about the widespread starvation on the island so as to depose the government at the next election. Currently the weight of opinion was clustering behind the suggestion that they buy a freight dirigible and airlift packages of synthetic food to the worst-hit areas. So far nobody seemed to have pointed out that the cost of a suitable airship would run into seven figures and Jamaica was as usual bankrupt.

*Not tonight! I can't face any more stupidity!*

But when he rejected that, the screen went dark. Could there really be nothing else on all the multifarious channels of the three-vee which held any interest for the Reverend Lazarus? He cut out the monitor and tried manual switching.

First he found a coley group, all blue-skin makeup and feathers in their hair, not playing instruments but moving among invisible columns of weak microwaves and provoking disturbances which a computer translated into sound . . . hopefully, music. They were stiff and awkward and their coordination was lousy. His own amateur group, composed of kids fresh out of high school, was better at keeping the key and homing on the tonic chord.

Changing, he found a scandal bulletin, voicing unprovable and slanderous—but by virtue of computerized editing not actionable—rumors designed to reassure people by convincing them the world really was as bad as they suspected. In El Paso, Texas, the name of the mayor had been mentioned following the arrest of a man running an illegal Delphi pool taking bets on the number of deaths, broken limbs and lost eyes during hockey and football games; it wasn't the pool *per se* that was illegal, but the fact that it had been returning less than the statutory fifty percent of

11

money staked to the winning bettors. Well, doubtless the mayor's name had indeed been mentioned, several times. And over in Britain, the secretary of the Racial Purification Board had invited Princess Shirley and Prince Jim to become joint patrons of it, because it was known they held strong views on immigration to that unhappy island. Given the rate at which poverty was depopulating all but the areas closest to the Continent, one could scarcely foresee Australians or New Zealanders being impressed. And was it true that last week's long-range rocket attack on tourist hotels in the Seychelles had been financed by a rival hotel chain, not by irredentist members of the Seychellois Liberation Party?

The hell with that.

But what he got next was circus—as everybody called it, despite the official title 'experiential reward and punishment complex." He must have hit on a field-leader—perhaps the most famous of all, which operated out of Quemadura CA taking advantage of some unrepealed local statute or other—because it was using live animals. Half a dozen scared, wide-eyed kids were lining up to walk a plank no more than five centimeters wide spanning a pool where restless alligators gaped and writhed. Their eager parents were cheering them on. A bold red sign in the corner of the screen said that each step each of them managed to take before slipping would be worth $1000. He switched once more, this time with a shudder.

The adjacent channel should have been spare. It wasn't. A Chinese pirate satellite had taken it over to try and reach midwestern American émigrés. There was a Chinese tribe near Cleveland, so he'd heard, or maybe it was Dayton. Not speaking the language, he moved on, and there were commercials. One was for a life-styling consultancy that he knew maintained private wards for those clients whose condition was worsened instead of improved by the expensive suggestions they'd been given; another was for a euphoric claimed not to be addictive but which was—the company marketing it was being sued by the FDA, only according to the mouth-to-mouth circuit they'd reached the judge, he was good and clutched, and they'd have cleared their profit and would be willing to withdraw the product voluntarily before the case actually came to trial, leaving another few hundred thousand addicts to be cared for by the underfunded, overworked Federal Health Service.

Then there was another pirate broadcast, Australian by the accents, and a girl in a costume of six strategic bubbles was saying, "Y'know, if all the people with life-style crises were laid end to end . . . Well, I mean, who'd be left to actually *lay* them?"

That prompted him to a faint grin, and since it was rare to pick up an Australian show he had half-decided to stick with this for a while when a loud buzzer shrilled at him.

Someone was in the confessional booth at the main gate. And presumably at this time of night therefore desperate.

Well, being disturbed at all hours was one of the penalties he'd recognized as inescapable when he created the church. He rose, sighing, and shut off his screen.

*Memo to selves:* going into three-vee for a while might be a good idea. Get back in touch with the media. Or has priesthood used up the limited amount of public exposure the possessor of a 4GH can permit himself in a given span of time? If not, how much left?

Must find out. *Must.*

Composing his features into a benign expression, he activated the three-vee link to the confessional. He was apprehensive. It was no news to the few who kept in circuit that the Billykings and the Grailers had counted seven dead in last week's match, and the latter had come out ahead. As one might expect; they were the more brutal. Where the Billykings were normally content to disable their captives and leave them to struggle home as best they might, the Grailers' habit was to rope and gag them and hide them in some convenient ruin to die of thirst.

13

So the caller tonight might not be in need of counsel or even medication. It might be someone sussing out the church with a view to razing it. After all, in the eyes of both tribes it was a pagan shame.

But the screen showed him a girl probably too young to be inducted in either tribe: at a glance, no older than ten, her hair tousled, her eyes red-rimmed with weeping, her cheeks stained with dust down which tears had runneled. A child who had over-reached her ability to imitate an adult, presumably, lost and frightened in the dark— Oh! No! Something more, and worse. For he could see she was holding a knife, and on both its blade and her green frock there were smears so red they could well be fresh blood.

"Yes, little sister?" he said in a neutral tone.

"Father, I got to make confession or I'll be damned!" she sobbed. "I shivved my mom—cut her all to bits! I guess I must have killed her! I'm *sure* I did!"

Time seemed to stop for a long moment. Then, with what calm he could summon, he uttered what had to be said for the benefit of the record . . . because, while the booth itself was sacrosanct, this veephone circuit like all such was tied into the city police-net, and thence to the tireless federal monitors at Canaveral. Or wherever. There were so many of them now, they couldn't all be in the same place.

*Memo to selves:* would be worth knowing where the rest are.

His voice as gritty as a gravel road, he said, "My child"—aware as ever of the irony in the phrase—"you're welcome to unburden your conscience by confiding in me. But I must explain that the secrecy of the confessional doesn't apply when you're talking to a microphone."

She gazed at his image with such intensity he fancied for a moment he could see himself from her point of view: a lean dark man with a broken nose, wearing a black jerkin and a white collar ornamented with little gilt crosses. Eventually she shook her head, as though her mind were too full of recent horror to leave room for any new shocks.

Gently he explained again, and this time she connected.

"You mean," she forced out, "you'll call the croakers?"

"Of course not. But they must be looking for you now in any case. And since you've admitted what you did over my mikes . . . Do you understand?"

Her face crumpled. She let fall her knife with a tinkling sound that the pickups caught, faint as fairy bells. A few seconds, and she was crying anew.

"Wait there," he said. "I'll be with you in a moment."

## RECESS

A sharp wind tasting of winter blew over the hills surrounding Tarnover and broke red and gold leaves off the trees, but the sky was clear and the sun was bright. Waiting his turn in line at the best of the establishment's twenty restaurants, redolent of old-fashioned luxury up to and including portions of ready-heated food on open display, Hartz gazed admiringly at the view.

"Beautiful," he said at length. "Just beautiful."

"Hm?" Freeman had been pressing his skin on both temples toward the back of his head, as though attempting to squeeze out overpowering weariness. Now he glanced at the window and agreed, "Oh—yes, I guess it is. I don't get too much time to notice it these days."

"You seem tired," Hartz said sympathetically. "And I'm not surprised. You have a tough job on your hands."

"And a slow one. Nine hours per day, in segments of three hours each. It gets wearing."

"But it has to be done."

"Yes, it has to be done."

15

## HOW TO GROW DELPHINIUMS

It works, approximately, like this.

First you corner a large—if possible, a very large —number of people who, while they've never formally studied the subject you're going to ask them about and hence are unlikely to recall the correct answer, are nonetheless plugged into the culture to which the question relates.

Then you ask them, as it might be, to estimate how many people died in the great influenza epidemic which followed World War I, or how many loaves were condemned by EEC food inspectors as unfit for human consumption during June 1970.

Curiously, when you consolidate their replies they tend to cluster around the actual figure as recorded in almanacs, yearbooks and statistical returns.

It's rather as though this paradox has proved true: that while nobody knows what's going on around here, everybody knows what's going on around here.

Well, if it works for the past, why can't it work for the future? Three hundred million people with access to the integrated North American data-net is a nice big number of potential consultees.

Unfortunately most of them are running scared from the awful specter of tomorrow. How best to corner people who just do not want to know?

Greed works for some, and for others hope. And most of the remainder will never have any impact on the world to speak of.

Good enough, as they say, for folk music . . .

## A MOMENT FOR MILLSTONES

On the point of undogging his trailer's sealed door and disconnecting the alarms, he hesitated.

Sunday. A moderately good collection, if not a

record-breaker. (He sniffed. Hot air. From the smelter.)

And she *might* be a precociously good actress . . .

He pictured a tribe raiding, looting, vanishing before the croakers swooped, leaving behind no one but a minor immune from police interrogation, hysterical with laughter at the success of her "practical joke."

Therefore, prior to shutting down the alarms, he activated all the church's electronics except the coley music system and the automated collection trolleys. When he rounded the base of the altar—ex-screen— it was as though fire raged in the whale's-belly of the dome. Lights flashed all colors of the rainbow and a few to spare, while a three-vee remote over his head not only repeated his image monstrous on the face of the altar but also stored it, minutely detailed, in a recorder buried beneath a yard of concrete. If he were attacked, the recording would be evidence.

Moreover, he carried a gun . . . but he was never without it.

These precautions, slender though they were, constituted the maximum a priest was expected to take. More could easily worry the federal computers into assessing him as a potential paranoid. They'd been sensitive on such matters ever since, last summer, a rabbi in Seattle who had mined the approaches to his shul forgot to turn off the firing-circuit before a bar mitzvah.

Generally the Fedcomps approved of people with strong religious convictions. They were less likely than some to kick up a fuss. But there were limits, not to mention mavericks.

A few years ago his defenses would have been adequate. Now their flimsiness made him tremble as he walked down the wall-less aisle defined by the black rubber streaks car tires had left over decades. Sure, the fence at the base of the dome was electrified except where access had to be left for the confessional, and the booth itself was explosive-resistant and had its own air supply against a gas attack, but even so . . . !

*Memo to selves:* next time, a role where I can take

more care of life and limb. Privacy is fine, and I needed it when I arrived here. But this place was never meant to be operated by a single individual. I can't scan every shifting shadow, make sure no nimble shivver is using it for cover!

Thinking of which as I stare around: my vision is unaided. At forty-six??? Out of three hundred million there are bound to be some people that age who have never bought corrective lenses, most because they can't afford them. But suppose the Bureau of Health or some pharmo-medical combine decided there were few enough middlers without glasses to organize an exhaustive study of them? Suppose the people at Tarnover decided there must be a genetic effect involved? *Ow.*

*Memo to selves, in red italics:* stay closer to chronological age!

At that point in his musing he entered the confessional—and found that through its shatterproof three-centimeter window he was *not* looking at a little girl in a dress spattered with blood.

Instead, the exterior section of the booth was occupied by a burly blond man with a streak of blue in his tightly curled hair, wearing a fashionable rose-and-carmine shirt and an apologetic smile.

"So sorry you've been disturbed, Father," he said. "Though it's a stroke of luck that little Gaila found her way here. . . My name's Shad Fluckner, by the way."

This poker looked too young to be the girl's father: no more than twenty-five, twenty-six. On the other hand, his congregation included women married for the third or fourth time and now to men as much as twenty years younger. Stepfather?

In that case, why the smile? Because he'd used this kid he didn't give a plastic penny for to rid himself of a rich but dragsome older wife? Fouler things had been admitted in this booth.

Foggily he said, "Are you kin to—ah—Gaila, then?"

"Not in law, but you could say that after what we've been through together I'm closer to her than her legal kinfolk. I work for Anti-Trauma Inc., you see. Very sensibly, the moment Gaila's parents detected signs of deviant behavior in her, they signed her up for a full course of treatment. Last year we cured her sibling rivalry—classic penis-envy directed against her younger brother—and right now she's working into her Electra complex. With luck we'll progress her to Poppaea level this coming fall. . . . Oh, incidentally: she babbled something about you calling in the croakers. You don't need to worry. She's on file with the police computers as a non-act case."

"She told me"—slowly and with effort—"she'd stabbed her mother. Killed her."

"Oh, far as she's concerned, sure she did! Just like she's unconsciously wanted to ever since her mother betrayed her by letting her be born. But it was all a setup, naturally. We dosed her with scotophobin and shut her in a dark room, to negate the womb-retreat impulse, gave her a phallic weapon to degrade residual sexual envy, and turned an anonymous companion loose in there with her. When she struck out, we turned up the lights to show her mother's body lying all bloody on the floor, and then we gave her the chance to run like hell. With me trailing her, of course. Wouldn't have wanted her to come to any harm."

His slightly bored tone indicated that for him this was just another routine chore. But when he had concluded his exposition, he brightened as though a sudden idea had occurred to him. He produced a recorder from his pocket.

"Say, Father! My publicity department would welcome any favorable comment about our methods you may care to make. Coming from a man of the cloth, it would carry extra weight. Suppose you said something to the effect that enabling kids to act out their most violent impulses in a controlled situation is preferable to letting them commit such crimes in real life, thereby endangering their immortal—"

"Yes, I do have a comment you can record! If

there is anything more disgusting than war, it's what your company is doing. At least in warfare there is passion. What you do is calculated, and more likely by machines than men!"

Fluckner withdrew his head a fraction, as though afraid he might be punched through the intervening glass. He said defensively, "But what we've done is to enlist science in the service of morality. Surely you see—"

"What I see is the first person I ever felt justified in cursing. You have offended against our little ones, therefore a millstone shall be tied around your neck and you shall be cast into the depths of the sea. Depart from me into eternal darkness!"

Fluckner's face grew mottled-red on the instant, and harsh anger invaded his voice.

"You'll regret saying that, I promise you! You've insulted not just me but thousands of good citizens who rely on my company to save their children from hellfire. You'll pay for that!"

He spun on his heel and marched away.


## LIGHT AND POWER CORRUPT

"Yes, of course Gaila's doing fine! What happier discovery could a kid make—what more welcome re-inforcement can you offer her—than to find the mother she consciously loves, yet unconsciously hates, has been killed and in spite of that is still alive? We've been over that before!"

He had to wipe his forehead, hoping his mask of perspiration would be ascribed to the summer heat.

"And now may I use your phone? Alone, if you don't mind. It's best for the parents not to know too many details of our methods."

In a bright room with an underfloor pool reflecting sparkling random lights across an ecumenical array of a crucifix, a Buddha and a six-handed Kali draped with roses, Shad Fluckner composed the code of Continental Power and Light's anonymous-denunciation department.

When he heard the proper tone, he followed it with the code for the Church of Infinite Insight, then a group equating to "fraudulent misapplication of charitable donations," then another for "assets sequestered pending legal judgment," which would automatically deevee the minister's credit rating, and lastly one for "notify all credit-appraisal computers."

That should do the trick. He dusted his hands in satisfaction and left the room. There was effectively no chance of the call being traced to him. It had been two years since he worked for Power and Light, and their personnel was turning over at sixty-five percent annually, so any of half a million people might have fed in the false data.

By the time Reverend Lazarus fought his way through the maze of interlinked credit-appraisal computers and nailed the tapeworm that had just been hatched, he could well be ragged and starving.

Serve him right.


## ON LINE BUT NOT REAL TIME

During a lull in the proceedings, while a nurse was spraying the subject's throat to restore his voice, Hartz glanced at his watch.

"Even if this is a slow job," he muttered, "you can't run at this rate very often, obviously—less than a day per day."

Freeman gave his habitual skull-like smile. "If so, I'd still be questioning him about his experience as a life-style counselor. But remember: once we knew where to look, we were able to put all data concerning his earlier personae into store. We know what he *did*; now we need to find out how he *felt*. In some cases the connection between a key memory and his unusually strong reaction is fairly plain, and you've been lucky today in that we've hit on such a link."

"His identifying with the girl who was running in panic? A parallel with his own hunted life?"

"More than that. Much more, I'm afraid. Consider the curse he pronounced on this man Fluckner, and the trigger that provoked it. That was consistent with the attitudes of Reverend Lazarus, certainly. What we have to find out is how deeply it reflected his real self. Nurse, if you've finished, I'd like to carry on."

## MOVING DAY, OVERCAST AND HOT

Must MUST learn to control my temper even in face of an insult to humanity like—

*What the hell?*

He emerged with a gasp from coma-like sleep. Last night he had lain awake for hours with Fluckner's threat reverberating in memory, and ultimately resorted to a pill. It took a long time for an all-important fact to penetrate his muzzy mind.

The hum of the air compressor had stopped.

Rolling over, he checked the self-powered illuminated clock at the head of his bed. It showed 7:45 A.M. But the windows of his trailer were solidly dark, although by now the sun must be high in the sky, the forecast had been for more fine weather, and when it was stretched taut the plastic membrane of his roof was quite translucent.

Therefore the power had been cut off and the dome had collapsed. All twenty-two and a half tons of it.

Naked, feeling terribly vulnerable, he swung his feet out of bed and fumbled for the switch of the nearest lamp to confirm his deduction. The darkness was oppressive; worse, the air had grown foul already—no doubt from the deposit of dirt, grease and fetid moisture which while the dome was distended had formed an unnoticeable film but now had been condensed into a layer like the muck lining a sewer pipe.

The light duly failed to shine.

A strike? Hardly likely; those key workers who still had the leverage to close down the nation's auto-

mated power system always waited for frost and snow
before striking. An overload blackout? Scarcely more
probable. There hadn't been a summer overload since
1990. People had seemingly been cured of regarding
power as free like air.

Admittedly, a whole new generation had grown up
since 1990 . . . including himself.

A reactor meltdown?

After last year's triple-header of disasters, the Delphi boards currently showed much money riding on a
lapse of two full years before the next such. Nonetheless he grabbed his one and only battery radio. By
law an all-news monophonic station was still required
to broadcast in each conurbation of a million or more
people, so that the public could be warned of riots,
tribal matches and disasters. The cells were low on
power, but by placing the set close to his ear he
determined that the duty newscaster was talking about
record bets on today's football fatalities. If there had
been a meltdown, radiation warnings would have been
pouring out nonstop.

*So what in the world . . . ? Oh. Fluckner?*

He felt a shiver crawl down his spine, and realized
that he was gazing hungrily at the little blurred glow
from his clock, as though this darkness were symbolic
of the womb (echoes of Gaila and those like her,
condemned to grow up not as human beings but as
mules, offspring of a bastard mating between Freudian
psychoanalysis and behaviorism), and that mysterious
glimmer presaged his emergence into a strange new
world.

Which, as he admitted to himself with a pang of
disappointment, it obviously did.

At least, even though the air stank, it wasn't over-
full of $CO_2$; he had no headache, just a hint of
nausea. Somewhat reassured, he felt his way into the
living zone, where against emergencies he kept a big
battery lamp. Its cells were still powerful, being automatically recharged from the main supply. But when
he clicked it on its yellowish gleam made everything
around him menacing and unfamiliar. As he moved

it, shadows scuttered on the polished metal walls, mimics of those that last night he had imagined offering cover to teeners bent on the work of Baron Samedi, Saint Nicholas or even Kali.

He splashed his face with what should have been ice water from the middle faucet over his washbasin. It didn't help. The power had been off so long, the tank was tepid. Unrefreshed, he opened the trailer door and looked out. Under the graceful curve formed by the plastic as it slumped over the altar a distant glimmer of light suggested he might be able to escape unaided.

But it would be preferable to get his power back.

In his office the smelter was cold and the copper ingot lay ready for removal. The desk computer, with a more demanding task, had been caught before finishing it. The fourth—no, the fifth—of today's Delphi assessments protruded from it like a pale stiff tongue, duly stamped with his automatic notary's seal. That, however, was not important right now. What he had to discover was whether Fluckner (who else could or would have discredited him overnight?) had contrived to isolate his phone as well as his power supply.

The answer was yes. A sweet recorded voice told him his phone credit was in abeyance pending judgment in the lawsuit that was apt to end with all his assets being garnisheed. If he wanted service to be renewed he must furnish proof that the verdict had gone in his favor.

*Lawsuit? What lawsuit? Surely you can't take someone to court in this state for wishing a curse on you?*

Then the answer dawned on him, and he almost laughed. Fluckner had resorted to one of the oldest tricks in the store and turned loose in the continental net a self-perpetuating tapeworm, probably headed by a denunciation group "borrowed" from a major corporation, which would shunt itself from one nexus to another every time his credit-code was punched into a keyboard. It could take days to kill a worm like that, and sometimes weeks.

Unless the victim possessed a means to override the original command. This one did. Any 4GH code-holder—

His embryo laughter died. What if, since he last exploited its potential, the validity of a 4GH had been downgraded or even deeveed?

There was only one way to find out. Dutiful, the machinery was waiting for him to furnish the asked-for evidence. He punched his full code into the phone, added the standard group for "input error due to malicious malpractice," and tailed it with an order to give the reference number of the lawsuit he had allegedly been cited in.

The normal dial tone sounded within seconds.

He had been holding his breath, unaware, and let it go with a gasp that sounded terribly loud in the unfamiliar silence. (How many separate soft hums had ended? Computer, water cooler, water heater, air conditioner, alarm monitor . . . et cetera. It was not customary to recall offhand how many powered devices one owned; therefore he didn't.)

Promptly he sent a retaliatory worm chasing Fluckner's. That should take care of the immediate problem in three to thirty minutes, depending on whether or not he beat the inevitable Monday morning circuit overload. He was fairly sure he wouldn't. According to recent report, there were so many worms and counterworms loose in the data-net now, the machines had been instructed to give them low priority unless they related to a medical emergency.

Well, he'd know as soon as the lights came on.

Now it was time for Reverend Lazarus to commit suicide. Fortified by a glass of lukewarm mock orange juice, sickly-sweet but not actively harmful to his metabolism—he was careful about the brands he patronized—he pondered the details of his next incarnation.

Thirty minutes and the power returned. Sixty, and the dome was inflated. Ninety, and he started on his rebirth.

It was always a bad experience, this computerized parturition. Today, because he had not intended to give up the Lazarus role yet and in consequence had not properly prepared his mind, it was the worst ever. His skin crawled, his heart hammered, sweat made his palms slippery, and his buttocks—bare, since he had not wasted time on getting dressed—itched all over the area in contact with his chair.

Even having found out that his code remained valid, he had to break off twice while priming the Fed-comps with his new lies. His fingers were trembling so badly, he was afraid of mis-hitting the phone buttons, and regular phones like this weren't equipped with a "display-last-five" facility.

But eventually he punched the final group to activate the phage that would eliminate all trace of Lazarus, the super-tapeworm compared to which Fluckner's was negligible, and he was able to stretch and scratch and do all the other things he had to forgo in order not to interrupt the invention of his new self.

No one below congressional level was entitled to call for a printout of the data stored behind a 4GH. It must have been devised for people with official permission to live other lives than their own. More than once he had been tempted to try to discover just what sort of person his code in theory made him —an FBI operative on undercover assignment, a counter-espionage agent, a White House special representative mopping up the mess his boss had left. . . . But he had never actually been so foolish. He was like a rat, skulking in the walls of modern society. The moment he showed his nose, the exterminators would be sent for.

He dressed in the wrong clothes and collected what he felt he need not leave behind, a single bagful of oddments like transferable Delphi tickets and his new copper ingot. He also pocketed two inhalers of tranquilizer, which he knew he would require before the day was out.

Finally he set a bomb under his desk and wired it to the phone so that he could trigger it whenever he chose.

The destruction of the church might figure in the media's daily crime list—murders so many, robberies so many, rapes so many—but quite often they didn't get down as far as arson because there wasn't time. That, so long as nobody filed a claim for insurance money, would be that. With ready-made suspects at hand in the shape of the Grailers and the Billykings, the harried local police would be content to treat the case as open and shut.

He gave one final glance around as he prepared to quit the plastic dome for the last time. Traffic hummed on the highway, but there was nobody in sight who might have paid special attention to him. In some ways, he reflected, this was a much less complex century to live in than the twentieth must have been.

If only it were as simple as it looked.


## THE NUMBER YOU HAVE REACHED

Back when it was still TV and not three-vee, a famous, crusty, cynical historian named Angus Porter, who had survived long enough to become a Grand Old Man and whose lifelong leftist views were in consequence now tolerated as forgivable eccentricity, had put the matter in a nutshell.

Or, as some would-be wit promptly said, in a nut case.

Invited to comment on the world nuclear disarmament treaty of 1989, he said, "This is the third stage of human social evolution. First we had the legs race. Then we had the arms race. Now we're going to have the brain race.

"And, if we're lucky, the final stage will be the human race."

## THE PERSONIFICATION OF A TALENT

"So that's how he managed it!" Hartz said, marveling. He stared at the shaven body in the steel chair as though he had never seen this man before. "I'd never have believed it possible to punch a whole new identity into the net from a domestic phone—certainly not without the help of a computer larger than he owned."

"It's a talent," Freeman said, surveying the screens and lights on his console. "Compare it to the ability of a pianist, if you like. Back before tape, there were soloists who could carry twenty concerti in their heads, note-perfect, *and* could improvise for an hour on a four-note theme. That's disappeared, much as poets no longer recite by the thousand lines the way they apparently could in Homer's day. But it's not especially remarkable."

Hartz said after a moment, "Know something? I've seen a good few disturbing things, here at Tarnover, and been told about a great many more. But I don't think anything has . . ." He had to force himself to utter the next words, but with a valiant effort he made the confession. "So frightened me as hearing you say that."

"I'm not sure I follow you."

"Why, calling this amazing talent 'not especially remarkable'!"

"But it isn't." Freeman leaned back in his padded chair. "Not by our standards, at any rate."

"That's just it," Hartz muttered. "*Your* standards. Sometimes they don't seem altogether . . ."

"Human?"

Hartz nodded.

"Oh, but I assure you they are. We're a very gifted species. Most of what we're doing here is concerned with the recovery of talents we've neglected. We've been content to remain shockingly ignorant about some of our most precious mental resources.

Until we've plugged those gaps in our knowledge, we can't plan our path toward the future." He glanced at his watch. "I think we've had enough for today. I'll call the nurse and have him taken away for feeding and cleansing."

"That worries me, too. Hearing you speak about him in—in such depersonalized terms. While I admire your thoroughness, your dedication, I have reservations about your methods."

Freeman rose, stretching slightly as he did so to relieve his cramped limbs.

"We use those methods which we've found to work, Mr. Hartz. Moreover, please recall we're dealing with a criminal, a deserter who, if he'd had the chance, would willingly have evolved into a traitor. There are other people engaged in projects similar to ours, and some of them are not just single-minded but downright brutal. I'm sure you wouldn't wish people of that stamp to outstrip us."

"Of course not," Hartz said uncomfortably, running his finger around his collar as though it had suddenly grown too tight.

Freeman smiled. The effect was that of a black turnip-ghost.

"Shall I have the pleasure of your company tomorrow?"

"No, I have to get back to Washington. But—uh . . ."

"Yes?"

"What did he do after leaving Toledo in such a hurry?"

"Oh, he took a vacation. Very sensible. In fact, the best thing he could possibly have done."


FOR PURPOSES OF RE-IDENTIFICATION

At present I am being Sandy (short, as I admit to people when I get stonkered and confidential, not for good old Alexander but for *Lysander*, of all things!) P. (worse yet, for *Pericles*!!!) Locke, aged thirty-two,

29

swingle and in view of my beardless condition probably skew. However, I'm trying to give that up and might even consider getting married one of these years.

I shall remain Sandy Locke for a while at least, even after I finish my vacation at this resort hotel in the Georgia Sea Islands, medium-fashionable, not so boringly up-to-the-second as some even if it does boast an underwater wing for womb-retreat therapy and the manager is a graduate psychologist. At least there's no obligatory experiential R&P.

It's my second vacation this year and I shall take at least one further in late fall. But I'm among people who aren't likely to mistake "taking another vacation" for "surpled and unemployable," as some would that I can think of. Many of my fellow guests are taking their third this year already and plan to make the total five. These latter, though, are considerably older, shut of the care and cost of kids. To be a triple-vacationer at thirty-two marks me as a comer . . . in all three senses. Right now the third kind matters; I need a job.

I've picked a good age, not so difficult as forty-six to put on when you're chronologically twenty-eight (the sudden recollection of spectacles! Ow!) and youthful enough to attract the middlers while being mature enough to impress the teeners. *Memo to selves*: could thirty-two be stretched until I'm actually, say, thirty-six? Keep eyes and ears ajar for data.

## WINED AND DENIED

Past forty but not saying by how much, beautiful and apt to stay so for a long while yet, currently looking her best by reason of a bright brown tan, hair bleached by sun instead of shampoo, and an hour more sleep per night than she'd enjoyed for ages, Ina Grierson was also tough. Proof lay in the fact that she was heading the transient-executive recruitment dept at the Kansas City HQ of Ground-to-Space Industries Inc., world's largest builders of orbital factories.

The question was, though: tough *enough?*

She thought of the old saying about being promoted to your level of incompetence—what was it called, the Peter-Pays-Paul Principle, or something like that?—and fumed and fretted. Her daughter kept declining to quit school, just signed up year after year for weirder and wilder courses of study (and all at the same university, for heaven's sake! Wouldn't be so bad if she'd consent to go someplace else). Ina felt tied, wanted to break away, move to the Gulf or Colorado or even the Bay Area, given that the slippage techniques were as efficient as the seismologists claimed and there wasn't going to be another million-victim quake, not ever . . . or at least for fifty years.

On her own terms, of course—no one else's.

Last year she'd rejected five offers. This year, so far only one. Next year?

Having a daughter out of step like Kate—hell! Why couldn't the stupid slittie act normal like everybody else, dig up her roots and plug them in some other socket, preferably on a different continent?

*If Anti-Trauma Inc. had started up soon enough . . . !*

Tactless people sometimes wondered publicly why Ina insisted on remaining in the same city as her daughter who was, after all, twenty-two and had had her own apt since entering college and was not noticeably clinging or dependent. But Ina hated to be asked about that.

She never like being asked questions she couldn't answer.

One week into her two-week vacation Ina wanted to be cheered up but the man she'd kept company with since arrival had left today. That meant dining alone. Worse and worse. Eventually, with much effort she put on her favorite red-and-gold evening gear and went to the open-air dining terrace where soft music mingled with the hush of waves. She felt a little better after two drinks. To put the regular sparkle back in her world, what about champagne?

And a minute later she was shouting at the waiter (this being an expensive and exclusive establishment instead of the cast-from-a-mold type where you dealt always with machines that kept going wrong . . . not that human beings were immune from *that*): "What the hell do you mean, there isn't any?"

Her shrill voice caused heads to turn.

"That gentleman over there"—pointing—"just ordered the last bottle we have in stock."

"Call the manager!"

Who came, and explained with regret that was probably unfeigned (who likes to find his pride and joy deeveed by a mere bunch of circuitry?) why there was nothing he could do. The computer in charge of resources utilization at the HQ of the chain controlling this and a hundred other hotels had decided to allot what champagne was available to resorts where it could be sold at twice the price the traffic in the Sea Islands could bear. The decision was today's. Tomorrow the wine list would have been reprinted.

Meanwhile the waiter had faded in response to a signal from another table, and when he returned Ina was struggling not to scream with fury.

He laid a slip of paper in front of her. It bore a message in firm clear handwriting, unusual now that most literate kids were taught to type at seven. She read it at a glance:

*The lucky shivver with the champagne has an idea. Share the bottle? —Sandy Locke*

She raised her eyes and found grinning at her a man in a fashionable pirate shirt open to the waist, a gaudy headband, gilt wristers, one long lean finger poised at arm's length on the cork.

She felt her anger fade like mist at sunrise.

He was a strange one, this Sandy. He dismissed her complaint about how ridiculous it was never to have any more champagne at this hotel and steered the conversation into other channels. That made her

32

ill-tempered all over again, and she went to bed alone.

But when the breakfast-trolley rolled automatically to her bedside at 0900, there was a bottle of champagne on it tied with a ribbon and accompanied by a posy. When she met Sandy by the pool at eleven, he asked whether she had enjoyed it.

"So it was you who fixed it! Do you work for this hotel chain?"

"This slumpy linkage? I'm insulted. Third-rank operations aren't my framework. Shall we swim?"

The next question died on her lips. She had been going to ask what pull he had, whether it was government or a hypercorp. But another explanation fitted, and if that were the right one, the implications were so enticing she dared not broach the matter without a buildup. She said, "Sure, let's." And peeled off her clothes.

The wine list was not reprinted after all, and the manager wore a very puzzled expression. That convinced Ina her guess might be correct. Next morning while they were breakfasting in bed she put it squarely to Sandy.

"Poker, I think you must be a CSC."

"Only if this bed isn't bugged."

"Is it?"

"No. I made sure. There are some things I simply don't care to let computers know."

"How right you are." She shivered. "Some of my colleagues at G2S, you know, live at Trianon, where they test new life-styles. And they boast about how their actions are monitored night and day, compare the advantages of various ultramodern bugs . . . I don't know how they can stand it."

"Stand?" he echoed sardonically. "Not a matter of standing, except social standing, I guess. More, it kind of props them up. A few years and they'll forget they have feet of their own."

All day Ina was near to shaking with excitement. To think that by pure chance she had bumped into a genuine three-vee tactile-true member of that prestigious elite, the tiny secretive tribe of computer-sabotage consultants . . . ! It was a perfectly legal discipline, provided its practitioners didn't tamper with data reserved to a government dept under the McBann-Krutch "greatest-good-of-the-greatest-number" act, but its experts didn't advertise themselves any more than industrial spies, and it would have been politer to ask whether he was into DDR, "difficult data retrieval." Luckily he'd taken no offense.

Delicately she hinted at what was worrying her. How much longer was she still going to be able to move upward, not crosswise, when she changed jobs? At first his response was casual: "Oh, turn freelance, why not, the way I did? It's not so much different from the regular plug-in life-style. When you get adjusted to it."

Echoes underlying "freelance" resounded in her head: the lone knight riding out to champion his lady fair and Christian justice, the King's Messenger, the secret agent, the merchant venturer . . .

"I've thought about it, naturally. But I'd dearly like to know what G2S has added to my file before I decide."

"You could try asking me to find out."

"You mean"—hardly daring to hope—"you're for rent?"

"Right now?" He put the nip into nipple with sharp well-cared-for teeth. "No, my jiggle-oh rating is strictly O. This kind of thing I do for free."

"You know what I mean!"

He laughed. "Don't slidewise out of control. Of course I know. And it might be kind of fun to poke G2S."

"Are you serious?"

"I could be, when my vacation's over. Which it isn't."

Musingly, at two in the morning—her sleeping time was being eroded, but what the hell?—she said, "It isn't knowing that the machines know things about you which you wouldn't tell your straightener, let alone your spouse or chief. It's not knowing what the things *are* which they know."

"Sweedack. The number of people I've seen destabled by just that form of uncertainty, clear into paranoia!"

"Sweedack?"

"Ah, you don't follow hockey."

"Now and then, but I'm not what you'd call a 'fish for it."

"Nor me, but you have to stay in circuit. It's French. Came south with Canadian hockey players. Short for *je suis d'accord*. Thought everybody had picked up on it."

Before she could guard her tongue she had said, "Oh, yes! I've heard Kate say it to her friends."

"Who?"

"Uh . . . My daughter." And she trembled, imagining the inevitable sequence:

*I didn't know you had a daughter. She in high school?*

*No—uh—at UMKC.*

Followed by the brief silence full of subtraction which would all too closely betray her location on the age scale.

But this man, ultimately tactful, merely laughed. "Quit worrying. I know all about you. Think I'd have generated so much champagne on spec?"

That figured. In seconds she was laughing too. When she recovered, she said, "Would you really come to KC?"

"If you can afford me."

"G2S can afford anybody. What do you usually click on as?"

"A systems rationalizer."

She brightened. "Fantastic! We lost our head-of-dept in that area. He broke his contract and— Say, you didn't know that too, did you?" Suddenly suspicious.

He shook his head, stifling a yawn. "Never had any reason to probe G2S until I met you."

"No. No, of course not. What attracted you to
your line of work, Sandy?"

"I guess my daddy was a phone freak and I inherited the gene."

"I want a proper answer."

"I don't know. Unless maybe it's a sneaking feeling
that people are wrong when they say human beings
can't keep track of the world any more, we have to
leave it up to the machines. I don't want to be hung
out to dry on a dead branch of the evolutionary tree."

"Nor do I. Right, I'll get you to KC, Sandy. I
think your attitude is healthy. And we could do with a
blast of fresh air."


## SOLD TO THE MAN AT THE TOP

"I am not bleating you. This shivver is escape-
velocity type. And we've been short one systems rash
since Kurt bailed out and not wishing to cast nasturti-
ums at George she hasn't made my job any less of a
bed of nails—let alone yours, hm?

"Sure, he asked for a trial period himself. Eight
weeks, maybe twelve, see how he meshes with the
rest of us.

"Right now he's on vacation. I told you: I met
him in the Sea Islands. You can reach him there.

"Great. Here, take down his code. 4GH . . ."


## UNSETTLEMENT PROGRAM

The palisade of thousand-meter towers around Mid-
Continental Airport had two gaps in it, memorializing
not—for once—buildings that had been riot-blown
or tribaled but the crash sites of two veetol airliners,
one taking off and one landing, which had slidewised
simultaneously off their repulsors last week. Rumor
had it the reason might be found in the launch of
Ground-to-Space's latest orbital factory from their
field westward in the cross-river state of Kansas; al-

legedly someone had omitted to notify the airlines of the volume and extent of the blast wave. But an inquiry was still in progress, and anyhow G2S was far too much of a Power in the Land hereabouts for any negligence charge to emerge from the hearings.

Nonetheless the outcome was a popular subject for bets on illegal short-term Delphi pools. Legal pools, naturally, were forbidden to pre-guess a court's verdict.

The façades of the remaining towers, whether homes or offices, were as blank as ancient gravestones and as gloomy. They had mostly been erected during the shitabrick phase architecture had suffered through in the early nineties. There was a more flattering term for the style—antideco—but it was too lame to have caught on. Such structures were as dehumanized as the coffins employed to bury the victims of the Great Bay Quake, and stemmed from the same cause. The damage sustained when San Francisco, plus most of Berkeley and Oakland, collapsed overnight had come close to bankrupting the country, so that everything but *everything* had to be designed with the fewest possible frills.

In a desperate attempt to make a virtue of necessity, all such buildings had been made "ecofast"—in other words, they were heavily insulated, they incorporated elaborate garbage-reclamation systems, every apartment was supplied with a flat area outside that caught at least some sunlight, allegedly large enough to be hydroponically planted with sufficient vegetables and fruit to meet the requirements of an average family. The consequence had been to fix in the public mind the impression that any genuinely efficient building must be stark, ugly, undesirable and dull.

It seemed that necessity was too hateful for anybody to enjoy being virtuous.

Thanks to some smart route adjustment by his airline's computers, his plane was a few minutes early. Ina had agreed to meet him on the main concourse, but when he emerged, tingling slightly, from the static-discharge chamber by the plane gate, she wasn't in sight.

It would be out of character for him to waste spare minutes. Rubbing his arms, reflecting that even if electric lift for aircraft was efficient, economical and non-polluting it was damnably hard on the passengers when they had to shed their accumulated volts, he caught sight of a sign pointing the way to the public Delphi boards.

Most of his belongings, bought to fit his new identity, were on their way direct to G2S's recruit-settlement block. But he did have a travel bag weighing nine kaygees. From under the nose of a sour woman who favored him with a string of curses he nabbed an autoporter and—after consulting the illuminated fee table on its flank—credded the minimum: $35 for an hour's service. Rates were higher here than at Toledo, but that was to be expected; the cost of living at Trianon, a hundred kilometers away, was the second highest in the world.

From now until his credit expired the machine would carry his bag in its soft plastic jaws and follow him as faithfully as a well-trained hound, which indeed it resembled, down to the whimper it was programed to utter at the 55-minute mark, and the howl at 58.

At 60 it would drop the bag and slink away.

With it at his heels he stood surveying the high-slung display, tracking the shifting figures with the ease of much practice. He looked first at his favorite sector, social legislation, and was pleased to see he had two won bets due to be collected shortly. Despite all the pressure that had been applied, the president would not after all be able to make jail sentences mandatory for slandering his personal aides—it would cost him his majority if he tried. And Russian math-teaching methods were definitely going to be introduced here, given that money was still piling in when the odds had shortened to five-to-four. Well, if the U.S.

team were ever to make a decent showing in the Mathematical Olympiads, there was no alternative.

Odds, though, were poor on that sector of the board, except ten-to-one against the adoption of the proposed new amendment to the Constitution which would redefine electoral zones in terms of professions and age groups rather than geographical location. It might make sense, but people were scarcely ready for it yet. Next generation, maybe.

He turned his attention to social analysis, which was offering many double and a few treble figures. He put a thousand on the chance that the mugging-per-adult rate in New York City would break ten percent this year; it had been hovering around eight for an improbably long time and people were losing their enthusiasm, but there was a new police chief in the Bronx with a get-tough reputation and that ought to sew the matter up.

And the technical breakthrough odds were also nice and fat. For old time's sake he put another thousand on the introduction of an Earth-Moon gravislide before 2025. That was a perennial disappointment. The idea was to haul cargo off the Moon on a cable stretching past the neutral point and spill it direct into Earth's gravity-well so it could coast to a landing free of charge. It had failed twice already. But someone in New Zealand was on the track of mile-long single-crystal filaments. Given those . . .

A couple of hungry-faced old men, one black and the other white, who clearly were not here to travel but merely to pass the time, noticed him placing the wager. They studied his expensive clothes, assessed his air of financial well-being, and after some argument agreed to risk fifty apiece.

"It beats horse racing," he heard one of them say.

"I used to like the horses!" the other objected, and they moved on, their voices querulous as though both craved the tension discharge of a quarrel but dared not start one for fear of losing an only friend.

*Hmm! I wonder whether the Delphi systems in Russia, or East Germany, are patterned on stock*

*markets and totalizators the way ours obviously are.
One knows that in China they—*

But at that moment he caught sight of odds being
quoted which he simply didn't believe. One gets three
in favor of genetic optimization becoming a commercial service by 2020, instead of a privilege reserved
to government officials, hypercorp execs and billion-
aires? Last time he saw a board it had been up around
200, regardless of the fact that the public was clearly
hungry for it. Such a violent crash in the odds must
surely be due to inside information. One of the thou-
sand-and-some staff and "students" at Tarnover must
have yielded to the temptation to go sell his headful
of data, and company scientists somewhere must be
busily trying to turn a vague hope into a self-fulfilling
prophecy.

Unless . . .

*Oh, no! It can't be that they know somebody did
get away? After all this time, after these six mortal,
hateful years, has the precious secret of my escape
leaked out?*

There couldn't possibly be a connection! Even
so—!

The world swam around him for the space of half
a dozen thumping heartbeats. Some one jostled him
roughly; he was barely able to perceive that it was an
economist, wearing a sewn-on badge in bright green
and white saying UNDERPOWER!—one of the people
who on principle declined to use up their full power
allotment and did their utmost to prevent others from
using theirs. There were alleged to be a great many
economists at KC.

Then a bright voice was saying, "Sandy, good to
see you— Is something wrong?"

Vast effort pulled him back together, smiling, calm,
in a condition to note how changed Ina was from the
image she'd presented at the resort. She wore a light
but severe coverall in plain black and white, and her
long hair was in a snood. She was very much the
head-of-dept doing a special favor to this recruit who

40

was slotting into a higher-than-average level of the hierarchy.

Therefore he didn't kiss her, didn't even take her hand, simply said, "Hello. No, nothing's wrong. Except I just saw what the odds are on my favorite long shot. One of these mornings I'll wake to find my credit well and truly docked."

As he spoke, he started toward the exit. Ina, and the autoporter, kept pace.

"You have baggage?" she inquired.

"Just this. I sent the rest direct. I hear you have a great settlement block."

"Oh, yes. It has a fine record. Been in use for ten years and so far not one environmental psychosis. Speaking of accommodation, I should have asked if you plan to bring a house with you. Currently we have room for one on site; we don't start building our next factory until September."

"No, I've had my house four years so I decided to trade it in. Matter of fact, I might get my next built here. I'm told there are good architects around KC."

"Well, I wouldn't know. I prefer to plug into an apt, but someone at the party might advise you."

"I'll ask around. What time is it set for?"

"Eight o'clock. The welcome suite is right on the entrance floor. All your signifying colleagues will be there."

## PARADOX, NEXT STOP AFTER THE BOONDOCKS

"It's not because my mind is made up that I don't want you to confuse me with any more facts.

"It's because my mind isn't made up. I already have more facts than I can cope with.

"So SHUT UP, do you hear me? SHUT UP!"

## YOU'RE BEING FRAMED

Although this was strictly transient accommodation, it differed subtly from a hotel suite. He noted

41

with approval the touches that made it more like a
smart private apartment. Retractable textured walls
could subdivide the main room in half a dozen ways,
according to taste. The decor on his arrival was in
neutral shades: beige, pale blue and white. He made
use at once of the switch by the door to change that
to rich dark green, russet and old gold. It was done
with lights behind translucent paneling. The conveniences, such as the three-vee, the polarity-reversal
clothing cleaner and the electrotoner attached to the
bathtub, were not the basic hotel-chain type but the
more expensive home-use version. Perhaps most important of all, you could not only draw back the curtains but even open the windows. That was a facility
not found in hotels nowadays.

Out of curiosity he did open one, and found he was
looking over treetops toward the source of a roaring
noise which a moment ago had been inaudible thanks
to superefficient soundproofing.

*What in the world—?*

Followed a moment later by the wry contradiction:
*What out of this world—?*

A brilliant light, dazzling as a magnesium flare, rose
into sight above the trees and to the roar was added
the impact of blast. He just managed to discern the
needle-form of a one-man orbital ship before the glare
compelled him to shut his eyes and turn away, groping for the window-closure again.

No doubt that would be one of G2S's troubleshooters on his way to orbit. The company was proud of
its prompt and efficient after-sales service, and since
even now three out of four orbital factories were one-
off projects—new industries kept deciding to jump up
there every other week—that was an essential element
in preserving its field-leader rating.

Which was not, in fact, as stable as the G2S board
wished the public to believe. He'd investigated. Among
the tasks he expected to be assigned, even though Ina
hadn't mentioned it, was penetration of a rival corporation's research into so-called olivers, electronic alter
egos designed to save the owner the strain of worry-

ing about all his person-to-person contacts. A sort of
twenty-first-century counterpart to the ancient Roman
nomenclator, who discreetly whispered data into the
ear of the emperor and endowed him with the reputation of a phenomenal memory. G2S was badly in need
of diversification, but before picking up the option it
had on a small independent company's work in this
area, it wanted to make certain nobody else had
reached the stage of commercial launching.

It would be a good-sized feather in his cap if he
produced the answer within a few days of starting
work.

Continuing his tour of inspection he discovered,
neatly tucked away under the bed, a tension reliever
with a reversible proboscis which a woman could let
stand out and a man could simply push inward . . .
or not, according to taste. Above it was a small but
fine-detail screen, the images fed to which were
changed—said a little label—on an eight-day rota;
there were also headphones and a mask offering
twenty odors.

Replacing the instrument in its sanitizing case, he
decided he'd have to experiment with it at least once
or twice; it was appropriate to the plug-in life-style,
after all. But at most two or three times. Corpora-
tions like G2S were wary of people who relied excessively on machines in place of person-to-person contact. They would be watching.

He sighed. To think that some people were (had to
be?) content with mechanical gratification. . . . But
maybe it was best in certain special cases: for instance, for those who had to establish deep emotional
attachments or none at all, who suffered agonies when
a change of employment or a posting to another city
shattered their connections, who were safest when
keeping their chance colleagues at a distance.

Not for the first time he reflected on the good fortune—heavily disguised—which had stunted his own
capacity for intense emotional involvement to the
point where he was content with mere liking. It was

so much superior to the transitory possessiveness he had been exposed to in childhood, the strict impersonality maintained during his teener years at Tarnover.

Best not to think about Tarnover.

Showering down, he relished his new situation. Much would depend on the personalities of the people he was about to meet at the welcome party, but they were bound to be good stable plug-in types, and certainly the nature of the job was ideal for his talents. Most commercial systems were sub-logical and significantly redundant, so he'd have no trouble tidying up a few tangles, saving G2S a couple of million a year, by way of proving he really was a systems rash. They'd regard him within weeks as an invaluable recruit.

Meantime, taking advantage of the corporation's status, he could gain access to data-nets that were ordinarily secure. That was the whole point of coming to KC. He wanted—more, he needed—data that as a priest he'd never have dared to probe for. Six years was about as far ahead as he'd been able to plan when he escaped from Tarnover, so . . .

He was stepping out of the shower compartment, dried by blasts of warm air, when he heard the sound of his circulation enormous in his ears: thud, thud, thud-thud-thud-thud, faster with each passing second. Giddy, furious, he clutched at the rim of the handbasin to steady himself and caught a glimpse of Sandy Locke's face in the mirror above it—haggard, aged by decades on the instant—before he realized he wasn't going to make it to the tranquilizers he'd left in the main room. He was going to have to stay right here and fight back with yoga-style deep breathing.

His mouth was dry, his belly was drum-taut, his teeth wanted to chatter but couldn't because his jaw muscles were so tense, his vision wavered and there was a line of cramp as brutal as a knife-cut all the way up his right calf. And he was *cold*.

But luckily it wasn't a bad attack. In less than ten

minutes he was able to reach his inhalers, and he was only three minutes late joining the party.

## BETWEEN 500 AND 2000 TIMES A DAY

Somewhere out there, a house or an apartment or a hotel or motel room: beautiful, comfortable, a living hell.

Stonkered or clutched or quite simply going insane, someone reaches for the phone and punches the most famous number on the continent: the ten nines that key you into Hearing Aid.

And talks to a blank though lighted screen. It's a service. Imposing no penances, it's kinder than the confessional. Demanding no fees, it's affordable where psychotherapy is not. Offering no advice, it's better than arguing with that son (or daughter) of a bitch who thinks he/she knows all the answers and goes on and on and *on* until you want to SCREAM.

In a way it's like using the I Ching. It's a means of concentrating attention on reality. Above all, it provides an outlet for all the frustration you've struggled to digest for fear that, learning of it, your friends would brand you *failure*.

It must help some of the unhappy ones. The suicide rate is holding steady.

## FLESHBACK SEQUENCE

Today, said the impersonal instruments, it would be advisable to waken the subject fully; too long spent in the trance-like state of recall that he had endured for the past forty-two days might endanger his conscious personality. The recommendation was not unwelcome to Paul Freeman. He was growing more and more intrigued by this man whose past had been mapped along so improbable a course.

On the other hand there was a diktat in force, straight from the Federal Bureau of Data Processing, which instructed him to produce a full report in the shortest possible time. Hence Hartz's flying visit. And that had lasted a whole working day, moreover, when one might have expected the typical "hello-how-interesting-goodbye" pattern. Someone in Washington must have a hunch . . . or at any rate have gone out so far on a limb as to need results regardless of what they were.

He compromised. For a single day he would talk person-to-person instead of merely replaying facts from store in a living memory.

He quite looked forward to the change.

"You know where you are?"

The totally shaven man licked his lips. His gaze flickered around the stark white walls.

"No, but I figure it must be Tarnover. I always pictured rooms like this in that faceless secret block on the east side of the campus."

"How do you feel about Tarnover?"

"It makes me want to be scared stiff. But I guess you dose me with something so I can't."

"But that wasn't how you felt when you first came here."

"Hell, no. In the beginning it seemed wonderful. Should it not to a kid with my background?"

That was documented: father disappeared when he was five, mother stood the strain for a year and vanished into an alcoholic haze. But the boy was resilient. They decided he would make an ideal rent-a-child: obviously bright, rather quiet, tolerably well mannered and cleanly in his habits. So, from six to twelve, he lived in a succession of modern, smart, sometimes luxurious company homes occupied by childless married couples posted in on temporary assignment from other cities. He was generally well liked by these "parents" and one couple seriously considered adopting him but decided against landing themselves permanently with a boy of another color. Anyhow, they consoled themselves, he was getting a terrific introduction to the plug-in life-style.

He appeared to accept the decision with good grace.

But several times after that, when left alone in the house for an evening (which was in fact often, for he was a good boy and to be trusted), he went to the phone—with a sense of dreadful guilt—and punched the ten nines as he dimly recalled seeing his mother do, his real mother, during the last terrible few months before something went wrong inside her head. To the blank screen he would pour out a nonstop volley of filth and curses. And wait, shaking, for the calm anonymous voice to say, "Only I heard that. I hope it helped."

Paradoxically: yes, it did.

"What about school, Haflinger?"

"Was it really my name . . . ? Don't bother to answer; that was rhetorical. I just didn't like it. Overtones of 'half,' as though I was condemned never to become a finished person. And I didn't care for Nick, either."

"Do you know why not?"

"Sure I do. In spite of anything it may say to the contrary on my record, I have excellent juvenile recall. Infantile too, in fact. I found out early about Auld Nick, the Scottish term for the devil. Also 'to nick,' meaning to arrest or sometimes to steal. And above all Saint Nick. I never did manage to find out how the same figment could give rise to both Santa Claus and Saint Nicholas, the patron saint of thieves."

"Maybe it was a matter of giving with one hand and taking away with the other. Did you know that in Holland Sinter Klaas brought gifts to children in the company of a black man who whipped the ones who hadn't behaved well enough to deserve a present?"

"That's news to me, and very interesting, Mr.— Mr. Freeman, isn't it?"

"You were going to tell me how you remember school."

"Should have known better than to try and strike up a brotherly chat. Yes, school. Much the same— the teachers turned over even faster than my temporary parents, and every new arrival seemed to have a new theory of education, so we never did learn very much. But of course in most respects it was a hell of a lot worse than—uh—*home.*"

The high walls. The guarded gates. The classrooms where the walls were lined with broken teaching machines, waiting for the engineers who never seemed to come, inevitably vandalized after a couple of days and rendered unrepairable. The stark corridors where so often sand greeted the soles with a gritty kiss, marking a spot where blood had been shed. The blood on the floor was his only once; he was clever, to the point of being considered odd because he kept trying to learn when everybody else knew the right thing to do was sit tight and wait to be eighteen. He contrived to avoid all the shivs, clubs and guns bar one, and his wound was shallow and left no scar.

The one thing he was not clever enough to do was escape. Authoritatively the State Board of Education had laid it down that there must be one major element of stability in the life of a rent-a-child; therefore he must continue at this same school regardless of where he currently happened to reside, and none of his temporary parents remained in the vicinity long enough to fight that ruling to the bitter end.

When he was twelve a teacher arrived named Adele Brixham, who kept on trying same as he did. She noticed him. Before she was ambushed and gang-raped and overloaded, she must have filed some sort of report. At any rate, a week or so later the classroom and the approach corridor were invaded by a government platoon, men and women in uniform carrying guns, webbers and fetters, and for a change the roll was called complete bar one girl who was in the hospital.

And there were tests which for a change could not be ignored, because someone with hard eyes and a holster stood by you to make sure. Nickie Haflinger sank all his frustrated lust for achievement into the six hours they lasted: three before, three after a supervised lunch eaten in the classroom. Even to visit the can you were escorted. It was a new thing for those of the kids who hadn't been arrested yet.

After IQ and EQ—empathic quotient—and perceptual and social tests, like the regular kind only more so, came the kickers: laterality tests, double-take tests, open-dilemma tests, value-judgment tests, wisdom tests . . . and those were fun! For the final thirty minutes of the session he was purely drunk on the notion that when something happened which had never happened before one human being could make a right decision about the outcome, and that person might be Nickie Haflinger!

The government people had brought a portable computer with them. Little by little he grew aware that each time it printed out, more and more of the gray-garbed strangers looked at him rather than the other children. The rest realized what was going on, too, and that expression came to their faces which he had long ago learned to recognize: *Today, after class, he's the one we'll carve the ass off!*

He was shaking as much from terror as excitement when the six hours ended, but he hadn't been able to stop himself from applying all he knew and all he could guess to the tests.

But there was no attack, no sanding along the streets between here and his current home. The woman in overall charge switched off the computer and jerked her head his way, and three men with guns drawn closed on him and one said in a kindly tone, "Stay right there, sonny, and don't worry."

His classmates drifted away, giving puzzled backward glances and kicking the doorposts with fury as they left. Later someone else was sanded—the term came from "S-and-D," search and destroy—and lost an eye. But by then he had arrived home in a government limo.

It was carefully explained, to him and his "parents," that he was being requisitioned in the service of his country under special regulation number such-and-such issued by the Secretary of Defense as authorized by clause number whatever of some or other

Act of Congress. . . . He didn't take in the details. He was giddy. He'd been promised that for the first time in his life he could stay where he was going as long as he liked.

Next morning he woke at Tarnover, and thought he had been transported halfway to heaven.


"Now I realize I was in hell. Why are you alone? I had the vague impression that when you woke up I'd find there were two of you, even though you were doing all the talking. Is there usually someone else in here?"

Freeman shook his head, his eyes watchful.

"But there has been. I'm sure of it. He said something about the way you regard me. Said he felt scared."

"Yes, that's so. You had a visitor, who sat in on one day's interrogation, and he did say that. But he doesn't work at Tarnover."

"The place where you take the improbable for granted."

"So to speak."

"I see. I'm reminded of one of my favorite funny stories when I was a kid. I haven't told it in years. With luck it'll have gone far enough out of style not to bore you. Seems that an oil company, back in— oh—the thirties of last century would fit, wanted to impress a sheikh. So they laid on a plane when they were few and far between in that part of the world."

"And when he was at ten thousand feet, perfectly calm and collected, they said, 'Aren't you impressed?' And the sheikh said, 'You mean it's not supposed to do this?' Yes, I know the story. I learned it from your dossier."

There was a short pause full of veiled tension. Eventually Freeman said, "What convinced you that you were in hell?"

*After the legs race, the arms race; after the arms race . . .*


Angus Porter's epigram was not just a slick crack

to be over-quoted at parties. But few people realized how literally true the *bon mot* had become.

At Tarnover, at Crediton Hill, at some hole in the Rockies he had never managed to identify beyond the code name "Electric Skillet," and at other places scattered from Oregon to Louisiana, there were secret centers with a special task. They were dedicated to exploiting genius. Their ancestry could be traced back to the primitive "think tanks" of the mid-twentieth century, but only in the sense that a solid-state computer was descended from Hollerith's punched-card analyzer.

Every superpower, and a great many second- and third-rank nations, had similar centers. The brain race had been running for decades, and some countries had entered it with a head start. (The pun was popular, and forgivable.)

In Russia, for example, great publicity had long attended the Mathematical Olympiads, and it was a signal honor to be allowed to study at Akadiemgorodok. In China, too, the sheer pressure of population had forced an advance from ad hoc improvisation along predetermined Marxist-Maoist guidelines to a deliberate search for optimal administrative techniques, employing a form of cross-impact matrix analysis for which the Chinese language was peculiarly well adapted. Well before the turn of the century a pattern had been systematized that proved immensely successful. To every commune and small village was sent a deck of cards bearing ideograms relevant to impending changes, whether social or technical. By shuffling and dealing the symbols into fresh combinations, fresh ideas could automatically be generated, and the people at a series of public meetings discussed the implications at length and appointed one of their number to summarize their views and report back to Peking. It was cheap and amazingly efficient.

But it didn't work in any Western language except Esperanto.

The U.S.A. entered the race on the grand scale very late. Not until the nation was reeling under the impact of the Great Bay Quake was the harsh lesson learned that the economy could not absorb disasters of even this magnitude—let alone a nuclear strike which would exterminate millions plural. Even then it took years for the switch from brawn to brain to become definitive in North America.

In some ways the change remained incomplete. At Electric Skillet the primary concern was still with weaponry . . . but at least the stress was on defense in its literal meaning, not on counterstrike or pre-emptive strategies. (The name, of course, had been chosen on the frying-pan-and-fire principle.)

Newer concepts, though, were embodied at Crediton Hill. There, top-rank analysts constantly monitored the national Delphi pools to maintain a high social-mollification index. Three times since 1990 agitators had nearly brought about a bloody revolution, but each had been aborted. What the public currently yearned for could be deduced by watching the betting, and steps could be taken to ensure that what was feasible was done, what was not was carefully deeveed. It was a task that taxed the skills of top CIMA experts to ensure that when the government artificially cut Delphi odds to distract attention from something undesirable no other element in the mix was dragged down with it.

And newest of all was the ultra-secret work of Tarnover and those other centers whose existence, but not whose names, one was aware of. The goal?

To pin down before anybody else did the genetic elements of wisdom.

"You make wisdom seem like a dirty word, Haflinger."

"Maybe I'm ahead of my time again. What you people are doing is bound to debase the term, and soon at that."

"I won't waste time by saying I disagree. If I didn't I wouldn't be here. But perhaps you'd define what you understand by the term."

"My definition is the same as yours. The only difference is that I mean what I say, and you manipulate it. What a wise man can do, that can't done by some-one who's merely clever, is make a right judgment in an unprecedented situation. A wise man would never be overloaded by the plug-in life-style. He'd never need to go get mended in a mental hospital. He'd adjust to shifts of fashion, the coming-and-going of fad-type phrases, the ultrasonic-blender confusion of twenty-first-century society, as a dolphin rides the bow wave of a ship, out ahead but always making in the right direction. And having a hell of a good time with it."

"You make it sound eminently desirable. So why are you opposed to our work?"

"Because what's being done here—and elsewhere —isn't motivated by love of wisdom, or the wish to make it available to everyone. It's motivated by terror, suspicion, and greed. You and everybody above and below you from the janitor to—hell, probably to the president himself and beyond that to the people who pull the president's strings!—the *lot* of you are afraid that by taking thought someone else may already have added a cubit to his wisdom while you're still fiddling around on the foolishness level. You're so scared that they may have hit on the answer in Brazil or the Philippines or Ghana, you daren't even go and ask. It makes me sick. If there is a person on the planet who has the answer, if there's even the shadow of a chance he does, then the only sane thing to do is go sit on his doorstep until he has time to talk to you."

"You believe there is *an* answer—one, and only one?"

"Hell, no. More likely there are thousands. But I do know this: as long as you're determined to be the first to reach the—or a—solution, just so long will you fail to find it. In the meantime, other people with other problems will be humbly pleased because things aren't so bad this year as they were last."

In China . . . One always began with China. It was

the most populous country on the planet, hence the logical starting point.

Once there had been Mao. Then followed The Consortium, which was more like an interregnum, the Cultural Revolution redoubled in no trumps (except that the stock translation "Cultural Revolution" was ludicrously wrong and the people involved understood by the term something more like "agonizing reappraisal"), and then there was Feng Soo Yat . . . very suddenly, and with so little warning that on foreign-affairs Delphi boards high odds in favor of China crumbling into anarchy and violence swung to three hundred against in three days. He was the epitome of the Oriental wise man: young, reputedly still in his thirties, yet capable of running his goverment with such delicate touches and so keen an insight that he never needed to explain or justify his decisions. They simply worked.

He might have been trained to display such powers of judgment; he might have been specially bred to possess them. One thing was sure: he hadn't lived long enough to grow into them.

Not if he started from where most people had to.

Also in Brazil there had been no religious warfare since Lourenço Pereira seized power—whoever he might be—and that was a welcome contrast to the turn-of-the-century period when Catholics and Macumbans had fought pitched battles in the streets of São Paulo. And in the Philippines the reforms introduced by their first-ever woman president, Sara Castaldo, had slashed their dreadful annual murder rate by half, and in Ghana when Premier Akim Gomba said to clean house they started cleaning house and laughed and cheered, and in Korea since the *coup* by Inn Lim Pak there had been a remarkable fall-off in the crap-and-screw charter flights which formerly had come in from Sydney, Melbourne and Honolulu at the rate of three or four a day, and . . . and generally speaking in the most unlikely places wisdom appeared to be on the increase.

"So you're impressed by what's been happening in other countries. Why don't you want your own homeland to benefit from—shall we call it a shot in the arm of wisdom?"

"My homeland? I was born here, sure, but . . . Never mind; that's a stale argument these days, I guess. The point is that what's being peddled here as wisdom isn't."

"I sense a long debate ahead. Perhaps we should start again tomorrow."

"Which mode are you going to put me in?"

"The same as today. We're drawing closer to the point at which you ultimately overloaded. I want to compare your conscious and unconscious recollections of the events leading up to the climax."

"Don't try and bleat me. You mean you're bored with talking to an automaton. I'm more interesting when I'm fully awake."

"On the contrary. Your past is far more intriguing than either your present or your future. Both of those are completely programed. Good night. There's no point in my saying 'sleep well'—that's programed too."

## KNOWN FACTORS CONTRIBUTING TO HAFLINGER'S DESERTION

The shy, quiet, reserved boy who came to Tarnover had spent so much of his childhood being traded from one set of "parents" to the next that he had developed a chameleon-like adaptability. He had liked almost all his "fathers" and "mothers"—small wonder, given the computerized care with which child was matched to adult—and he had been, briefly, exposed to an enormous range of interests. If his current "dad" enjoyed sports, he spent hours with a baseball or a football; if his "mom" was musical he sang to her accompaniment, or picked his way up and down a keyboard . . . and so on.

But he had never let himself become deeply engaged in anything. It would have been dangerous, as

55

dangerous as coming to love somebody. At his next home it might not have been possible to continue.

At first, therefore, he was unsure of himself: diffident with his fellow students, among whom he was one of the youngest—most were in their mid-teens—and excessively formal when talking to members of the staff. He had a vague mental picture of government establishments, which was based on three-vee and movie portrayals of cadet schools and army bases. But there was nothing in the least military about Tarnover. There were rules, naturally, and among the students some customary traditions had already grown up although the place had been founded a mere decade earlier, but they were casually observed, and the atmosphere was—not friendly, but comradely. There was a sense of people banded together for a common purpose, undertaking a shared quest; in sum, there was a feeling of solidarity.

It was so novel to Nickie that he took months to realize how much he liked it.

Above all, he relished meeting people, not only adults but kids too, who obviously enjoyed knowing things. Accustomed to keeping his mouth shut in class, to imitating the sullen obstinacy of his fellow pupils because he had seen what happened to those who showed off their knowledge, he was astonished and for a while badly disturbed by this. Nobody tried to push him. He knew he was being watched, but that was all. He was told what was available for him to do, and his instructions stopped there. Provided he did one of the dozen or twenty choices, that was enough. Later he wouldn't even be obliged to choose from a list. He could make his own.

Suddenly he clicked on. His mind buzzed like a hive of bees with new and fascinating concepts: minus one has a square root, there are nearly a billion Chinese, a Shannon tree compresses written English by fifteen percent, so *that's* how a tranquilizer works, the word "okay" comes from the Wolof *wawkay* meaning "by all means" or "certainly" . . .

His comfortable private room was equipped with a

computer remote; there were hundreds of them around the campus, more than one for each person living there. He used it voraciously, absorbing encyclopedias of data.

Very quickly he became convinced how necessary it was for his country and no other to be the first to apply wisdom to the running of the world. With change so radical and swift, what else would serve? And if a repressive, unfree culture got there ahead . . .

Shuddering when he recalled what life under a non-wise system had done to him, Nickie was ripe to be persuaded.

He didn't even mind the twice-yearly sampling of his cerebellar tissue which he and all the students had to undergo. (Only later did he start putting quote marks around "student" and thinking of himself and the others more as "inmates.") It was done with a microprobe and the loss was a negligible fifty cells.

And he was impressed to the point of awe by the single-mindedness of the biologists who worked in the anonymous-looking group of buildings on the east side of the campus. Their detachment was incredible and a little alarming, but their purpose seemed admirable. Organ grafts were routine to them—heart, kidney, lung, they made the transplant as impersonally as a mechanic would fit a spare part. Now they were after more ambitious goals: limb replacement complete with sensor and motor functions, restoration of vision to the blind, external gestation of the embryo . . . Now and then, without realizing what the slogans implied, Nickie had read advertisements in bold type headed BUY BABY BUNTING and IF YOU ABORT THEN WE'LL SUPPORT! But not until he arrived at Tarnover did he actually see one of the government fetus-trucks making its delivery of unwanted incomplete babies.

That troubled him a little, but it wasn't hard for him to decide that it was better for the not-yet-children to come here and be useful in research than for them to burn in a hospital incinerator.

After that, however, he wasn't quite as interested

in genetics as he had begun to be. It could well have been coincidence, of course; most of the time he was hungrily rounding out his incomplete picture of the modern world, concentrating on history, sociology, political geography, comparative religion, linguistics and fiction in every possible form. His instructors were pleased and his fellow students were envious: here was one of the lucky ones, who was certain to go a long, long way.

There were graduates from Tarnover out in the larger world now. Not many. To build the student body up to its present total of seven hundred plus had taken nine years, and a good deal of the early work done here had gone to waste on the error side of the trial-and-error methods inevitable with any system as radically new as this. That was over. Sometimes a graduate returned for a short visit and expressed pleasure at the smoothness with which the establishment now ran, and told half-sad, half-funny stories about mistakes made when he or she was still a student. Most centered on the original assumption that an element of rivalry was indispensable if the people here were to function at maximum efficiency. On the contrary; one of the basic characteristics of a wise person is the ability to see how competition wastes time and effort. Some ludicrous contradictions had arisen before that problem was straightened out.

Existence at Tarnover was isolated. Vacations were naturally permitted—many of the students had living families, unlike Nickie. Pretty often one of his friends would take him home over Christmas or Thanksgiving or Labor Day. But he was well aware of the danger inherent in talking freely. No formal oath was administered, no security clearance issued, but all the kids were conscious, indeed proud, that their country's survival might depend on what they were doing. Besides, being a guest in another person's home reminded him uncomfortably of the old days. So he never accepted an invitation lasting more than a week, and always returned thankfully to what he now regarded as his ideal environment: the place where the air was constantly crackling with new ideas, yet the day-to-day pattern of life was wholly stable.

Naturally there were changes. Sometimes a student, less often an instructor, went away without warning. There was a phrase for that; it was said they had "bowed out"—bowed in the sense of an overstressed girder, or a tree before a gale. One instructor resigned because he was not allowed to attend a conference in Singapore. No one sympathized. People from Tarnover did not attend foreign congresses. They rarely went to those in North America. There were reasons not to be questioned.

By the time he was seventeen Nickie felt he had made up for most of his childhood. He had learned affection, above all. It wasn't just that he'd had girls —he was a presentable young man now, and a good talker, and according to what he was told an enterprising lover. More important was the fact that the permanence of Tarnover had allowed him to go beyond merely liking adults. There were many instructors to whom he had become genuinely attached. It was almost as though he had been born late into a vast extended family. He had more kinfolk, more dependable, than ninety percent of the population of the continent.

And then the day came when . . .

Most of the education imparted here was what you taught yourself with the help of computers and teaching machines. Logically enough. Knowledge that you wanted to acquire before you knew where to look for it sticks better than knowledge you never even suspected in advance. But now and then a problem arose where personal guidance was essential. It had been two years since he'd dug into biology at all, and in connection with a project he was planning in the psychology of communication he needed advice on the physiological aspects of sensory input. The computer remote in his room was not the same one he had had when he arrived, but a newer and more efficient model which by way of a private joke he had baptized Roger, after Friar Bacon of the talking head.

It told him within seconds that he should call on Dr. Joel Bosch in the biology section tomorrow at 1000. He had not met Dr. Bosch, but he knew about him: a South African, an immigrant to the States seven or eight years ago, who had been accepted on the staff of Tarnover after long and thorough loyalty evaluation, and reputedly was doing excellent work.

Nickie felt doubtful. One had heard about South Africans . . . but on the other hand he had never met one, so he suspended judgment.

He arrived on time, and Bosch bade him enter and sit down. He obeyed more by feel than sight, for his attention had instantly been riveted by—by a *thing* in one corner of the light and airy office.

It had a face. It had a torso. It had one normal-looking hand set straight in at the shoulder, one withered hand on the end of an arm straw-thin and almost innocent of muscle, and no legs. It rested in a system of supports that held its overlarge head upright, and it looked at him with an expression of indescribable jealousy. It was like a thalidomide parody of a little girl.

Portly, affable, Bosch chuckled at his visitor's reaction. "That's Miranda," he explained, dropping into his own chair. "Go ahead, stare all you like. She's used to it—or if she isn't by now, then she's damned well going to have to get used to it."

"What . . . ?" Words failed him.

"Our pride and joy. Our greatest achievement. And you're accidentally privileged to be among the first to know about it. We've kept her very quiet because we didn't know how much input she could stand, and if we'd let even the faintest hint leak out people would have been standing on line from here to the Pacific, demanding a chance to meet her. Which they will, but in due time. We're adjusting her to the world by slow degrees, now we know she really is a conscious being. Matter of fact, she probably has at least an average IQ, but it took us a while to figure out a way of letting her talk."

Staring, hypnotized, Nickie saw that a sort of bellows mechanism was pumping slowly in and out alongside her shrunken body, and a connection ran from it to her throat.

"Of course even if she hadn't survived this long she would still have been a milestone on the road," Bosch pursued. "Hence her name—Miranda, 'to be wondered at.'" He gave a broad grin. "We built her! That's to say, we combined the gametes under controlled conditions, we selected the genes we wanted and shoved them to the right side during crossover, we brought her to term in an artificial womb—yes, we literally built her. And we've learned countless lessons from her already. Next time the result should be independently viable instead of relying on all that gadgetry." An airy wave.

"Right, to business. I'm sure you don't mind her listening in. She won't understand what we're talking about, but she's here, as I said, to accustom her to the idea that there are lots of people in the world instead of just three or four attendants taking care of her. According to the computers you want a fast rundown on . . ."

Mechanically Nickie explained the reason for his visit, and Bosch obliged him with the titles of a dozen useful recent papers on relevant subjects. He barely heard what was said. When he left the office he stumbled rather than walked back to his room.

Alone that night, and sleepless, he asked himself a question that was not on the program, and agonized his way to its answer.

Consciously he was aware that not everyone would have displayed the same reaction. Most of his friends would have been as delighted as Bosch, stared at Miranda with interest instead of dismay, asked scores of informed questions and complimented the team responsible for her.

But for half his life before the age of twelve, for six of his most formative years, Nickie Haflinger had been more furniture than person and willy-nilly had been forced to like it.

As though he had come upon the problem in a random test of the type that formed a standard element in his education—training people to be taken by surprise and still get it right was an integral part of Tarnover thinking—he saw it, literally saw it, in his mind's eye. It was spelled out on the buff paper they used for "this section to be answered in terms of the calculus of morality," marking it off from the green used for administration and politics, the pink for social prognostication, and so on.

He could even imagine the style of type it was printed in. And it ran:

*Distinguish between (a) the smelting of ore which could have become a tool in order to make a weapon and (b) the modification of germ plasm which might have been a person in order to make a tool. Do not continue your answer below the thick black line.*

And the answer, the hateful horrible answer, boiled down to this.

*No difference. No distinction. Both are wicked.*

He didn't want to believe that conclusion. Taking it at face value implied giving up all that had been most precious in his short life. Tarnover had become his home in a more total sense than he had previously imagined possible.

But he felt insulted, clear down to the marrow of his bones.

*I thought I was here to become myself with maximum perfection. I'm no longer sure that I was right. Suppose, just suppose, I'm here to become the person who's regarded as most usable. . . .*

Miranda died; her life supports were less than perfect. But she was reincarnated in numerous successors, and even when there was none of them around, her image continued to haunt Nickie Haflinger.

Privately, because he was afraid he would fail to explain himself if he talked about this to his friends, he wrestled with the ramifying tentacles of the problem.

The word *wicked* had sprung to his mind unbidden;

it had been learned in infancy, most likely from his mother whom he dimly remembered as having been devout, a Pentecostalist or Baptist or the like. His later temporary parents had all been too enlightened to use such loaded terms around a child. Their homes contained computer remotes giving access to all the newest data concerning kids.

So what did the word mean? What in the modern world could be identified as evil, an abomination, *wrong?* He groped his way toward a definition, and found the final clue in his recollection of what Bosch had said. Having discovered that Miranda was a conscious being with an average IQ, they had not given her merciful release. They had not even kept her ignorant of the world, so that she could have had no standard of comparison between her existence and that of mobile, active, free individuals. Instead, they brought her out in public to "get used to being stared at." As though their conception of personality began and ended with what could be measured in the labs. As though, capable themselves of suffering, they granted no reality to the suffering of others. "The subject exhibited a pain response."

But not, under any circumstances, *we hurt her.*

Outwardly his conduct during his second five years at Tarnover was compatible with how he had previously behaved. He took tranquilizers, but they were prescribed for him as for most of his age group. He was sometimes called for counseling sessions after arguing with his instructors, but so were at least half of his peers. Having been jilted by a girl, he teetered on the verge of turning skew, but the typical emotional tempests of adolescence were magnified in this closed environment. All quite within the parameters laid down.

Once—literally once—he found he could stand the pressure no longer, and did something which, had he been found out, would have ensured his expulsion and very likely an operation to blank his memory. (It was rumored . . . One could never pin the rumor down.)

From a public veephone at the railcar terminal linking Tarnover to the nearest town he called Hearing Aid, for the first time in years, and for one dark lonely hour poured out the secrets of his heart. It was a catharsis, a purgation. But long before he had regained his room he was shaking, haunted by the fear that Hearing Aid's famous promise ("Only I heard that!") might not be true. How could it be? It was absurd! From Canaveral the tendril-ears of federal computers wove through his society like mycelia. No place could possibly be immune. All night he lay awake in fear, expecting his door to be flung open and stern silent men to take him under arrest. By dawn he was half-minded to kill himself.

Miraculously, there followed no disaster, and a week later that awful impulse had receded in memory, growing vague as a dream. What he recalled all too vividly, though, was his terror.

He resolved it was the last time he'd be such a fool.

Shortly thereafter he began to concentrate on data processing techniques at the expense of his other study subjects, but about one in four of his contemporaries had by then also evinced a preference for some specialty, and this was a valuable talent. (It had been explained to him that in terms of n-value mean-path theory administering the three hundred million people of North America was a determinate problem; however, as with chess or fencing, it was no good to be told that there must be a perfect game if the universe wouldn't last long enough for it to be found by trial and error.)

He had been reserved and self-contained when he arrived. It was not inconsistent that after a gesture in the direction of greater openness he should revert to his old solitary habits. Neither his teachers nor his friends guessed that he had revised himself for a purpose. He wanted out, and there was not supposed to be an out.

The point was never labored, but there were constant reminders that to support one student at Tarnover cost the federal budget approximately three million dollars per year. What had been spent in the last century on missiles, submarines, the maintenance of forward bases overseas, was now lavished on these secret establishments. And it was known in the subtle way such things can be known that a condition of being here was that ultimately one must offer the government a return on its investment. All the graduates who came back to visit were doing so.

But the conviction had gradually grown in Nickie's mind that something was amiss. Were these people dedicated . . . or insensitive? Were they patriotic . . . or power-hungry? Were they single-minded . . . or purblind?

He was determined that somehow, sooner or later, before committing himself to the lifetime repayment they were bound to demand of him, he must break loose long enough to take a detached view and make his mind up about the rights and wrongs of the brain race.

That was what set him on the trail of what he later found to be a 4GH code.

He deduced from first principles that there must be a way of allowing authorized persons to drop an old identity and assume a new one, no questions asked. The nation was tightly webbed in a net of interlocking data-channels, and a time-traveler from a century ago would have been horrified by the degree to which confidential information had been rendered accessible to total strangers capable of adding two plus two. ("The machines that make it more difficult to cheat on income tax can also ensure that blood of the right group is in the ambulance which picks you up from a car crash. *Well?*")

Yet it was known that not merely police informers, FBI agents and counterspies continued to go about their secret business, but also commercial spies—party agents shepherding million-dollar bribes—procurers serving the carnal purposes of the hypercorps. It was still true that if you were rich enough or had the ear of the proper person, you could avoid and evade.

Most people were resigned to living wholly on the public level. He was not. He found his code.

A 4GH contained a replicating phage: a group which automatically *and consistently* deleted all record of a previous persona whenever a replacement was keyed in. Possessed of one, an individual could rewrite him- or herself via any terminal connected to the federal data banks. That meant, since 2005, any veephone including a public one.

This was the most precious of all freedoms, the plug-in life-style raised to the *n*th power: freedom to become the person you chose to be instead of the person remembered by the computers. That was what Nickie Haflinger desired so keenly that he spent five years pretending he was still himself. It was the enchanted sword, the invulnerable shield, the winged boots, the cloak of invisibility. It was the ultimate defense.

Or so it seemed.

Therefore, one sunny Saturday morning, he left Tarnover, and on Monday he was a life-style counselor in Little Rock, ostensibly aged thirty-five and—as the data-net certified—licensed to practice anywhere in North America.

## THE TANGLED WEB

"Your first career went well for a while," Freeman said. "But it came to an abrupt and violent end."

"Yes." A harsh chuckle. "I was nearly shot by a woman I advised to go screw someone of a different color. The massed computers of half a continent were in agreement with me, but she wasn't. I concluded I'd been overoptimistic and rethought myself."

"Which was when you became an instructor with a three-vee cassette college. I note that for your new post you dropped down to twenty-five, much nearer your real age, even though the bulk of the clientele was forty or over. I wonder why."

"The answer's simple. Think what lured most of

those clients on to the college's reels. It was a sense of losing touch with the world. They were hungry for data supplied by people fifteen or twenty years younger, usually because they'd done what they thought best for their children and been repaid with rejection and insults. They were pathetic. What they wanted was not what they claimed to want. They wanted to be told yes, the world really is pretty much as it was when you were young, there aren't any objective differences, there's some magic charm you can recite and instantly the crazy moiling framework of the modern world will jell into fixed familiar patterns. . . . The third time a complaint was filed about my tapes I was surpled despite my rigorous proof that I was right. Being right was at a discount in that context, too."

"So you tried your skill as a full-time Delphi gambler."

"And made a fortune in next to no time and grew unspeakably bored. I did nothing that anybody else couldn't do, once he realized the government manipulates Delphi odds to keep the social-mollification index high."

"Provided he had access to as much computer capacity as you did."

"But in theory everybody does, given a dollar to drop into a pay phone."

There was a pause. Freeman resumed in a brittle tone, "Did you have a clearly defined goal in mind which guided you in your choice of roles?"

"You didn't already dig that out of me?"

"Yes, but when you were regressed. I want your contemporary conscious opinion."

"It's still the same; I never hit on a better way of phrasing it. I was searching for a place to stand so that I could move the Earth."

"Did you ever consider going overseas?"

"No. The one thing I suspected a 4GH might not be good for was a passport, so if I found the right spot it would have to be in North America."

"I see. That puts your next career into much clearer

THE SHOCKWAVE RIDER

perspective. You spent a full year with a utopia-design consultancy."

"Yes. I was naïve. It took me that long to realize that only the very rich and the very stupid imagine happiness can be bought tailor-made. What's more, I should have discovered right away that it was company policy to maximize variety from one project to the next. I designed three very interesting closed communities, and in fact the last I heard all were still operating. But trying to include in the next utopia what seemed to be most promising in the previous one was what got me redunded again. You know, I sometimes wonder what became of last century's hypothetical life-style labs, where a serious effort was to be made to determine how best human beings can live together."

"Well, there are the simulation cities, not to mention the paid-avoidance zones."

"Sure, and there are the places like Trianon where you get a foretaste of tomorrow. But don't bleat me. Trianon couldn't exist if G2S didn't subsidize it with a billion dollars a year. Simulation cities are only for the children of the rich—it costs nearly as much to send the kids back to the past for a year as it does to keep them at Amherst or Bennington. And the paid-avoidance areas were created as a way of economizing on public expenditure after the Great Bay Quake. It was cheaper to pay the refugees to go without up-to-the-minute equipment. Which they couldn't have afforded anyhow."

"Maybe mankind is more adaptable than they used to believe. Maybe we're coping well enough without such props."

"In a day and age when they've quit covering individual murders on three-vee, where they just say bluntly, 'Today there were so many hundred killings,' and change the subject? That's not what I call coping!"

"You don't seem to have coped too well yourself. Each of your personae led to failure, or at any rate it didn't lead to fulfillment of your ambition."

"Partly true, but only partly. In the enclosed environment of Tarnover I didn't realize how apathetic most people have become, how cut off they feel from the central process of decision-making, how utterly helpless and resigned. But remember: I was doing in my middle twenties what some people have to wait another decade, even two decades, to achieve. You people were hunting for me with all the resources at your command. You still didn't spot me, not even when I changed roles, which was my most vulnerable moment."

"So you're blaming others for your failure and seeking consolation in your few and shallow successes."

"I think you're human after all. At any rate that sounded as though you're trying to needle me. But save your breath. I admit my worst mistake."

"Which was—?"

"To assume that things couldn't possibly be as bad as they were painted. To imagine that I could undertake constructive action on my own. I'll give you an example. A dozen times at least I'd heard the story of how a computer purchased by one of the hypercorps exclusively—on their own admission—to find means whereby they could make tax-immune payments to government officials for favors received, had been held an allowable business expense. I was convinced it must be folklore. And then I found there really was such a case on record." A sour chuckle. "Faced with things like that, I came to accept that I couldn't get anywhere without supporters, sympathizers, colleagues."

"Which you were hoping to obtain via your church?"

"Two more personae intervened before I hit on that idea. But, broadly speaking, yes."

"Wasn't it galling to have to rethink yourself so often because of outside circumstances?"

There was another pause, this time a long one.

"Well, to be candid, I sometimes regarded myself as having escaped into the biggest prison on the planet."

## DEAN INGE HE SAY

"There are two kinds of fool. One says, 'This is old, and therefore good.' And one says, 'This is new, and therefore better.' "

## RECEPTION TODAY IS OF
## AVERAGE QUALITY

"This is Seymour Schultz, who's one of our orbital troubleshooters."

A lean dark man wearing blue, smiling and proffering, according to custom, a card bearing his name and code. Projected image: man of action, no-nonsense type.

"Ah, I saw one of your colleagues taking off just now."

"Yes, that would have been Harry Leaver."

"And this is Vivienne Ingle, head-of-dept for mental welf."

Fat in gray and green, never pretty. Projecting: got here on merit, I know more than you do about yourself.

"And Pedro Lopez, and Charlie Verrano, and . . ."

Plug-in people as predicted, which meant he could switch off half his attention and still be sure he'd do and say the right conformist things.

". . . Rico Posta, veep i/c long-term planning—"

*Snap back. Vice-presidents count, often stay put instead of bouncing around.* So for this tall bearded man in black and yellow a specially warm handshake and:

"Great to meet you, Rico. Guess you and I will be in circuit quite a lot over this diversification you have in mind."

"And—oh, yes, my daughter Kate, and over there is Dolores van Bright, asshead of contract law dept, whom you absolutely must meet right away because . . ."

70

But somehow he wasn't at Ina's side any more as
she crossed the room to make the introduction. He
was smiling at Kate, and that was ridiculous. Because
on top of not even being pretty she was bony—damn
it, scrawny! Moreover, her face was too sharp: eyes,
nose, chin. And her hair: tousled, of no special color,
mousy-brown.

But looking at him with a degree of speculative interest he found dreadfully disturbing.

*This is crazy. I don't like thin women. I like them
cuddly. Ina, for example. And that's true in all versions of myself.*

"So you're Sandy Locke." With a curious husky in-
tonation.

"Mm-hm. Large as life and twice as."

There was an appraising pause. He was vaguely
aware of Ina, who was on the far side of the floor now
—and this was a big room, of course—as she glanced
around in surprise to relocate him.

"No. Larger, and half," Kate said unaccountably,
and pulled an amusing face that made her nose woffle
like a rabbit's. "Ina's making wild signals at you. Better catch up. I'm not supposed to be here—I just have
nothing else to do this evening. But suddenly I'm glad
I came. Talk to you later."

"Hey, Sandy!" Loud over the omnipresent soothing
music, bland as the decor warranted to offend nobody. "This way!"

*What the hell happened just now?*

The question kept leaping back into his mind even
when "just now" was an hour old, distracting him
constantly without warning from the prescribed display of interest in the affairs of these new colleagues
of his. It cost him much effort to maintain a veneer of
politeness.

"Say, I hear your kid had to go be straightened,
poor thing. How's she doing?"

"We collect her Saturday. Good as new or better,
so they say."

71

"Should have signed her with Anti-Trauma Inc. like us. Don't you agree, Sandy?"

"Hmm? Oh! It's no use asking me. I'm strictly swingle, so for me you're into a no-go zone."

"Yeah? Shame. Was going to ask your view on fifty-fifty schools—know, where pupils pick half, staff the other half of the curriculum? Fair compromise on the face; in the guts I wonder . . ."

"At Trianon?"

"No. Try live the future today, get it all wrong."

And:

"—wouldn't take on a secondhand home. Too big a clog, reprograming the automatics. Short end to a friendship, inviting someone over and having him webbed solid to the driveway because the moronic machinery misunderstood you."

"Mine you can update with no more than the poker's code. Tough it isn't at Trianon. Sandy here's a smart shiver—bet he's into the same type thing, right?"

"Presently between houses, friend. Next time maybe I'll move up where you are. Maybe I'll go clear back instead. I'm still sussing the aroma."

And:

"You were tribed in teentime, Sandy? Hmm? Son of mine wants in the Assegais! Sure their solidarity and morale are great, but—uh . . ."

"Fatality rate kind of high? I heard that too. Since they switched from Baron Samedi to Kali. Me, I'm trying to plug Donna into the Bold Eagles. I mean what's it worth to get custody of a kid from a cross-marriage where she got to take some oath about shivving any white the warlord says?"

"Bold Eagles? Not a hope. Signing up kids at birth now. Go find some nice quiet tribe that follows Saint Nick. The life-assurance rates are lower, to begin with."

And so on.

But at alarmingly frequent intervals he kept finding that his eyes had strayed past the shoulder of the Important Person he was chatting with and come to rest on the untidy hair or the pointed profile of Ina's daughter.

Why?

Eventually Ina said in a tart tone, "Kate seems to have you mezzed, Sandy!"

*Yes, mesmerized would be a good name for it.*

"Takes after you in that respect," he answered lightly. "Mainly I'm puzzled to find her here. I thought this was strictly a meet-the-folks deal."

That was convincing; the girl was one jarring element in an otherwise predictable milieu. Ina softened a little.

"Should have guessed. Should say sorry, too. But she knows quite a lot of the staff, and she called up today to ask if I was doing anything this evening or could she drop by for dinner, so I said there was this party and she could ride my back."

"So she isn't with the corp. I thought maybe. What's she doing with her life?"

"Nothing."

"What?"

"Oh, nothing worth mentioning. Going back next fall for *another* course of study. Right here at UMKC, *again*. And she's twenty-two, damn it!" In a lower voice—but Sandy already knew that damaging number, no extra harm involved. "I could peg it if she wanted to go study in Australia, or even Europe, but . . . And she blames it all on this cat her father gave her!"

At which point she caught sight of Rico Posta signaling for her to go talk with him and Dolores van Bright, and separated with a mutter of excuses.

A few seconds, and while he was still debating whether to pay another call on the autobar, Kate was at his side. The room was crowded now—fifty-odd guests were present—and last time he saw her she had been the far side of the floor. It followed she had been watching him as keenly as Vivienne. (No, not any more. Hooray. Mental welfare was taking time out.)

*What do I do—run?*

"How long are you going to be in KC?" Kate demanded.

"The usual. As long as G2S and I agree I should."

"You're claiming to be the bounce-around type?"

"It's bounce or break," he said, trying to make the cliché sound like what it was supposed to be: a flip substitute for a proper answer.

"You're the first person I've met who can say that as though he means it," Kate murmured. Her eyes, dark brown and very piercing, were constantly on his face. "I knew the moment you came in there was something unusual about you. Where did you bounce in from?"

And, while he was hesitating, she added, "Oh, I know it's rude to pry into people's pasts. Ina's been telling me since I learned to talk. Like you don't stare, you don't point, you don't make personal remarks. But people do have pasts, and they're on file at Canaveral, so why let machines know what your friends don't?"

"Friends are out of fashion," he said, more curtly than he had intended . . . and how long was it since he had been taken that much off his guard? Even pronouncing that curse on Fluckner—already the encounter felt as though it lay ages behind him—had not been as disturbing as his casual party conversation. Why? Why?

"Which doesn't mean nonexistent," Kate said. "You'd be a valuable friend. I can sense it. That makes you rare."

A sudden possibility struck him. It could be that this plain, thin, unprepossessing girl had found a way to reach men who would not otherwise regard her as attractive. The offer of friendship, deeper than the commonplace acquaintanceships of the plug-in lifestyle, might well appeal to those who hungered for solid emotional fare.

He almost voiced the charge, but he seemed to taste in advance the flavor of the words. They were like ashes on his tongue. Instead, with reluctance, he said, "Thank you. I take that as a compliment though thousands wouldn't. But right now I'm thinking more of the future than the past. I didn't enjoy my last position too much. What about you? You're studying. What?"

"Everything. If you can be enigmatic, so can I."

He waited.

"Oh! Last year, water ecology, medieval music and Egyptology. The year before, law, celestial mechanics and handicrafts. Next year, probably— Is something the matter?"

"Not at all. I'm just trying to look impressed."

"Don't bleat me. I can tell you're not wondering why anybody should waste time on such a mishmosh. I see that look all the time on Ina's face, and her so-called friends' here at the company." She paused, pondering. "Maybe . . . Yes, I think so. Envious?"

*My God! How did she catch on so quickly? To have the chance without being fettered by the demands of Tarnover, without having it drummed into your mind nonstop that every passing year sees you three million further into the government's debt. . . .*

It was 2130. A thudding sound announced the issue from wall vents of a cold buffet supper. Ina returned to ask whether he wanted her to bring him a plateful. He was glad. He could use the distraction to formulate not his but Sandy Locke's proper response.

"Ah, you don't have to know everything. You just have to know where to find it."

Kate sighed. As she turned away an odd look came into her eyes. He only glimpsed it, but he was quite certain how best to define it.

Disappointment.


## AMONG THE MOST HIGHLY PRAISED
## OF ALL THREE-VEE COMMERCIALS

*1:* Dead silence, the black of empty space, the harsh bright points of the stars. Slowly into field orbits the wreckage of a factory. Obviously an explosion has opened it like a tin can. Spacesuited figures are seen drifting around it like fetuses attached to the umbilical

75

cords of their regulation life lines. Hold for a beat. Pan to a functioning factory operating at full blast, glistening in the rays of the naked sun and swarming with men and women loading unmanned freight capsules for dispatch to Earth. Voice over: "On the other hand . . . *this* factory was built by G2S."

*2*: Without warning we are plunging through the outer atmosphere, at first on a steady course, then vibrating, then wobbling as the ablation cone on the capsule's nose starts to flare. It spins wildly and tumbles end-for-end. Explosion. Cut to half a dozen men in overalls staring furiously at a dying streak of brightness on the night sky. Cut again, this time to a similar group walking across a concrete landing pan toward a smoking capsule that targeted so close to home they don't even need to ride to reach it. Voice over: "On the other hand . . . *this* capsule was engineered by G2S."

*3*: Deep space again, this time showing a bulky irregular mass of asteroid rock drifting toward a smelting station, recognizable by its huge mirror of thin mylar. Jets blaze on the asteroid's nearer side, men and women in suits gesticulate frantically. Sound over, faint, of confused yells for help and angry orders to "do something!" But the asteroid rock plows its solemn way clear through the mirror and leaves it in shreds that float eerily on nothing. Cut to another smelting station whose mirror is focused on an even larger chunk of ore. Magnetic vapor-guides tidily collect the gas as it boils off, separators—each shining with a different shade of reddish white—deliver valuable pure metals into cooling chambers on the shadow side of the rock. Voice over: "On the other hand . . . *this* orbit was computed at G2S."

## THE KINGDOMS OF THE WORLD

"How did you enjoy working at G2S?" Freeman inquired.

"More than I expected. Being a sort of export agency for frontline technology, it attracts top men and women from every field, and lively minds are always fun to have around. I was most closely in contact with Rico Posta, and in fact it was because of what I did under his instructions that G2S didn't lay an enormous egg by going into olivers at the same time as National Panasonic. Their model would have been twice the price with half the advantages, *and* they wouldn't have wanted to amortize their research over twenty-seven years, either."

"Something to do with the structure of Japanese society," Freeman said dryly. "Nipponside, the things must be invaluable."

"True!"

Today the atmosphere was comparatively relaxed. There was an element of conversation in the dialogue.

"How about your other colleagues? You began by disliking Vivienne Ingle."

"Began by being prepared to dislike them all. But though in theory they were standard plug-in types, in practice they were the cream of the category, moving less often than the average exec and prepared to stay where interesting research was going on rather than move from sheer force of habit."

"You investigated them by tapping the data-net, no doubt."

"Of course. Remember my excuse for getting hired."

"Of course. But it can't have taken you long to find out what you originally intended to confirm: your 4GH was still usable. Why did you stay, even to the point of their offering you tenure?"

"That . . . That's hard to explain. I guess I hadn't encountered so many people functioning so well before. In my previous personae I chiefly contacted people who were dissatisfied. There's this kind of low-grade paranoia you find all the time and everywhere because people know that people they don't know can find out things about them they'd rather keep quiet. Are you with me?"

"Naturally. But at G2S the staff were different?"

"Mm-hm. Not in the sense of having nothing to hide, not in the sense of being superbly secure—witness Ina, for one. But in general they were enjoying the wave of change. They groused pretty often, but that was a safety valve. Once the pressure blew off, they went back to using the system instead of being used by it."

"Which is what you find most admirable."

"Hell, yes. Don't you?"

There was a pause, but no answer.

"Sorry, next time I'll know better. But you exaggerate when you say they were set to offer me tenure. They were prepared to semi-perm me."

"That would have evolved into tenure."

"No, I couldn't have let it. I was tempted. But it would have meant slipping into the Sandy Locke role and staying in it for the rest of my life."

"I see. It sounds as though role-switching can become addictive."

"What?"

"Never mind. Tell me what you did to make such a good impression."

"Oh, apart from the oliver bit I sorted out some snarls, saved them a few million a year. Routine stuff. Anybody can be an efficient systems rash if he can mouse around in the federal net."

"You found that easy?"

"Not quite, but far from difficult. A G2S code heading the inquiry was a key to open many doors. The corp has a max-nat-advantage rating at Canaveral, you know."

"Did you do as you promised for Ina Grierson?"

"Pecked away at it when I remembered. I lost my enthusiasm when I realized why she hadn't turned freelie already, cut loose and left her daughter to her own devices. So long as she was in reach of her ugly duckling, her confidence was reinforced. Knowing she was far the more conventionally beautiful of the two . . . She must have hated her ex-husband."

"You found out who he was, of course."

"Only when I got tired of her pestering and finally

dug deep into her file. Poor shivver. It must have been a horrible way to die."

"Some people would call it a lesson in nemesis."

"Not at Tarnover."

"Maybe not. However, you were saying you enjoyed yourself at G2S."

"Yes, I was amazingly content. But for one problem. It was spelt K-A-T-E, as if you hadn't guessed."

## STALKED

The university was closed for summer vacation, but instead of taking off for a remote corner of the world or even, like some students, going on a package tour to the Moon, Kate stayed in KC. Next after the welcomefest he met her at a coley club patronized by the more frameworked execs of G2S.

"Sandy, come and dance!" Seizing his arm, almost dragging him away. "You haven't seen my party trick!"

"Which is—?"

But she was doing it, and he was genuinely startled. The ceiling projectors were invisible; it took fantastic kinaesthetic sensibility to dance one chorus of a simple tune without straying off key, and more still to come back and repeat it. That though was exactly what she did, and the clamorous discord generated by the other dancers was overriden by her strongly-gestured theme, mostly in the bass as though some celestial organ had lost all its treble and alto couplers but none of its volume: the *Ode to Joy* in a stately majestic tempo. From the corner of his eye he noticed that four European visitors sitting at a nearby table were uneasy, wondering whether to stand in honor of their continental anthem.

"How in the—?"

"Don't talk! Harmonize!"

Well, if the last note was from *that* projector and the one adjacent is now delivering *that* note . . . He had never taken much interest in coley, but Kate's enthusiasm was infectious; her face was bright, her eyes sparkled. She looked as though some other age might have judged her beautiful.

He tried this movement, that one, another different . . . and suddenly there was a chord, a true fifth. Which slipped a little, and had to be corrected, and— *got it!* A whole phrase of the melody in two meticulously harmonizing parts.

"I'll be damned," she said in a matter-of-fact tone. "I never met anyone before over about twenty-five and capable of proper coley. We should get together more often!"

And then someone on the far side of the floor who looked no more than fifteen wiped the music of Beethoven and substituted something new, angular, acid —probably Japanese.

After the madrigal concert where he also met her, and the lakeside fish fry where he also met her, and the target-archery meet where he also met her, and the swimming gala where he also met her, and the lecture on advances in the application of topology to business administration where he also met her, he could hold back his challenge no longer.

"Are you following me or something?"

Tonight she was wearing something sexy and diaphanous, and she had had her hair machine-coiffed. But she was still plain, still bony, still disturbing.

"No," was her answer. "Pre-guessing you. I don't have you completely pegged yet—I went to the wrong place last night—but I'm closing in fast. You, Sandy Locke, are trying far too hard to adhere to a statistical norm. And I hate to see a good man go to waste."

With which she spun on her heel and strode—one might almost have said marched—to rejoin her escort, a plump young man who scowled at him as though virulently jealous.

He simply stood there, feeling his stomach draw drumhead-tight and sweat break out on his palms.

To be sought by federal officials: that was one thing. He was accustomed to it after six years, and his precautions had become second nature. But to have his persona as Sandy Locke penetrated with such rapidity by a girl he barely knew . . . !

*Got to switch her off my circuit! She makes me feel the way I felt when I first quit Tarnover—as though I was certain to be recognized by everyone I passed on the street, as though a web were closing that would trap me for the rest of my life. And I thought that poor kid Gaila had problems . . . STOP STOP STOP! I'm being Sandy Locke, and no child ever came sobbing out of the night to beg his help!*

## SEE ISAIAH 8:1-2

Make speed to the spoil, for the prey hasteneth.

## YEARSHIFT

"I thought you'd never show," Kate said caustically, and stood back from the door of her apartment. He had caught her wearing nothing but shorts, baggy with huge pockets, and a film of dust turning here and there to slime with perspiration. "Still, you picked a good time. I'm just getting rid of last year's things. You can give me a hand."

He entered with circumspection, vaguely apprehensive of what he might find inside this home of hers: the upper floor of what at the turn of the century must have been a desirable one-family house. Now it was subdivided, and the area was on the verge of ghettohood. The streets were deep in litter and tribe-signs were plentiful. Bad tribes at that—the Kickapoos and the Bent Minds.

Four rooms here had been interconnected by enlarging doorways into archways; only the bathroom remained isolated. As he glanced around, his attention was immediately caught by a splendidly stuffed mountain lion on a low shelf at the end of the hallway, warmed by a shaft of bright sunlight—

Stuffed?

It came back in memory as clear as though Ina were here to speak the words: "She blames it all on that cat her father gave her. . . ."

Regarding him almost as steadily as her unlikely pet, Kate said, "I wondered how you would react to Bagheera. Congratulations; you get full marks. Most people turn and run. You've just gone a trifle pale around the gills. To answer all your questions in advance—yes, he is entirely tame except when I tell him to be otherwise, and he was a present from my father, who saved him from being used up in a circus. You know who my father was, I presume."

His mouth very dry, he nodded. "Henry Lilleberg," he said in a croaking voice. "Neurophysiologist. Contracted degenerative myelitis in the course of a research program and died about four years ago."

"That's right." She was moving toward the animal, hand outstretched. "I'll introduce you, and after that you needn't worry."

Somehow he found himself scratching the beast behind his right ear, and the menace he had originally read in those opal eyes faded away. When he withdrew his hand Bagheera heaved an immense sigh, laid his chin on his paws and went to sleep.

"Good," Kate said. "I expected him to like you. Not that that makes you anything special. . . . Had you heard about him from Ina, by the way? Is that why you weren't surprised?"

"You think I wasn't? She said you had a cat, so I assumed—Never mind. It all comes clear now."

"Such as what?"

"Why you stay on at UMKC instead of sampling other universities. You must be very attached to him."

"Not especially. Sometimes he's a drag. But when I was sixteen I said I'd accept responsibility for him, and I've kept my word. He's growing old now—won't last more than eighteen months—so . . . But you're right. Dad had a license to transport protected species interstate, but I wouldn't stand a hope in hell of getting one, let alone a permit to keep him on residential premises anywhere else. I'm not exactly tied hand and foot, though. I can take vacations for a week or two, and the girls downstairs feed and walk him for me, but that's about his limit, and eventually he gets fretful and they have to call me back. Annoys my boyfriends . . . Come on, this way."

She led him into the living room. Meter-high freehand Egyptian hieroglyphs marched around three of its walls; over the fourth, white paint had been slapped.

"I'm losing this," Kate said. "It's from the Book of the Dead. Chapter Forty, which I thought was kind of apt."

"I'm afraid I never read the . . ." His voice trailed away.

"Wallis Budge titles it 'The Chapter of Repulsing the Eater of the Ass.' I bleat you not. But I quit repulsing that fiercely." She gave a mocking grin. "Anyhow, now you see what you can lend a hand with."

No wonder she was wearing a layer of dust. The whole apartment was being bayquaked. In the middle of the floor here three piles of objects were growing, separated by chalked lines. One contained charitable items, like clothing not yet past hope; one contained what was scrapworthy, like a last-year's stereo player and a used typewriter and such; one contained stuff that was only garbage, though it was subdivided into disposable and recyclable.

Everywhere shelves were bare, closets were ajar, boxes and cases stood with lids raised. This room had a south aspect and the sun shone through large open windows. The smell of the city blew in on a warm breeze.

Willing to play along he peeled off his shirt and hung it on the nearest chair. "I do what?" he inquired.

"As I tell you. Mostly help with the heavier junk. Oh, plus one other thing. Talk about yourself while we're at it."

He reached for his shirt and made to put it back on.

"Point," she said with an exaggerated sigh, "taken. So just help."

Two sweaty hours later the job was finished and he knew a little about her which he hadn't previously guessed. This was the latest of perhaps five, perhaps six, annual demolitions of what was threatening to turn from a present into a past, with all that that implied: a fettering, hampering tail of concern for objects at the expense of memories. Desultorily they chatted as they worked; mostly he asked whether this was to be kept, and she answered yes or no, and from her pattern of choice he was able to paradigm her personality—and was more than a little frightened when he was through.

*This girl wasn't at Tarnover. This girl is six years younger than I am, and yet . . .*

The thought stopped there. To continue would have been like holding his finger in a flame to discover how it felt to be burned alive.

"After which we paint walls," she said, slapping her hands together in satisfaction. "Though maybe you'd like a beer before we shift modes. I make real beer and there are six bottles in to chill."

"*Real* beer?" Maintaining Sandy Locke's image at all costs, he made his tone ironical.

"A plastic person like you probably doesn't believe it exists," she said, and headed for the kitchen before he could devise a comeback.

When she returned with two foam-capped mugs, he had some sort of remark ready, anyway. Pointing at the hieroglyphs, he said, "It's a shame to paint these over. They're very good."

"I've had them up since January," was her curt reply. "They've furnished my mind, and that's what counts. When you've drunk that, grab a paint-spray."

He had arrived at around five P.M. A quarter of ten saw them in a freshly whitened framework, cleansed of what Kate no longer felt to be necessary, cleared of what the city scrap-and-garbage team would remove from the stoop come Monday morning and duly mark credit in respect of. There was a sense of space. They sat in the spacefulness eating omelets and drinking the last of the *real* beer, which was good. Through the archway to the kitchen they could see and hear Bagheera gnawing a beefbone with old blunt teeth, uttering an occasional *rrrr* of contentment.

"And now," Kate said, laying aside her empty plate, "for the explanations."

"What do you mean?"

"I'm a virtual stranger. Yet you've spent five hours helping me shift furniture and fill garbage cans and redecorate the walls. What do you want? To plug into me by way of payment?"

He sat unspeaking and immobilized.

"If that were it . . ." She was gazing at him with a thoughtful air. "I don't think I'd say no. You'd be good at it, no doubt about that. But it isn't why you came."

Silence filled the brightly whitened room, dense as the feathers in a pillow.

"I think," she said eventually, "you must have come to calibrate me. Well, did you get me all weighed and measured?"

"No," he said gruffly, and rose and left.


## INTERIM REPORT

"Bureau of Data Processing, good afternoon!"

"The Deputy Director, please. Mr. Hartz is expecting my call. . . . Mr. Hartz, I thought you should know that I'm approaching a crisis point, and if you care to come back and—

"Oh. I see. What a pity. Then I'd better just arrange for my tapes to be copied to your office.

"Yes, naturally. By a most-secure circuit."


## IMPERMEABLE

It was a nervous day, very nervous. Today they were boarding him: not just Rico and Dolores and Vivienne and the others he had met but also august remote personages from the intercontinental level. Perhaps he should not have shown a positive reaction when Ina mentioned the corp's willingness to semi-perm him, hinted that eventually they might give him tenure.

Stability, for a while at any rate, was tempting. He had no other plans formulated, and out of this context he intended to move when *he* chose, not by order of some counterpart to Shad Fluckner. Yet a sense of risk grew momently more agonizing in his mind. To be focused on by people of such power and influence—what could be more dangerous? Were there not at Tarnover people charged with tracking down and dragging back in chains Nickie Haflinger on whom the government had lavished thirty millions' worth of special training, teaching, conditioning? (By now perhaps there were other fugitives. He dared not try to link up with them. If only . . . !)

Still, facing the interview was the least of countless evils. He was preening prior to departure, determined to perfect his conformist image to the last hair on his head, when the buzzer called him to the veephone.

The face showing on the screen belonged to Dolores van Bright, with whom he had got on well during his stay here.

"Hi, Sandy!" was her cordial greeting. "Just called to wish you luck when you meet the board. We prize you around here, you know. Think you deserve a long-term post."

"Well, thanks," he answered, hoping the camera wouldn't catch the gleam of sweat he felt pearling on his skin.

"And I can strew your path with a rose or so."

"Hm?" Instantly, all his reflexes triggered into fight-or-flight mode.

"I guess I shouldn't, but . . . Well, for better or worse. Vivienne dropped a hint, and I checked up, and there's to be an extra member on the selection board. You know Viv thinks you've been overlooked as kind of a major national resource? So some fed-

eral twitch is slated to join us. Don't know who, but
I believe he's based at Tarnover. Feel honored?"

How he managed to conclude the conversation, he
didn't know. But he did, and the phone was dead,
and he was . . .

On the floor?

He fought himself, and failed to win; he lay
sprawled, his legs apart, his mouth dry, his skull
ringing like a bell that tolls nine tailors, his guts
churning, his fingers clenched and his toes attempting to imitate them. The room swam, the world
floated off its mooring, everything EVERYTHING dissolved into mist and he was aware of one sole fact:

*Got to get up and go.*

Weak-limbed, sour-bellied, half-blind with terror
he could no longer resist, he stumbled out of his
apartment (*Mine? No! Their apartment!*) and headed
for his rendezvous in hell.

## THE CONVICTION OF HIS COURAGE

After pressing the appropriate switches Freeman
waited patiently for his subject to revert from regressed
to present-time mode. Eventually he said, "It seems
that experience remains peculiarly painful. We shall
have to work through it again tomorrow."

The answer came in a weak voice, but strong
enough to convey venomous hatred. "You devil! Who
gave you the right to torture me like this?"

"You did."

"So I committed what you call a crime! But I was
never put on trial, never convicted!"

"You're not entitled to a trial."

"Anybody's entitled to a trial, damn you!"

"That is absolutely true. But you see you are *not*
anybody. You are *nobody*. And you chose to be so
of your own free will. Legally—officially—you simply
don't exist."

# BOOK 2

## THE DELPHI CORACLE

## SHALLOW MAN IN ALL HIS GORY WAS NOT DISMAYED BY ONE OF THESE

Take no thought for the morrow; that's your privilege. But don't complain if when it gets here you're off guard.

## ARARAT

With a distant . . . Too weak a word. With a *remote* part of his mind he was able to observe himself doing all the wrong things: heading in a direction he hadn't chosen, and running when he should and could have used his company electric car, in sum making a complete fool of himself.

In principle he had made the correct decisions. He would turn up for his appointment with the interview board, he would outface the visitor from Tarnover, he would win the argument because you don't, simply *don't*, haul into custody someone who is being offered permanent employment by a corporation as powerful as G2S. Not without generating a continental stink. And if there's one thing they're afraid of at Tarnover, it's having the media penetrate their guise of feigned subimportance.

The road to hell is paved with good intentions. His were fine. They simply had no effect on his behavior.

"Yes, who is it?" In a curt voice from the speaker under the veephone camera. And then, almost in the same breath, "Sandy! Hey, you look sick, and I don't mean that as a compliment! Come right on up!"

Sound of antithief locks clicking to neutral.
*Sick?*

He pondered the word with that strange detached portion of his awareness which was somehow isolated from his body at present, yet continued to function as though it were hung under a balloon trailed behind this fleshly carcass now ascending stairs not by legs alone but by arms clutching at the banister to stop from falling over. Legs race combines with arms race to make brain race and his brain was definitely racing. An invisible tight band had clamped on his head at the level of his temples. Pain made him giddy. He was double-focusing. When the door of Kate's apt opened he saw two of it, two of her in a shabby red wrap-around robe and brown sandals . . . but that wasn't so bad, because her face was eloquent of sympathy and worry and a double dose of that right now was to be welcomed. He was sweating rivers and imagined that he could have heard his feet squelching in his shoes but for the drumming of his heart, which also drowned out the question she shot at him.

Repeated louder, "I said, what the hell have you taken?"

He hunted down his voice, an elusive rasp in the caverns of a throat which had dried like a creek bed in a bad summer all the way to his aching lungs.

"No-uh-thing!"

"My God. In that case have you ever got it strong. Come quickly and lie down."

As swiftly and unreally as in a dream, with as much detachment as though he were viewing these events through the incurious eyes of old Bagheera, he witnessed himself being half-led, half-carried to a couch with a tan cover. In the Early Pleistocene he had sat on it to eat omelets and drink beer. It was a lovely sunny morning. He let his lids fall to exclude it, concentrated on making the best use of the air, which was tinted with a faint lemony fragrance.

She drew drapes against the sun by touching a button, then came in twilight to sit by him and hold his hand. Her fingers sought his pulse as expertly as a trained nurse.

"I knew you were straining too hard," she said.

"I still can't figure out why—but get the worst of it over and then you can tell me about it. If you like."

Time passed. The slam of his heart lessened. The sweat streaming from his pores turned from hot to cool, made his smart clothing clammy. He began to shiver and then, with no warning, found he was sobbing. Not weeping—his eyes were dry—but sobbing in huge gusting gasps, as though he were being cruelly and repeatedly punched in the belly by a fist that wasn't there.

At some stage she brought a thick woolen blanket, winterweight, and laid it on him. It had been years since he felt the rough bulk of such a fabric—now, one slept on a pressure bed, insulated by a directed layer of air. It evoked thousands of inchoate childhood memories. His hands clamped like talons to draw it over his head and his knees doubled into the fetal posture and he rolled on his side and miraculously was asleep.

When he awoke he felt curiously relaxed. He felt purged. In the . . . How long? He checked his watch. In the at-most hour since he dozed off, something more than calm had occupied his mind.

He formed a word silently and liked its taste.

Peace.

*But—!*

He sat up with a jerk. There was no peace—must be none—*could* be none! It was the wrong world for peace. At the G2S HQ someone from Tarnover must now be adding—correction, must already have added —two plus two. This person Sandy Locke "overlooked as kind of a national resource" might have been identified as the lost Nickie Haflinger!

He threw aside the blanket and stood up, belatedly realizing that Kate was nowhere to be seen and perhaps Bagheera had been left on guard and . . .

But his complicated thought dissolved under a wave of dizziness. Before he had taken as much as one pace away from the couch, he'd had to lean an outstretched hand against the wall.

Upon which came Kate's voice from the kitchen. "Good timing, Sandy. Or whatever your real name is. I just fixed some broth for you. Here."

It approached him in a steaming cup, which he accepted carefully by the less-hot handle. But he didn't look at it. He looked at her. She had changed into a blue and yellow summer shirt and knee-long cultoons also of yellow with the blue repeated in big Chinese ideograms across the seat. And he heard himself say, "What was that about my name?"

Thinking at the same time: *I was right. There is no room for peace in this modern world. It's illusory. One minute passes, and it's shattered.*

"You were babbling in your sleep," she said, sitting down on a patched old chair which he had expected her to throw out yet perversely had been retained. "Oh, please stop twitching your eyes like that! If you're wondering what's become of Bagheera, I took him downstairs; the girls said they'd look after him for a while. And if you're trying to spot a way of escape, it's too soon. Sit down and drink that broth."

Of the alternatives open, the idea of obeying seemed the most constructive. The instant he raised the cup he realized he was ravenous. His blood-sugar level must be terribly debased. Also he was still cold. The warmth of the savory liquid was grateful to him.

At long last he was able to frame a one-word question.

"Babbling . . . ?"

"I exaggerate. A lot of it made sense. That was why I told G2S you weren't here."

"*What?*" He almost let go of the cup.

"Don't tell me I did the wrong thing. Because I didn't. Ina got them to call me when you didn't show for your interview. I said no, of course I haven't seen him. He doesn't even like me, I told them. Ina would believe that. She's never realized that men can like me, because I'm all the things she didn't want her daughter to be, such as studious and intelligent and mainly plain. She never dug deeper into any man's

personality than the level she dealt with you on:
looks good, sounds good, feels good and I can use
him." She gave a harsh laugh, not quite over the
brink of bitterness.

He disregarded that comment. "What did I—uh—
let slip?" he demanded. And trembled a little as he
awaited the answer.

She hesitated. "First off . . . Well, I kind of got
the impression you never overloaded before. Can
that be true?"

He had been asked often by other people and had
always declared, "No, I guess I'm one of the lucky
ones." And had believed his claim to be truthful.
He had seen victims of overload; they hid away, they
gibbered when you tried to talk to them, they screamed
and struck out and smashed the furniture. These occasional bouts of shaking and cramp and cold, aborted
in minutes with one tranquilizer, couldn't be what
you'd call overload, not really!

But now he had sensed such violence in his own
body, he was aware that from outside his behavior
must have paralleled that of a member of his Toledo
congregation, and his former chief at the utopia
consultancy, and two of his colleagues at the three-vee
college, and . . . Others. Countless others. Trapped
in fight-or-flight mode when there was no way to
attain either solution.

He sighed, setting aside his cup, and drove himself
to utter an honest answer.

"Before, drugs have always straightened me in no
time. Today—well, somehow I didn't want to think
of taking anything . . . if you see what I mean."

"You never sweated it out before? Not even once?
Small wonder this is such a bad attack."

Nettled, he snapped back. "It happens to you all
the time, hm? That's why you're so knowledgeable?"

She shook her head, expression neutral. "No, it
never did happen to me. But I've never taken tranquilizers, either. If I feel like crying myself to sleep,
I do. Or if I feel like cutting classes because it's such
a beautiful day, I do that too. Ina overloaded when I

was about five. That was when she and Dad split up. After that she started riding constant herd on my mental state as well as her own. But I got this association fixed in my mind between the pills she took and the way she acted when she broke down—which wasn't pleasant—so I always used to pretend I'd swallowed what she gave me, then spit it out when I was alone. I got very good at hiding tablets and capsules under my tongue. And I guess it was the sensible thing to do. Most of my friends have folded up at least once, some of them two or three times beginning in grade school. And they all seem to be the ones who had—uh—special care taken of them by their folks. Care they'll never recover from."

Somehow a solitary fly had escaped the defenses of the kitchen. Sated, heavy on its wings, it came buzzing in search of a place to rest and digest. As though a saw blade's teeth were adding an underscore to the words, he felt his next question stressed by the sound.

"Do you mean the sort of thing Anti-Trauma does?"

"The sort of thing parents hire Anti-Trauma to do to their helpless kids!" There was venom in her tone, the first strong feeling he had detected in her. "But they were far from the first. They're the largest and best-advertised, but they weren't the pioneers. Ina and I were having a fight last year, and she said she wished she'd given me that type of treatment. Once upon a time I quite liked my mother. Now I'm not so sure."

He said with weariness born of his recent tormented self-reappraisal, "I guess they think they're doing the right and proper thing. They want their kids to be able to cope, and it's claimed to be a way of adjusting people to the modern world."

"That," Kate said, "is Sandy Locke talking. Whoever you are, I now know for sure that you're not him. He's a role you've put on. In your heart you know what Anti-Trauma does is monstrous . . . don't you?"

He hesitated only fractionally before nodding. "Yes. Beyond any hope of argument, it's evil."

"Thank you for leveling with me at last. I was sure nobody who's been through what you have could feel otherwise."

"What am I supposed to have been through?"

"Well, in your sleep you moaned about Tarnover, and since everybody knows what Tarnover is like—"

He jerked as though he had been kicked. "Wait, wait! That can't be true! Most people don't know Tarnover exists!"

She shrugged. "Oh, you know what I mean. I've met several of their so-called graduates. People who could have been individuals but instead have been standardized—filed down—straitjacketed!"

"But that's incredible!"

It was her turn to be confused and startled. "What?"

"That you've met all these people from Tarnover."

"No, it's not. UMKC is crawling with them. Turn any wet stone. Oh, I exaggerate, but there are five or six."

The sensations he had been victim of when he arrived threatened to return. His mouth dried completely, as though it had been swabbed with cottonwool; his heart pounded; he instantly wanted to find a bathroom. But he fought back with all the resources at his command. Steadying his voice was as exhausting as climbing a mountain.

"So where are they in hiding?"

"Nowhere. Stop by the Behavioral Sciences Lab and— Say, Sandy!" She rose anxiously to her feet. "You'd better lie down again and talk about this later. Obviously it hasn't penetrated that you're suffering from shock, just as surely as if you'd walked away from a veetol crash."

"I do know!" he barked. "But there was someone from Tarnover sitting in with the G2S selection board, and if they think to make a physical check of this place . . . They thought of calling you up, didn't they?"

She bit her lip, eyes scanning his face in search of clues that were not to be found.

"Why are you so afraid?" she ventured. "What did they do to you?"

"It's not so much what they did. It's what they will do if they catch me."

"Because of something you did to them? What?"

"Quit cold after they'd spent thirty million on trying to turn me into the sort of shivver you were just describing."

During the next few seconds he was asking himself how he could ever have been so stupid as to say that. And with surprise so terrific it was almost worse than what had gone before he then discovered he hadn't been stupid after all.

For she turned and walked to the window to peer out at the street between the not-completely-closed curtains. She said, "Nobody in sight who *looks* suspicious. What's the first thing they'll do if they figure out who you are—deevee your code? I mean the one you've been using at G2S."

"I let that out too?" he said in renewed horror.

"You let a lot out. Must have been stacking up in your head for years. Well?"

"Uh—yes, I guess so."

She checked her watch and compared it with an old-fashioned digital clock that was among the few ornaments she had not disposed of. "There's a flight to Los Angeles in ninety minutes. I've used it now and then; it's one that you can get on without booking. By tonight we could be at—"

He put his hands to his head, giddy again. "You're going too fast for me."

"Fast it's got to be. What can you do apart from being a systems rash? Everything?"

"I . . ." He took an enormous grip on himself. "Yes, or damn nearly."

"Fine. So come on."

He remained irresolute. "Kate, surely you're not going to—"

"Forget about school next year, abandon friends and home and mother, and Bagheera?" Her tone was scathing. "Shit, no. But how are you going to make out if you don't have a usable code to prop you up while you're building another they don't know about? I guess that must be how you work the trick, hm?"

"Uh—yes, more or less."

"So move, will you? My code is in good standing, and the girls downstairs will mind Bagheera for a week as willingly as for an evening, and apart from that all I have to do is leave a note for Ina saying I've gone to stay with friends." She seized the nearest phone and began to compose the code for her mother's mail-store reel.

"But I can't possibly ask you to—"

"You're not asking, I'm offering. You damn well better grab the chance. Because if you don't you'll be as good as dead, won't you?" She waved him silent and spoke the necessary words to mislead Ina.

When she had finished he said, "Not as good as. Worse than." And followed her out the door.


## IN THE BEGINNING WAS THE HERD

At Tarnover they explained it all so reasonably!

Of course everybody had to be given a personal code! How else could the government do right by its citizens, keep track of the desires, tastes, preferences, purchases, commitments and above all location of a continentful of mobile, free individuals?

Granted, there was an alternative approach. But would you want to see it adopted here? Would you like to find your range of choice restricted to the point where the population became predictable in its collective behavior?

So don't dismiss the computer as a new type of fetters. Think of it rationally, as the most liberating device ever invented, the only tool capable of serving the multifarious needs of modern man.

Think of it, for a change, as *him*. For example, think of the friendly mailman who makes certain your letters reach you no matter how frequently you move or over what vast distances. Think of the loyal secretary who always pays your bills when they come due, regardless of what distractions may be on your mind. Think of the family doctor who's on hand at the hospital when you fall sick, with your entire medical history in focus to guide the unknown specialist. Or if you want to be less personal and more social, think of computers as the cure for the monotony of primitive mass-production methods. As long ago as the sixties of last century it became economic to turn out a hundred items in succession from an assembly line, of which each differed subtly from the others. It cost the salary of an extra programer and—naturally— a computer to handle the task . . . but everybody was using computers anyhow, and their capacity was so colossal the additional data didn't signify.

(When he pondered the subject, he always found himself flitting back and forth between present and past tense; there was that sensitive a balance between what had been expected, indeed hoped for, and what had eventuated. It seemed that some of the crucial decisions were still being made although generations had elapsed since they were formulated.)

The movement pattern of late twentieth-century America was already the greatest population flow in history. More people moved annually at vacation time than all the armies led by all the world's great conquerors put together, plus the refugees they drove from home. What a relief, then, to do no more than punch your code into a public terminal—or, since 2005, into the nearest veephone, which likely was in the room where you were sitting—and explain *once* that because you'd be in Rome the next two weeks, or surfing at Bondi, or whatever, your house should be watched by the police more keenly than usual, and your mail should be held for so many days unless marked "urgent," in which case it should be redirected to so-and-so, and the garbage truck needn't come by on its next weekly round, and—and so forth. The muscles of the nation could be felt flexing with joyous new freedom.

Except . . .

The theory was and always had been: this is the thing the solid citizen has no need to worry about.

Important, later all-important question: what about the hollow citizen?

Because, liberated, the populace took off like so many hot-air balloons.

"Okay, let's!"—move, take that job in another state, go spend all summer by the lake, operate this winter out of a resort in the Rockies, commute by veetol over a thousand miles, see how island living suits us and forget the idea if it's a bust . . .

Subtler yet, more far-reaching: let's trade wives and children on a monthly rota, good for the kids to get used to multiple parents because after all you've been married twice and I've been married three times, and let's quit the city fast before the boss finds out it was me who undercut him on that near-the-knuckle deal, and let's move out of shouting distance of that twitch you were obsessed with so you can cool down, and let's go someplace where the word isn't out on the mouth-to-mouth circuit that you're skew else you'll never have the chance to give up men, and let's see if it's true about those fine dope connections in Topeka and let's—let's—let's . . .

Plus, all the time and everywhere, the sneaking suspicion: *don't look now, I think we're being followed.*


Two years after they spliced the home-phone service into the continental net the system was screaming in silent agony like the limbs of a marathon runner who knows he can shatter the world's best time provided he can make the final mile.

But, they asked at Tarnover in the same oh-so-reasonable tones, what else could we have done?

## LET'S ALL BE DIFFERENT
## SAME AS ME

"That," Freeman said thoughtfully, "sounds like a question you still have found no answer to."

"Oh, shut up. Put me back in regressed mode, for God's sake. I know you don't call this torture—I know you call it stimulus-response evaluation—but it feels like torture all the same and I'd rather get it over and done with. Since there isn't an alternative."

Freeman scanned his dials and screens.

"Unfortunately it's not safe to regress you again at the moment. It will take a day or so for the revived effects of your overload at KC to flush out of your system. It was the most violent experience you've undergone as an adult. Extremely traumatizing."

"I'm infinitely obliged for the data. I suspected so, but it's nice to have it confirmed by your machines."

"Sweedack. Just as it's good to have what the machines tell us confirmed by your conscious personality."

"Are you a hockey 'fish?"

"Not in the sense of following one particular team, but the game does offer a microcosm of modern society, doesn't it? Group commitment, chafing against restrictive rules, enactment of display-type aggression more related to status than hate or fear, plus the use of banishment as a means of enforcing conformity. To which you can add the use of the most primitive weapon, the club, albeit stylized."

"So that's how you view society. I've been wondering. How trivial! How oversimplified! You mention restrictive rules . . . but rules only become restrictive when they're obsolescent. We've revised our rules at every stage of our social evolution, ever since we learned to talk, and we're still making new ones that suit us better. We'll carry right on unless fools like you contrive to stop us!"

Leaning forward, Freeman cupped his sharp chin in his right palm.

"We're into an area of fundamental difference of opinion," he said after a pause. "I put it to you that no rule consciously invented by mankind since we acquired speech has force equivalent to those inherited from perhaps fifty, perhaps a hundred thousand generations of evolution in the wild state. I further suggest that the chief reason why modern society is in turmoil is that for too long we claimed that our special human talents could exempt us from the heritage written in our genes."

"It's because you and those like you think in strict binary terms—'either-or'—as though you've decided machines are our superiors and you want to imitate them, that I have to believe you not only don't have the right answer but can never find it. You treat human beings on the black-box principle. Cue this reflex, that response ensues; cue another and get something different. There's no room in your cosmos for what you call special talents."

"Come, now." Freeman gave a faint, gaunt smile. "You're talking in terms at least two generations old. Have you deleted from your mind all awareness of how sophisticated our methodology has become since the 1960s?"

"And have you suppressed all perception of how it's rigidified, like medieval theology, with your collective brilliance concentrated on finding means to abolish any view not in accord with yours? Don't bother to answer that. I'm experiencing the reality of your black-box approach. You're testing me to destruction, not as an individual but as a sample that may or may not match your idealized model of a person. If I don't react as predicted, you'll revise the model and try again. But you won't care about *me*."

"*Sub specie aeternitatis*," Freeman said, smiling anew, "I find no evidence for believing that I matter any more than any other human being who ever existed or who ever will exist. Nor does any of them matter more than I do. We're elements in a process that began in the dim past and will develop through who knows what kind of future."

"What you say reinforces my favorite image of Tarnover: a rotting carcass, pullulating with indistinguishable maggots, whose sole purpose in life is to grab more of the dead flesh more quickly than their rivals."

"Ah, yes. The conqueror worm. I find it curious that you should have turned out to be of a religious bent, given the cynicism with which you exploited the trappings of your minister's role at Toledo."

"But I'm not religious. Chiefly because the end point of religious faith is your type of blind credulity."

"Excellent. A paradox. Resolve it for me." Freeman leaned back, crossing his thin legs and setting his thin fingers tip to tip with elbows on the side of his chair.

"You believe that man is comprehensible to himself, or at any rate you act as though you do. Yet you refer constantly to processes that began back then and will continue for ever and ever amen. What you're trying to do is step out of the flow of process, just as superstitious savages did—do!—by invoking divine forces not confined by human limitations. You give lip service to the process, but you won't accept it. On the contrary, you strive to dominate it. And that can't be done unless you stand outside it."

"Hmm. You're an atavism, aren't you? You have the makings of a schoolman! But that doesn't save you from being wrong. We are trying not to want to step out of the flow, because we've recognized the nature of the process and its inevitability. The best that can be hoped for is to direct it into the most tolerable channels. What we're doing at Tarnover is possibly the most valuable service any small group ever performed for mankind at large. We're diagnosing our social problems and then deliberately setting out to create the person who can solve them."

"And how many problems have been solved to date?"

"We haven't yet exterminated ourselves."

"You claim credit for that? I knew you had gall, but this is fantastic! You could just as well argue that in the case of human beings it took the invention of nuclear weapons to trigger the life-saving response most species show when faced with the fangs and claws of a tougher rival."

"That in fact appears to be true."

"If you believed that you wouldn't be working so hard to universalize the new conformity."

"Is that a term you coined yourself?"

"No, I borrowed it from someone whose writings aren't particularly loved at Tarnover: Angus Porter."

"Well, it's a resounding phrase. But does it mean anything?"

"I wouldn't bother to answer except that it's better to be talking in present time than sitting back inside my head while you interrogate my memory . . . because you know damned well what it means. Look at yourself. You're part of it. It's a century old. It began when for the first time people in a wealthy country started tailoring other cultures to their own lowest common denominator: people with money to spend who were afraid of strange food, who told the restaurateur to serve hamburgers instead of enchiladas or fish and chips instead of couscous, who wanted something pretty to hang on the wall at home and not what some local artist had sunk his heart and soul in, who found it too hot in Rio and too cold in Zermatt and insisted on going there anyhow."

"We're to be blamed because that's how people reacted long before Tarnover was founded?" Freeman shook his head. "I remain unconvinced."

"But this is the concept you started with, the one you've clung to! You walked straight into a trap with no way out. You wanted to develop a generalized model of mankind, and this was the handiest to build on: more general than pre–World War I European royalty despite the fact that that was genuinely cosmopolitan, and more homogeneous than the archetypal peasant culture, which is universal but individualized. What you've wound up with is a schema where the people who obey those ancient evolutionary principles you cite so freely—as for example by striking roots in one place that will last a lifetime—are regarded by their fellows as 'rather odd.' It won't be long before they're persecuted. And then how will you justify your claim that the message in the genes overrides consciously directed modern change?"

"Are you talking about the so-called economists, who won't take advantage of the facilities our technology offers? More fool them; they choose to be stunted."

"No, I'm talking about the people who are surrounded by such a plethora of opportunity they dither and lapse into anxiety neurosis. Friends and neighbors rally round to help them out, explain the marvels of today and show them how, and go away feeling virtuous. But if tomorrow they have to repeat the process, and the day after, and the day after that . . . ? No, from the patronizing stage to the persecuting stage has always been a very short step."

After a brief silence Freeman said, "But it's easy to reconcile the views I really hold, as distinct from the distorted versions you're offering. Mankind originated as a nomadic species, following game herds and moving from one pasture to another with the seasons. Mobility of similar order has been reintegrated into our culture, at least in the wealthy nations. Yet there are advantages to living in an urban society, like sanitation, easy communications, tolerably cheap transportation . . . And thanks to our ingenuity with computers, we haven't had to sacrifice these conveniences."

"One might as well claim that the tide which rubs pebbles smooth on a beach is doing the pebbles a service because being round is prettier than being jagged. It's of no concern to a pebble what shape it is. But it's very important to a person. And every surge of your tide is reducing the variety of shapes a human being can adopt."

"Your extended metaphors do you credit," Freeman said. "But I detect, and so do my monitors, that you're straining after them like a man at a party who's desperately pretending that he's not quite drunk. Today's session is due to end in a few minutes; I'll cut it short and renew the interrogation in the morning."

## THE RIGHT-ON THING FOR THE
## WRONG-OFF REASON

The experience was exactly like riding in a car when the driver, seeing ahead a patch of bad road with a lot of potholes, tramps hard on the accelerator in preference to slowing down. There was a drumming sound, and certain landmarks beside the route were noticeable, but essentially it was a matter of being *there then* and subsequently *here now*.

Just about enough time was perceived as having elapsed for the passenger to realize *he* wouldn't have traveled so fast on such a lousy bumpy bit of road . . . and ask himself why not, since it gave excellent results.

Then, very abruptly, it stopped.

"Where the hell have you brought me?"

Looking around a room with rough brown walls, an old-style spring bed, carpet on the floor which wasn't even fitted, a view of sunset through broad shallow windows that distracted him before he could enumerate other objects like chairs and a table and so forth. They registered as belonging in the sort of junk store whose owner would label as ANTIQUE anything older than himself.

"You poor shivver," Kate said. She was there too. "You have one hell of a bad case. I asked you, did you think it was a good idea to head for Lap-of-the-Gods? And you said yes."

He was sitting on a chair which happened to be near him. He closed his hands on its arms until his knuckles were almost white. With much effort he said, "Then I was crazy. I thought of coming to a town like this long ago and realized it was the first place they'd think of looking."

Theoretically, for somone trying to mislay a previous identity, no better spot could be found on the continent than this, or some other of the settlements created by refugees from Northern California after the Great Bay Quake. Literally millions of traumatized fugitives had straggled southward. For years they survived in tents and shanties, dependent on federal handouts because they were too mentally disturbed to work for a living and in most cases afraid to enter a building with a solid roof for fear it would crash down and kill them. They were desperate for a sense of stability, and sought it in a thousand irrational cults. Confidence-tricksters and fake evangelists found them easy prey. Soon it was a tourist lure to visit their settlements on Sunday and watch the running battles between adherents of rival—but equally lunatic—beliefs. Insurance extra.

There had been nothing comparable in western civilization since the Lisbon Earthquake shook the foundations of Christianity across half of Europe in 1755.

Now some semblance of regular government was in effect and had been for a quarter-century. But the scars left by the quake were cicatrized into the names of the new cities: Insecurity, Precipice, Protempore, Waystation, Transience . . . and Lap-of-the-Gods.

Inevitably, because these were new cities in a nation that had lacked a frontier these hundred years, they had attracted the restless, the dissident, sometimes the criminal elements from elsewhere. Up-to-date maps showed them dotted like accidental inkblots from Monterey to San Diego and inland over a belt almost two hundred miles wide. They constituted a nation within a nation. Tourists could still come here. But most often they decided not to. It felt more like home in Istanbul.


"Sandy!" Sitting down in a chair facing him, Kate tapped his knee. "You're out of it so don't slip back. Talk! And this time make sense. What makes you so terrified of Tarnover?"

"If they catch me they'll do what they meant to do in the first place. What I fled from."

"That being—?"

"They'll make me over in a version of myself I don't approve."

"That happens to everybody all the time. The lucky ones win, the others suffer. There's something deeper. Something worse."

He gave a weary nod. "Yes, there is. My conviction that if they get the chance to try they'll do it, and I won't have a hope in hell of fighting back."

There was a dull silence. At last Kate nodded, her face grave.

"I got there. You'd know what was being done to you. And later you'd be fascinated by the tape of your reactions."

With a humorless laugh he said, "I think you lie about your age. Nobody could be that cynical so young. Of course you're right."

Another pause, this time full of gray depression. She broke it by saying, "I wish you'd been in a fit state to talk before we left KC. You must have been just going through the motions. But never mind. I think we came to a right place. If you've been avoiding towns like Lap-of-the-Gods for—what is it?—six years, then they won't immediately start combing California for you."

It was amazing how calmly he took that, he thought. To hear his most precious secret mentioned in passing . . . Above all, it was nearly beyond belief that someone finally was on his side.

Hence the calmness? Very probably.

"Are we in a hotel?" he inquired.

"Sort of. They call it an open lodge. You get a room and then fend for yourself. There's a kitchen through there"—a vague gesture toward the door of the bedroom—"and there's no limit on how long you can stay. Nor any questions asked when you check in, luckily."

"You used your code?"

"Did you expect me to use yours? I have lots of credit. I'm not exactly an economist, but I'm blessed with simple tastes."

"In that case the croakers will come calling any moment."

"Shit on that. You're thinking in contemporary terms. Check into a hotel, ten seconds later the fact's on file at Canaveral, right? Not here, Sandy. They still process credit by hand. It could be a week before I'm debbed for this room."

Hope he had almost ceased to believe in burgeoned in his eyes. "Are you sure?"

"Hell, no. Today could be the day the desk clerk makes up his bills. All I'm saying is it isn't automatic. You know about this town, don't you?"

"I know about so many paid-avoidance areas . . ." He rubbed his forehead with the heel of his hand. "Is this one that's settled down to about a 1960 level?"

"I guess that would be fairly close. I haven't been here before, though I have been to Protempore, and I'm told the two are comparable. That's why I hit on it. I didn't want to take you anywhere I might be recognized."

She leaned toward him. "Now let's concentrate, shall we? The dobers *aren't* howling at the door, and it's long past time for me to learn the rest of your history. You seem to have spent a long while at Tarnover. Think you're fettered by a posthypnotic?"

He drew a deep breath. "No. I wondered about that myself and concluded that I can't be. Hypnosis isn't one of their basic tools. And if it were, the command would have been activated long ago, when I first quit the place. Of course, by now they may well use posthypnotics to stop others copying my example. . . . But what I'm hamstrung by is in myself."

Kate bit her lower lip with small and very white teeth. She said at length, "Funny. Meeting those grads from Tarnover that I mentioned, I felt sure they'd been treated with some quasi-hypnotic technique. They make my skin crawl, you know. They give the impression that they've learned everything, they could never possibly be wrong. Kind of inhuman. So my

assumption has always been that Tarnover is some
sort of behavioral-intensive education center for bright
deprived kids, where they use extreme forms of stimulation as an inducement to learn. Zero-distraction
environments—drugs, maybe—*I* don't know."

He picked on one key word. "You said . . . deprived?"

"Mm-hm." With a nod. "I noticed that at once.
Either they were orphaned, or they made no bones
about hating their parents and family. It gave them a
curious solidarity. Almost like White House aides. Or
maybe more like the Jesus bit: 'Who is my father
and my mother?' " She spread her hands.

"When did you first hear about Tarnover?"

"Oh, it was news when I graduated from high
school and went to UMKC four years ago. There was
no publicity, at least not the drums-and-trumpets type.
More kind of, 'We got the answer to Akadiemgorodok
—we think.' Low-key stuff."

"Shit, but they're clever!" he said savagely. "If I
didn't hate them I'd have to admire them."

"What?"

"It's the ideal compromise. You just described what
they obviously want the world to think about Tarnover; how did you put it? An intensive education
center for bright deprived kids? Very admirable!"

"And it isn't?" Her sharp eyes rested on his face
like sword points.

"No. It's where they're breeding the elite to run the
continent."

"I wish," she said, "I didn't suspect you of being
literal."

"Me too! But . . . Look, you're in power. Think
what's the most dangerous thing about a kid with no
parents and a high IQ."

She stared at him for a long moment, then suggested, "He won't look at things the way the men in
charge do. But he could be more right than they
are."

He slapped his thigh in delight. "Kate, you impress
the hell out of me! You've hit on it. Who are the

people recruited to Tarnover and Crediton Hill and the rest of the secret centers? Why, those who might invent sides of their own if the government doesn't enroll them on its side while they're still tractable. Yes, *yes*! But on top of that— Say, did you check this room for bugs?"

The exclamation was overdue; what had become of his customary caution? He was half out of his chair before she said with a trace of scorn, "Of course I did! And I have a damned good bug detector. One of my boyfriends built it for me. He's a post-grad in the UMKC school of industrial espionage. So relax and keep talking."

He sank back in relief and mopped his forehead.

"You said these Tarnover trainees you've met are mostly in the Behavioral Sciences Lab. Any of them in biology?"

"I met a couple but not at UMKC. Over the state line in Lawrence. Or they were. I loathed them and didn't keep in touch."

"Did they ever mention the pride and joy of Tarnover—the crippled kids they build with genius IQ?"

"*What?*"

"I met the first of them, who was called Miranda. Of course she was not a genius, so they counted it small loss when she died at four. But techniques have improved. The last example I heard about before I I quit still couldn't walk, or even eat, but she could use a computer remote with the best of us and sometimes she was quicker than her teachers. They specialize in girls, naturally. Men, embryonically speaking, are imperfect women, as you know."

There was never much color in Kate's face. In the next few seconds what little there was drained away, leaving the flesh of her forehead and cheeks as pale as candlewax.

In a tight, thin voice she said, "Give me the details. There must be a lot more to it than that."

He complied. When he had recited the full story, she shook her head with an incredulous expression.

"But they must be insane. We need a rest from

ultrarapid change, not an extra dose of it. Half the population has given up trying to cope, and the other is punch-drunk without knowing it."

"Sweedack," he said dully. "But of course their defense is that whether or not it's done here, it's bound to be done somewhere by somebody, so . . ." An empty shrug.

"That's okay. Maybe the people who come along second will profit from our example; maybe they won't repeat all our mistakes. But . . . Don't the people at Tarnover realize they could reduce our society to hysterics?"

"Apparently not. It's a prime example of Porter's Law, isn't it? They've carried over the attitudes of the arms race into the age of the brain race. They're trying to multiply incommensurables. You must have heard that applying minimax strategy to the question of rearmament invariably results in the conclusion that you must rearm. And their spiritual ancestors kept right on doing so even after H-bombs had written a factor of infinity into the equation of military power. They sought security by piling up more and more *irrelevant* weapons. At Tarnover today they're making the analogous error. They claim to be hunting for the genetic element of wisdom, and I'm sure most of them believe that's what they're really doing. They aren't, of course. What they're on the track of is the 200-plus IQ. And intelligence and wisdom aren't the same."

He clenched his fists. "The prospect terrifies me! They must be stopped. Somehow and at any cost. But I've been struggling for six years to think of a way, hoping that the thirty million they lavished on me won't go completely to waste, and I haven't achieved one goddamned thing!"

"Are you held back by fear of being—well, punished?"

He started. "You're sharp, aren't you? I guess I am!"

"Just for opting out?"

"Oh, I've committed a slew of federal crimes. Used

false identities, obtained a notary's seal by fraud, entered forged data in the continental net . . . Just take it for granted they could find plenty of reasons for me to go to jail."

"I'm surprised they let you get away in the first place."

"But they don't compel where they can persuade. They're not stupid. They're aware that one volunteer working his guts out on their behalf is worth a score of reluctant conscripts."

Gazing past him into nowhere, she said, "I see. Thinking you were trustworthy, they gave you too much rope. So when you did escape, what did you do?"

He summarized his careers.

"Hm! If nothing else, you took in a broad cross-section of society. What made you settle for a post at G2S after all that?"

"I needed to gain access to some restricted areas of the net. In particular I had to find out whether my code was still valid. Which it was. But now that they're closing on my identity at KC it's high time I made one last use of it and rewrote myself again. It costs, of course, but I have some won Delphi tickets to collect on, and I'm sure I can adopt a well-paid profession for the time being. Don't they go big for mystical things out here? I can run computerized horoscopes, and I can offer gene counseling —I think you can do that in California without a state license—and . . . Oh, anything that involves use of a computer terminal."

She gave him a level look.

"But you're in a paid-avoidance area," she said.

"Hell, so I am!" Suddenly he felt very much alone, unspeakably vulnerable. "Does the avoidance go deep? I mean even if you can't use any public phone to tap the net, do they forcibly exclude computers?"

"No, but you have to make special application to get time. And there's more cash in circulation than anywhere else on the continent, and veephone service is restricted: you can't dial out to the rest of the country, you have to cable and ask to be called back. Things like that."

"But if I can't rewrite myself, what am I going to do?" He was on his feet, shaking.

"Sandy!" She rose also, confronting him with a glare. "Have you never tried to outface the enemy?"

"What?" He blinked at her.

"I get the impression that every time one of your schemes went wrong, you abandoned it—and the identity that went with it—and switched to something else. Maybe that's why you've always failed. You've relied on this trick talent of yours to bail you out of trouble instead of seeing through what you started. The overload you've suffered today ought to be a warning to you. There's a limit to the number of times you can revise your personality. There's a limit to the load you can pile on your powers of reasoning. Your body just told you, loud and clear, you've gone too far at last."

"Oh, shit . . ." His voice was full of misery. "In principle I'm certain you're right. But is there any alternative?"

"Sure I have an alternative. One of the best things about a paid-avoidance area is you can still get manual cooking. I don't know what it's like here, but at Protempore it was delicious. We go find a good restaurant and a jug of wine."

## FENCED BUT NOT FOILED

*Inter alia* the Handbook of the National Association of Players at the Game of Fencing states:

The game may be played manually or electronically.

The field shall consist of 101 parallel equidistant lines coded AA, AB, AC . . . BA, BB, BC . . . to EA (omitting the letter I), crossed at 90° by 71 parallel equidistant lines 01 to 71.

The object is to enclose with triangles a greater number of coordinate points than the opponent.

The players shall toss or draw for red or blue; red begins.

At each turn each player shall claim two points, one by visibly marking it in the field, the other by entering its coordinates in a list concealed from the opponent (but subject to scrutiny by a referee in match play).

After at least 10 points (5 red, 5 blue) have been visibly claimed, having claimed his visible point for that turn either player may forego the option of claiming a concealed point and attempt to enclose a triangle by connecting three of his visibly claimed points. Prior to doing so he must require the opponent to enter his concealed points in the field. He may then enclose any triangle that does not include a point claimed by the opponent. A point claimed in a concealed list, which proves on inspection to have been claimed visibly by the opponent, shall be deleted from the concealed list. A triangle may enclose a point claimed by the same color. A point once enclosed may not be claimed. If a player claims such a point in error he shall forfeit both the visible and the concealed point due on that turn.

If a player finds, when the opponent's concealed points are entered in the field, he can enclose no valid triangle, he shall at once enter all his own concealed points, after which play shall proceed normally.

All triangles must have sides at least 2 units long, i.e. two adjacent coordinates cannot serve as apices of the same triangle, though they may serve as apices of two triangles of the same or different colors. No coordinate may serve as the apex of more than one triangle. No triangle may enclose a point enclosed by another triangle. A coordinate claimed by the opponent which lies on a horizontal or vertical line between apices of a proposed triangle shall be deemed included and renders the triangle invalid. A coordinate claimed by the opponent which lies on a true diagonal (45°) between apices of a proposed triangle shall be deemed excluded.

Scores shall be calculated in terms of coordinate

points enclosed by valid triangles. An approved device shall be employed such that as each triangle is validly enclosed its apices may be entered into the memory store of the device and upon entry of the third apex the device shall unambiguously display the number of points enclosed. It shall be the responsibility of the player to keep accurate record of his cumulative score, which he shall not conceal from the opponent, except in matches played for stake money or on which there has been wagering or by mutual agreement of the players, when the cumulative score may be kept by a referee or electronically or mechanically, but in such cases there shall be no grounds for appeal by either player against the score shown at the conclusion or at any stage of the game.

It is customary but not obligatory for any game in which one player's score exceeds that of the other by 100 points to be regarded as lost and won.

## METONYMIA

According to the instrument display the metabolic level of the subject remained satisfactory; however, his voice was weakening and his reaction times were slowing. It was becoming necessary to update him from regressed mode at ever-shorter intervals. Very probably this was due to the low-stimulus environment, excessively low for someone whose ability to tolerate rapid and extreme change had been graphically documented over the past several weeks. Accordingly Freeman indented for some equipment to ameliorate the situation: a large projection-type three-vee screen, an electrotoner and a personifactor which would give the illusion of one, two or three other people watching.

Waiting for the new machinery to be delivered, though, he perforce had to continue in the former manner, conversing with the subject in present time.

"You're a good fencing player, I believe."

"Care for a game to break the monotony?" A ghost of old defiance tinted the words.

"I'm a poor player myself; it would be a mismatch. But why did fencing appeal to you rather than, say, go, or even chess?"

"Chess has been automated," was the prompt reply. "How long is it since a world champion has done without computer assistance?"

"I see. Yes, I understand nobody has yet written a competent fencing program. Did you try it? You had adequate capacity."

"Oh, using a program to play chess is work. Games are for fun. I guess I could have spoiled fencing, if I'd spent a year or two on the job. I didn't want to."

"You wanted to retain it as a nondeterminate analogy of your own predicament, because of its overtones of captivity, enclosure, secure ground and the like—is that it?"

"Think of it in any way you choose. I say the hell with it. One of the worst things wrong with people like you is inability to enjoy themselves. You don't like the idea that there are processes that can't be analyzed. You're the lineal descendant, on the sociological side of the tree, of the researchers who pithed cats and dogs because even their personalities were too complex for comfort. Which is fine for studying synapse formation but no damned good for studying cats."

"You're a holist."

"I might have guessed that sooner or later you'd turn that word into an insult."

"On the contrary. Having studied, as you rightly say, the separate components of the nervous system, we finally feel we're equipped to attack their interaction. We declined to accept personality as a datum. Your attitude resembles that of a man content to gaze at a river without being interested in the springs and the watershed and the seasonal variations in rainfall and the silt it's carrying along."

"I notice you make no mention of fish in the river. Nor of taking a drink from it."

"Will watching from the bank inform you why there are no fish this year?"

"Will counting the liters-per-minute tell you why it's beautiful?"

Freeman sighed. "Always we reach the same sort of deadlock, don't we? I regard your attitude as complementary to mine. You on the other hand deny that mine has any validity. *Impasse.*"

"Wrong. Or at best only half right. Your problem's this: you want to file my attitude as a subcategory of yours, and it doesn't work because the whole can't be included in the part."


## GAME FOR ANYTHING

Venturing out on the streets of Lap-of-the-Gods, he felt a little like someone raised in an inhibited family braving a naturist beach, but the sensation did not last long. This was a surprisingly attractive little town. The architecture was miscellaneous because it had been thrown together in a hurry, yet the urgency had resulted in a basic unity enhanced now by reddish evening sunlight.

The sidewalks were crowded, the roadways not. The only vehicles they saw were bicycles and electric buses. There were many trees, bushes and flowering shrubs. Most of the people seemed to care little about dress; they wore uninspiring garments in blue, buff and tan, and some were shabby. But they smiled a lot and said hello to someone—even to himself and Kate, strangers—every half-dozen paces.

Shortly they came across a restaurant modeled on a Greek taverna, with tables on a terrace under a roof made of vines trained along poles and wires. Three or four games of fencing were in progress, each watched by a group of intent kibitzers.

"That's an idea," he muttered to Kate, halting. "Maybe I could pick up a bit of credit if they play for money."

"Are you a good player? Sorry. Stupid question. But I'm told competition here is stiff."

"But they're playing manually. Look!"

"Does that have to make them poor players?"

He gazed at her for a long moment. Eventually he said, "Know something? I think you're good for me."

"So I should hope," she answered tartly, and pulled the same face he'd seen at their first meeting, wrinkling her nose and raising her upper lip so her front teeth showed like a rabbit's. "Moreover I knew you liked me before you knew it, which is kind of rare and to be treasured. Come on, let's add fencing hustler to your list of occupations."

They found a table where they could watch the play while eating pizza and sipping a rough local wine, and about the time they finished their meal one of the nearest players realized he had just allowed his opponent to notch up the coveted hundred-point margin with a single slender triangle running almost the full width of the field. Swearing at his own incompetence, he resigned and strode away fuming.

The winner, a fat bald once-fair man in a faded pink singlet, complained to anybody who cared to listen, "But he didn't have to be such a sore loser, did he? I mean did he?" Appealing to Kate, who smiled and shook her head.

"And I can spare at least another hour before I have to go, and—Hey, would either of you care to take over? I noticed you were watching."

The tone and manner were unmistakable. Here was a full-timer, counterpart of those chess hustlers who used to sit around anonymously pretending to be no good until someone was fool enough to stake money on a game.

*Well, it's a way in. . . .*

"Sure I'll play you, and be glad to. This is Kate, by the way, and I'm—" He hoped the hesitation would go unremarked; one could convert to Alexander and since Kate was accustomed . . . "I'm Sandy."

"I'm Hank. Sit down. Want to think about odds? I'm kind of competent, as you may have gathered." The bald man tailed the words with a toothy grin.

"Let's play level, argue about odds when we have grounds for debate."

"Fine, fine! Would you care to let—uh—a little cash ride on the outcome?" A glint of greed lighted Hank's eyes.

"Cash? Uh . . . Well, we're fresh into town, so you'd have to take scrip, but if that's okay—? Good. Shall we say a hundred?"

"By all means," Hank purred, and rubbed his hands under the table. "And I think we ought to play the first one or two games blitz-tempo."

The first game aborted almost at once, a not uncommon happening. Attempting on successive turns to triangulate, both found it was impossible, and according to custom rather than rule agreed to try again. The second game was close and Hank lost. The third was even closer and he still lost, and the expiry of his hour gave him an excuse to depart in annoyance, two hundred the poorer. By then many more customers had arrived, some to play—a dozen games were now in progress—and some preferring to kibitz and assess a stranger's form. One of the newcomers, a plump girl carrying a baby, challenged the victor and went down in twelve turns. Two of the other watchers, a thin young black and a thin elderly white, whistled loudly, and the latter promptly took the girl's place.

*What is it that feels so weird about this evening . . . ? Got it. I'll be damned. I'm not playing Lazarus's game, or even Sandy Locke's; I'm playing mine, and I'm far better than I ever dreamed!*

The sensation was giddying. He seemed to be walking up steps inside his head until he reached a place where there was nothing but pure white light, and it showed him as plainly as though he were telepathic what his opponent was planning. Potential triangles outlined themselves on the board as though their sides were neon bars. The elderly man succumbed in twenty-eight turns, not beaten but content to resign on a margin of fifty points he was unlikely to make up, and ceded his place to the thin young black saying, "Morris, I think we finally found someone who can give you a hard time."

Faint warning bells began to sound at that stage, but he was having too much fun to pay attention.

The newcomer was good. He obtained a margin of twenty on the first triangulation and concentrated on preserving it. He did so for another six turns, growing more and more smug. But on the fifteenth turn his smugness vanished. He had tried another triangulation, and when the concealed points were entered there was nothing valid, and he had to post his own concealed list, and on the next turn found himself cut out of an entire corner worth ninety points. His face turned sour and he scowled at the score machine as though suspecting it of lying. Then he gathered his resources in an effort to regain the lost lead.

He failed. The game went to its bitter end and left him fourteen down. Whereupon he thrust his way through the bystanders—by now a couple of dozen strong—and stormed off, slamming fist into palm in impotent fury.

"I'll be damned," said the elderly man. "Well, *well!* Look—uh—Sandy, I didn't make too good a showing against you, but believe it or not I'm the area secretary of the Fencing Association, and if you can use a light-pen and screen as well as you use a manual board . . . !" Beaming, he made an all-embracing gesture. "I take it you have club qualifications where you come from? If you intend to shift your residential commitment to Lap-of-the-Gods, I can predict who'll win the winter championships. You and Morris together would make an unstoppable—"

"You mean that was *Morris Fagin?*"

All around the group of onlookers there were puzzled reactions: *this poker claims he didn't know?*

"Sandy," Kate murmured in the nick of time, "it's

getting late. Even later for us than it is for these nice people."

"I—uh . . . Yes, you're right. Excuse us, friends; we came a long way today." He rose, collecting the grimy unfamiliar bills which had accumulated on the corner of the table. It had been years since he handled this much of the generalized scrip known as paper money; at the church in Toledo it had been collected and counted automatically. For most people cash payments stopped at the number of dollar coins you would drop in a pocket without noticing their weight.

"I'm flattered," he said to the elderly man. "But you'll have to let me think about it. We may be only passing through. We have no plans to settle here."

He seized Kate's arm and hurried her away, terribly aware of the sensation he had caused. He could hear his feat being recounted already along the mouth-to-mouth circuit.

As they were undressing he said miserably, "I sabotaged that one, didn't I?"

Admitting the blunder was novel to him. The experience was just as unpleasant as he had imagined it would be. But in memory echoed Kate's description of the graduates from Tarnover: convinced they were incapable of error.

*That's not human. That's mechanical. It's machines whose view of the world is so circumscribed they go right on doing the only thing they can although it's wrong.*

"I'm afraid so." Her tone was matter-of-fact, devoid of criticism. "Not that you could help it. But to be spotted by an area secretary of the Fencing Association and then to beat the incumbent West Coast champion—yes, that is apt to provoke comment. I'm sorry; I didn't realize you hadn't recognized Fagin."

"You knew who he was?" In the middle of shedding his pants he stood ridiculous, one leg in and the other out. "So why the hell didn't you warn me?"

"Do me a favor? Before you pick your first quarrel

123

with me, get a little better acquainted. Then you can do it with justification."

He had been on the verge of anger. The inclination vanished. He completed undressing, as did she, and then took her in his arms.

"I like you very much as a person," he said, and bestowed a grave kiss on her forehead. "I think I'm going to like you just as much as a woman."

"I hope so," she answered with equal formality. "We may have to go a lot of places together."

He drew back to full stretch, hands on her shoulders.

"Where next? What next?"

As rare in his life as admitting mistakes was asking for advice. It too was disturbing. But it would have to become a habit if he was to stay afloat.

She shook her head. "Think about that in the morning. It has to be somewhere else, that's definite. But this town is already halfway right . . . No, too much has happened today. Let's overload it and sleep it out and worry about decisions afterwards."

With abrupt tigerish violence, as though she had borrowed from Bagheera, she clamped her arms around him and sank her sharp tongue—sharp as her gaze—between his lips.

## A LOAD OF CRYSTAL BALLS

In the twentieth century one did not have to be a pontificating pundit to predict that success would breed success and the nations that first were lucky enough to combine massive material resources with advanced knowhow would be those where social change would accelerate until it approximated the limit of what human beings can endure. By 2010, in the wealthiest countries, a classic category of mental patient was composed of boys and girls in their late teens who had come back for a first vacation from college to discover that "home" was unrecognizable, either because the parents had moved into a new framework, changed jobs and cities, or simply because—as they'd done a dozen times before—they had refurnished and redecorated . . . without realizing they were opening a door to what came to be termed the "final straw syndrome."

It was also not difficult to forecast that no matter how well endowed they were with material resources those countries where the Industrial Revolution arrived late would change proportionately more slowly. After all, the rich get richer and the poor get children. Which is okay so long as lots of them starve in infancy.

What many otherwise well-informed people apparently preferred to overlook was the phenomenon baptized by Angus Porter "the beetle and wedge," which retained its name long after even the poor nations found it uneconomic to split logs with a hammer and a chunk of steel. Even if your circular saws were pedal-driven, they were much less wasteful. Moreover, you could dictate a neat dividing line.

Beetling forward at full pelt split society. Some did their utmost to head the other way. A great many more decided to go sideways. And some simply dug in their heels and stayed put. The resultant cracks were unpredictable.

One and only one thing preserved even the illusion of national integrity. The gossamer strands of the datanet proved amazingly strong.

Unfortunately nothing came along to reinforce them.

People drew comfort from knowing there were certain objects near at hand, in the U.S.A. or the Soviet Union or Sweden or New Zealand, of which they could boast, "This is the biggest/longest/fastest frammistan on Earth!" Alas, however, tomorrow it might not be. Paradoxically, therefore, they derived even more emotional sustenance from being able to say, "This is the most primitive potrzebie, you know, still at work in any industrialized country!"

It was so precious to be able to connect with the calmer, stabler past.

The cracks spread. From national level they reached provincial level, from provincial they reached municipal, and there they met cracks going the other way, which had begun in the privacy of the family.

"We sweated blood to put the son-of-a-bitch through college! He ought to be paying us back, not sunning his ass in New Mexico!"

(For New Mexico read, at will, the Black Sea resort of Varna—or the beaches of Quemoy and Matsu where young Chinese by the thousand were content to pass their time practicing calligraphy, playing fan-tan, and smoking opium—or any of fifty other locations where *la dolce-far-niente vita* had spilled the contents of its seine-net after trawling through a nation, an ethnic grouping, or in the case of India a subcontinent. Sri Lanka had had no government to speak of for a generation.)

As much as anything else, it was the sense of exploitable talent going to waste that prompted the establishment of genius centers like Tarnover, funded on the scale previously reserved to weaponry. It was beyond the comprehension of those raised in traditional patterns of thinking that resources of whatever kind should not be channeled and exploited to dynamize ever-faster growth.

Secret, these centers—like the unseen points claimed in a fencing field—provoked consequences that now and then turned out to be disastrous.

## SCENT REFUGE

Even after two solid days in his company Ina Grierson couldn't get over how closely the man from Tarnover resembled Baron Samedi—very dark, very thin, head like a skull overlaid with parchment—so that one constantly expected a black tribe to march in and wreck the place. Some of his time had been devoted to Dolores van Bright, naturally, but she had admitted right away her attempt to help Sandy Locke by warning him there'd be an extra member of the interview board, and after that not even the influence of G2S was going to keep her out of jail.

But it was Ina the man from Tarnover was chiefly concerned to question. Sandy Locke had been hired on her say-so, whence the rest followed logically.

She grew terribly tired of saying over and over to the thin black man (whose name was Paul T. Freeman, but maybe only for the purposes of this assignment), "Of course I go to bed with men I know nothing about! If I only went to bed with men I *do* know about I'd never get any sex, would I? They all turn out to be bastards in the end."

Late on the afternoon of the second day of questioning the subject of Kate arose. Ina claimed to be unaware that her daughter had left the city, and the skull-faced man was obliged to believe her, since she had had no chance to go home and check her mail-store reel. Moreover, the girls in the apartment below Kate's, currently looking after Bagheera, insisted she had given no least hint in advance of her intention to travel.

Still, she'd done so. Gone west, and what was more with a companion. Very likely one of her fellow students, of course; many of her friends hailed from California. Besides, she'd talked freely about "Sandy Locke" to her downstairs neighbors, and called him plastic, artificial, and other derogatory terms. Her mother confirmed that she had said the same on various occasions both public and private.

There being no trace of Haflinger, however, and no other potential clue to his whereabouts, *and* no recent record of Kate's code being used—which meant she must have gone to a paid-avoidance area—Freeman, who was a thorough person, set the wheels in motion, and was rewarded by being able to advise the FBI that lodging for two people had been debbed against Kate Lilleberg in Lap-of-the-Gods.

Very interesting. Very interesting indeed.

## TODAY'S SPECIAL

He woke to alarm, recalling his gaffe of yesterday and along with that a great many details he'd have preferred to remain ignorant of concerning the habits of people in paid-avoidance areas. Their federal grants meant that few of them had to work at full-time jobs; they supplemented their frugal allowance by providing services—he thought of the restaurants where there were manual chefs and the food was brought by waiters and waitresses—or making handicrafts. Tourism in towns like this, however, was on the decline, as though people no longer cared to recall that this, the richest nation in history, had been unable to transcend a mere earthquake, so they spent much of their time in gossip. And what right now would offer a more interesting subject than the poker who blew out of nowhere and beat the local fencing champion?

"Sooner or later you're going to have to learn to live with one inescapable fact about yourself," Kate said over her shoulder as she sat brushing her hair before the room's one lighted mirror. Listening, he curled his fingers. The color of that hair might be nothing out of the ordinary, but its texture was superb. His fingertips remembered it, independently of his mind.

"What?"

"You're a very special person. Why else would they have recruited you to Tarnover? Wherever you go you're bound to attract attention."

"I daren't!"

"You can't help it." She laid aside her brush and swiveled to face him; he was sitting glum on the edge of the bed.

"Consider," she went on. "Would the people at G2S have offered to perm you if they didn't think you were special even disguised as Sandy Locke? And—and *I* realized you were special, too."

"You," he grunted, "just have more insight than is good for you."

128

"You mean: more than is good for you."

"I guess so." Now at last he rose to his feet, imagining he could hear his joints creak. To be this frustrated must, he thought, resemble the plight of being old: clearly recalling what it was like to act voluntarily and enjoy life as it came, now trapped in a frame that forbade anything except slow cautious movements and a diet prescribed by doctors.

"I don't want to go through life wearing fetters," he said abruptly.

"Tarnover talking!" she snapped.

"What?"

"Wear fetters? Wear *fetters*? I never heard such garbage. Has there ever been a time in the whole of history when someone with amazing exceptional gifts could be deluded into thinking they're a handicap?"

"Sure," he said at once. "How about conscripts who would rather maim themselves than obey a government order to go fight somebody they never met? Their gifts may have been no more than youth and health, but they were gifts."

"That's not being deluded. That's being compelled. A recruiting sergeant with a gun on his hip—"

"Same thing! They've merely brought it into finer focus!"

There was a brief electric silence. At length she sighed.

"I give in. I have no right to argue with you about Tarnover—you've been there and I haven't. And in any case it's too early for a row. Go get showered and shaved, and then we'll find some breakfast and talk about where we're going next."

## IS THIS YOU?

Did you have trouble last night in dropping off to sleep?

Even though you were tired in spite of doing nothing to exhaust yourself?

Did you hear your heart? Did it break its normal rhythm?

Do you suffer with digestive upsets? Get a feeling that your gullet has been tied in a knot behind your ribs?

Are you already angry because this advertisement hits the nail on your head?

*Then come to Calm Springs before you kill somebody or go insane!*

## COUNT A BLAST

"You're beginning to be disturbed by me," the dry hoarse voice announced.

Elbows on chair arms as usual, Freeman set his fingertips together. "How so?" he parried.

"For one thing, you've taken to talking to me in present-time mode for the last three-hour session every day."

"You should be grateful for small mercies. Our prognostications show it would be risky to maintain you in regressed mode."

"Half the truth. The rest can be found in your omission to use that expensive three-vee setup you had installed. You realized that I thrive on high levels of stimulus. But you're groping your way toward my lower threshold. You don't want me to start functioning at peak efficiency. You think that even pinned down like a butterfly on a board I may still be dangerous."

"I don't think of my fellow men as dangerous. I think of them as capable of occasional dangerous mistakes."

"You include yourself?"

"I remain constantly alert for the possibility."

"Being on guard like that itself constitutes aberrant behavior."

"How can you say that? So long as you were fully on guard we failed to catch you. In terms of your purposes that wasn't aberrant; it was functional. In the end, however . . . Well, here you are."

"Yes, here I am. Having learned a lesson you're incapable of learning."

"Much good may it bring you." Freeman leaned back. "You know, last night I was thinking over a new approach—a new argument which may penetrate your obstinacy. Consider this. You speak of us at Tarnover as though we're engaged in a brutal arbitrary attempt to ensure that the best minds of the current generation get inducted into government service. Not at all. We are simply the top end of a series of cultural subgroupings that evolved of their own accord during the second half of last century. Few of us are equipped to cope with the complexity and dazzling variety of twenty-first-century existence. We prefer to identify with small, easily isolable fractions of the total culture. But just as some people can handle only a restricted range of stimuli, and prefer to head for a mountain commune or a paid-avoidance area or even emigrate to an underdeveloped country, so some correspondingly not only cope well but actually require immensely strong stimuli to provoke them into functioning at optimum. We have a wider range of life-style choices today than ever before. The question of administration has been rendered infinitely more difficult precisely because we have such breadth of choice. Who's to manage this multiplex society? Must the lot not fall to those who flourish when dealing with complicated situations? Would you rather that people who demonstrably can't organize their own lives were permitted to run those of their fellow citizens?"

"A conventional elitist argument. From you I'd have expected better."

"Elitist? Nonsense. I'd expected better from you. The word you're looking for is 'aesthetic.' An oligarchy devoted by simple personal preference to the search for artistic gratification in government—that's what we're after. And it would be rather a good system, don't you think?"

131

"Provided you were in the top group. Can you visualize yourself in the lower echelons, a person who obeys instead of issuing orders?"

'Oh, yes. That's why I work at Tarnover. I hope that perhaps within my lifetime there will appear people so skilled in dealing with modern society that I and others like me can step out of their way with a clear conscience. In a sense I want to work myself out of a job as fast as possible."

"Resigning control to crippled kids?"

Freeman sighed. "Oh, you're obsessed with those laboratory-gestated children! Maybe it will relieve your mind to hear that the latest batch—six of them —are all physically whole and run and jump and feed and dress themselves! If you met them by chance you couldn't tell them from ordinary kids."

"So why bother to tell me about them? All that's registered in my mind is that they may look like ordinary kids . . . but they never will be ordinary kids."

"You have a positive gift for twisting things. No matter what I say to you—"

"I find a means of casting a different light on it. Let me do just that to what you've been saying. You, and the others you mentioned, acknowledge you're imperfect. So you're looking for superior successors. Very well: give me grounds for believing that they won't just be projections on a larger scale of your admittedly imperfect vision."

"I can't. Only results that speak for themselves can do that."

"What results do you have to date? You've sunk a lot of time and money in the scheme."

"Oh, several. One or two may impress even a skeptic."

"The kids that look like any other kids?"

"No, no. Healthy adults like yourself capable of doing things that have never been done before, such as writing a complete new identity into the data-net over a regular veephone. Bear in mind that before trying to invent new talents we decided to look for those that had been undervalued. The odds there were in our favor. We have records from the past—descriptions of lightning calculators, musicians capable of improvising without a wrong note for hours on end, mnemonists who commited whole books to memory by reading them through once . . . Oh, there are examples in every field of human endeavor from strategy to scrimshaw. With these for guidelines, we're trying to generate conditions in which corresponding modern talents can flourish."

He shifted casually in his chair; he sounded more confident by the minute.

"Our commonest current form of mental disorder is personality shock. We have an efficient way to treat it without machinery or drugs. We allow the sufferer to do something he long ago wanted to do and lacked either the courage or the opportunity to fit into his life. Do you deny the claim?"

"Of course not. This continent is littered coast to coast with people who were compelled to study business administration when they should have been painting murals or practicing the fiddle or digging a truck garden, and finally got their chance when it was twenty years too late to lead them anywhere."

"Except back to a sense of solid identity," Freeman murmured.

"In the case of the lucky few. But yes, okay."

"Then let me lay this on you. If you hadn't met Miranda—if you hadn't found out that our suspicions concerning the genetic component of personality were being verified by experiment—would you have deserted from Tarnover?"

"I think sooner or later I'd have quit anyhow. The attitude that can lead to using crippled children as experimental material would have disconnected me."

"You spin like a weather vane. You've said, or implied, repeatedly that at Tarnover we're conditioning people not to rebel. You can't maintain at the same time that what we're doing would have encouraged you to rebel."

Freeman gave his skull-like grin and rose, stretching his cramped limbs.

"Our methods are being tested in the only available lab: society at large. So far they show excellent results. Instead of condemning them out of hand you should reflect on how much worse the alternatives are. After what you underwent last summer, you of all people should appreciate what I mean. In the morning we'll rerun the relevant memories and see if they help to straighten you."

## CLIFFHANGER

They had to continue in a paid-avoidance zone. So, to supplement recollection, they bought a four-year-old tourist guide alleged to contain full details of all the post-quake settlements. Most rated four or even six pages of text, plus as many color pictures. Precipice was dismissed in half a page. On the fold-out map included with the booklet only one road— and that a poor one—was shown passing through it, from Quemadura in the south to Protempore thirty miles northwest, plus tracks for an electric railcar service whose schedule was described as irregular. The towns were graded according to what modern facilities could be found there; Precipice came bottom of the list. Among the things Precipicians didn't like might be cited the data-net, veephones, surface vehicles not running on tracks, heavier-than-air craft (though they tolerated helium and hot-air dirigibles), modern merchandising methods and the federal government. This last could be deduced from the datum that they had compounded to pay a flat-rate tax per year instead of income tax, though the sum appeared absurdly high considering there was no industry bar handicrafts (not available to wholesalers).

"It sounds like some sort of Amish setup," Kate commented, frowning over the brief entry in the guide.

"No, it can't be. They won't allow churches or

other religious buildings." He was gazing into no-where, focusing on facts casually encountered long ago. "I borrowed some ideas from the paid-avoidance zones while I was a utopia designer. I needed to figure a way of editing dogmatic religion into a com-munity without the risk of breeding intolerance. I checked out several of these towns, and I distinctly remember ignoring Precipice because in any case I couldn't spare the time to dig right down deep for more data. Almost nothing about the place, bar its location, was in store. Oh, yes: and a population limit of three thousand."

"Huh? A legally imposed limit, you mean?" On his nod: "Imposed by whom—the citizens or the state government?"

"The citizens."

"Compulsory birth control?"

"I don't know. I told you: when I found how little I could fish from the banks, I didn't bother to pursue the matter."

"Do they ride visitors out again on a rail?"

He gave a half-smile. "No, that's one other fact I remember. It's an open community, administered by some sort of town meeting, I think, and you may indeed go there to look it over or even to stay in-definitely. They just don't care for advertising, and apparently they regard noising their existence abroad as the same thing in principle."

"We go there, then," Kate said decisively, slapping shut the booklet.

"My choice would be the opposite. To be trapped in a backwater . . . But tell me why."

"Precisely because there's so little information in the banks. It's beyond belief that the government won't have tried—probably tried extremely hard—to tie Precipice into the net at least to the same extent as Protempore and Lap-of-the-Gods. If the citizens are dogged enough to stand out against such pressure, they might sympathize with your plight the way I do."

Appalled, he blurted out, "You mean you want me to march in and announce it?"

"Will you *stop* that?" Kate stamped her foot, eyes flashing. "Grow out of your megalomania, for pity's sake! Quit thinking in terms of 'Sandy Locke versus the world' and start believing that there are other people dissatisfied with the state of things, anxious to set it right. You know"—a level, caustic glare—"I'm beginning to think you've never sought help from others for fear you might wind up being the one who does the helping. You always like to be in charge, don't you? Particularly of yourself!"

He drew a deep breath and let it out very slowly, forcing his embryonic annoyance to go with it. He said at length, "I knew what they offered me under the guise of 'wisdom' at Tarnover wasn't the genuine article. It was so totally wrong it's taken me until now to realize I finally ran across it. Kate, you're a wise person. The first one I ever met."

"Don't encourage me to think so. If I ever come to believe it, I shall fall flat on my face."

## OUBLIETTE

By about then the lean black man from Tarnover was through with Ina Grierson and let her go home, stumbling with weariness. Before she fell asleep, however, she had to know one thing that Freeman had declined to tell her:

What the hell was so earthmoving about Sandy Locke?

She was not the most expert of data-mice; however, her position as head-of-dept for transient execs gave her access to the files of G2S employees. Trembling, she punched the code that started with 4GH.

The screen stayed blank.

She tried every route she could think of to gain access to the data, including some that were within the ace of being illegal . . . though they bent, rather than broke, the regulations laid down by the Bureau of Data Processing, and a blind eye was generally turned.

The result was invariably the same blank screen.

At first she only nibbled her nails; later, she started to gnaw them; finally, she had to cram her fingers into her mouth to stop herself whimpering in mingled terror and exhaustion.

If all her best attempts had failed, there was just one conclusion to be drawn. Sandy Locke, so far as the data-net was concerned, had been deleted from the human race.

For the first time since she broke her heart at seventeen, Ina Grierson cried herself to sleep.


## A SHOULDER TO BE WEPT ON
## BY THE WORLD

So they went to Precipice, where there wasn't one. The town had been founded on the levelest ground for miles, a patch of soft but stable silt due to some long-ago river which still had a few creeks meandering across it. Though hills could be seen on three sides, their slopes were gentle and any earthquake that shifted them in their eon-long slumber would be violent enough to cast loose California entire.

They rode toward it in the electric railcar with the irregular schedule, which they boarded at Transience. Small wonder the car didn't stick to a fixed timetable. As they were informed by the driver—a burly smiling man wearing shorts, sunglasses and sandals—a local ordinance obliged it to give precedence at all crossings to anyone on foot, cycle or horseback, as well as to farm animals and agricultural vehicles. Moreover, when making its final loop around Precipice proper it had to let passengers on or off at any point. Taking full advantage of this facility, local people boarded and descended every few hundred meters. All of them gazed with unashamed curiosity at the strangers.

Who became uncomfortable. Both of them had overlooked one problem involved in traveling around the paid-avoidance zones, being so used to the devices that in theory could eliminate the need for baggage from the plug-in life-style. At all modern hotels could be found ultrasonic clothing cleansers capable of ridding even the bulkiest garment of its accumulated dust and grime in five minutes, and when the cloth began to give way under repeated applications of this violent treatment, there were other machines that would credit you for the fiber, tease it apart, store it for eventual re-use, and issue another garment the same size but a different style and/or color, debbing the customer for the additional fiber and the work involved. Nothing like that was to be found at Lap-of-the-Gods.

Kate had snatched up toilet gear for them before departure, including an old-fashioned reciprocating-head razor left behind by one of her boyfriends, but neither had thought to bring spare clothing. Consequently they were by now looking, and even more feeling, dirty . . . and those strange eyes constantly scanning them made them fidget.

But things could have been a great deal worse. In many places people would have felt it their duty to put hostile questions to wanderers whose clothes looked as though they had been slept in and who carried almost no other possessions. Luggage might have dwindled; the list of what people felt to be indispensable had long ago reached the stage where both sexes customarily carried bulky purses when bound for any but their most regular destinations.

Yet until they were almost at the end of their journey no one in the railcar, except the informative driver, addressed anything but a greeting to them.

By then they had been able to look over the neighborhood, which they found impressive. The rich alluvial soil was being efficiently farmed; watered by irrigation channels topped up by wind-driven pumps, orchards and cornfields and half-hectare plots of both leaf and root vegetables shimmered in the sun. That much one could have seen anywhere. Far more remarkable were the buildings. They were virtually invisible. Like partridges hiding among rough grass, some of them eluded the eye altogether until a change of angle revealed a line too straight to be other than artificial, or a flash of sunlight on the black glass of a solar energy collector. The contrast with a typical modern farm, a factory-like place where standard barns and silos prefabricated out of concrete and aluminum were dumped all anyhow, was astonishing.

In a low voice he said to Kate, "I'd like to know who designed these farms. This isn't junk cobbled together by refugees in panic. This is the sort of landscaping a misanthropic millionaire might crave but not afford! Seen anything as good anywhere else?"

She shook her head. "Not even at Protempore, much as I liked it. I guess maybe what the refugees originally botched up didn't last. When it fell to bits they were calm enough to get it right on the second try."

"But this is more than just *right*. This is *magnificent*. The town itself can't possibly live up to the same standard. Are we in sight of it yet, by the way?"

Kate craned to look past the driver. Noticing, a middle-aged woman in blue seated on the opposite side of the car inquired, "You haven't been to Precipice before?"

"Ah . . . No, we haven't."

"Thought I didn't recognize you. Planning to stay, or just passing through?"

"Can people stay? I thought you had a population limit."

"Oh, sure, but we're two hundred under at the moment. And in spite of anything you may have heard"—a broad grin accompanied the remark—"we like to have company drop in. Tolerable company, that is. My name's Polly, by the way."

"I'm Kate, and—"

Swiftly inserted: "I'm Alexander—Sandy! Say, I was just wondering who laid out these farms. I never saw buildings that fit so beautifully into a landscape."

"Ah! Matter of fact, I was about to tell you, go see the man who does almost all our building. That's Ted Horovitz. He's the sheriff, too. You get off at Mean Free Path and walk south until you hit Root

Mean Square and then just ask for Ted. If he's not around, talk to the mayor—that's Suzy Dellinger. Got that? Fine. Well, nice to have met you, hope to see you around, this is where I get off."

She headed for the door.

Involuntarily Kate said, "Mean Free Path? Root Mean Square? Is that some kind of joke?"

There were four other passengers at this stage of the journey. All of them chuckled. The driver said over his shoulder, "Sure, the place is littered with jokes. Didn't you know?"

"Kind of rarefied jokes, aren't they?"

"I guess maybe. But they're a monument to how Precipice got started. Of all the people who got drove south by the Bay Quake, the ones who came here were the luckiest. Ever hear mention of Claes College?"

Kate exploded just as he began to say he hadn't.

"You mean *this* was 'Disasterville U.S.A.'?" She was half out of her seat with excitement, peering eagerly along the curved track toward the town that was now coming into view. Even at first glance, it promised that indeed it did maintain the standard set by the outlying farms; at any rate, there was none of the halfhearted disorganization found at the edge of so many modern communities, but a real sense of border: here, rural; there, urban. No, not after all a sharp division. A—a—

An ancient phrase came to mind: *dissolving view*.

But there was no chance to sort out his confused initial impressions; Kate was saying urgently, "Sandy, you must have heard of Claes, surely . . . ? No? Oh, that's terrible!"

She dropped back into her seat and gave him a rapid-fire lecture.

"Claes College was founded about 1981 to revive the medieval sense of the name, a community of scholars sharing knowledge regardless of arbitrary boundaries between disciplines. It didn't last; it faded away after only a few years. But the people involved left one important memorial. When the Bay Quake let go, they dropped everything and moved *en masse* to help with relief work, and someone hit on the idea of undertaking a study of the social forces at work in the post-catastrophe period so that if it ever happened again the worst tragedies could be avoided. The result was a series of monographs under the title 'Disaster-ville U.S.A.' I'm amazed you never heard of it."

She rounded on the driver. "Practically nobody has heard of it! I must have mentioned it a hundred times and always drawn a blank. But it's not only important —it's unique."

Dryly the driver said, "You didn't mention it at Precipice, that's for sure. We grow up on it in school. Ask Brad Compton the librarian to show you our first edition."

He applied the brakes. "Coming up to Mean Free now!"

Mean Free Path was indeed a path, winding among shrubs, trees and—houses? They had to be. But they were something else, too. Yes, they had roofs (although the roofs were never four-square) and walls (what one could see of them through masses of creeper) and doubtless doors, none of which happened to be visible from where they had left the railcar . . . already out of sight and sound despite its leisurely pace, lost in a tunnel of greenery.

"They are like the farms," Kate breathed.

"No." He snapped his fingers. "There's a difference, and I just figured out what it is. The farms—they're factors in landscape. But these houses *are* landscape."

"That's right," Kate said. Her voice was tinged with awe. "I have the most ridiculous feeling. I'm instantly ready to believe that an architect who could do this . . ." The words trailed away.

"An architect who could do this could design a planet," he said briefly, and took her arm to urge her onward.

Though the path wound, it was level enough to ride a cycle or draw a cart along, paved with slabs of rock conformable to the contour of the land.

Shortly they passed a green lawn tinted gold by slanting sunshine. She pointed at it.

"Not a garden," she said. "But a glade."

"Exactly!" He put his hand to his forehead, seeming dizzy. Alarmed, she clutched at him.

"Sandy, is something the matter?"

"No—yes—no . . . I don't know. But I'm okay." Dropping his arm, he blinked this way, then that. "It just hit me. This is *town*—yes? But it doesn't feel like it. I simply know it must be, because . . ." He swallowed hard. "Seeing it from the railcar, could you have mistaken this place for anything else?"

"Never in a million years. Hmm!" Her eyes rounded in wonder. "That's a hell of a trick, isn't it?"

"Yes, and if I didn't realize it was therapeutic I could well be angry. People don't enjoy being fooled, do they?"

"Therapeutic?" She frowned. "I don't follow you."

"Set-destruction. We use sets constantly instead of seeing what's there—or feeling or tasting it, come to that. We have a set 'town,' another 'city,' another 'village' . . . and we often forget there's a reality the sets were originally based on. We're in too much of a hurry. If this effect is typical of Precipice, I'm not surprised it gets so little space in the guidebook. Tourists would find a massive dose of double-take indigestible. I look forward to meeting this poker Horovitz. As well as being a builder and a sheriff I think he must be a . . ."

"A what?"

"A something else. Maybe something I don't know a word for."

The path had been a path. The square proved not to be a square, more a deformed cyclic quadrilateral, but it implied all the necessary elements of a public urban space. It was a great deal bigger than one might have guessed. They found this out by crossing it. Part of it, currently deserted, was paved and ornamented with flower-filled urns; part was park-like, though miniaturized, a severe formal garden; part sloped down to a body of water, less a lake than a pond, some three or four meters below the general level of the land, from whose banks steps rose in elegant curves. Here there were people: old folk on benches in the sun, two games of fencing in progress amid the inevitable cluster of kibitzers, while down by the water—under the indulgent but watchful eyes of a couple of teeners—some naked children were splashing merrily about in pursuit of a huge light ball bigger than any two of their heads.

And enclosing this square were buildings of various heights linked together by slanting roofs and pierced by alleyways but for which they would have composed a solid terrace. As it was, every alley was bridged at first-story level and every bridge was ornamented with delicate carvings in wood or stone.

"My God," Kate said under her breath. "It's incredible. Not town. Not here. This is *village.*"

"And yet it's got the city implicit in it—the Grand' Place, the Plaza Mayor, Old London Bridge . . . Oh, it's fantastic! And look a bit more closely at the houses. They're ecofast, aren't they? Every last one of them! I wouldn't be surprised to find they're running off ground heat!"

She paled a little. "You're right! I hadn't noticed. One thinks of an ecofast house as being—well, kind of one cell for a honeycomb, factory-made. There are ecofast communities around KC, you know, and they have no more character than an anthill!"

"Let's track down the sheriff at once. I can stand just so many unanswered questions at one go. Excuse me!" He approached the group around the fencing tables.

"Where do we find Ted Horovitz?"

"Through that alley," one of the watchers said, pointing. "First door on your right. If he's not there, try the mayor's office. I think he has business with Suzy today."

Again, as they moved away, they felt many curious eyes on them. As though visitors were a rarity at Precipice. But why weren't there thousands of them, millions? Why wasn't this little town famous the world around?

"Though of course if it were famous—"

"Did you say something?"

"Not exactly. This must be the door. Mr. Horovitz?"

"Come right in!"


They entered, and found themselves in an extraordinary room at least ten meters long. Conventionally enough furnished, with chairs and a desk and sundry cases crammed with books and cassettes, it was more like a forest clearing bright with ferns or a cave behind a waterfall hung with strands of glistening vegetation than anybody's office. Greenish light, reflected from wind-wavered panels outside irregular windows, flickered on flock-sprayed surfaces as soft as moss.

Turning to greet them from a carpenter's bench that had seen long service was a stocky man in canvas pants with big pockets full of tools, laying aside a wooden object whose outline was at first elusive, then suddenly familiar: a dulcimer.

In the same moment something moved, emerging from shadow beside the workbench. A dog. A vast, slow-moving graceful dog whose ancestry might have included Great Dane, Irish wolfhound, possibly husky or Chinook . . . plus something else, something strange, for its skull was improbably high-domed and its eyes, deep-set, looked disturbingly uncanine.

Kate's fingers clamped vise-tight on his arm. He heard her gasp.

"No need to be alarmed," the man rumbled in a voice half an octave nearer the bass than might have been guessed from his size. "Never met a dog like this before? You're in for an educational experience. His name is Natty Bumppo. Hold still a moment while he reads you. Sorry, but this is S.O.P. for any visitor. Nat, how do they rate? Any hard drugs— excessive liquor—anything apart from being a bit scared?"

The dog curled his wrinkled upper lip and inhaled a long slow breath, then gave a brisk headshake and a faint growl. Elegantly he lowered his massive hindquarters to the floor, keeping his eyes on the newcomers.

Kate's fingers relaxed, but she was trembling.

"He says you're clear," Horovitz announced. "I understand this poker pretty well, you know. Not as well as he understands us humans, maybe, but there it is. Right, sit down!" With a wave toward a nearby lounge; he himself dropped into an armchair facing it and produced an ancient charred pipe from one of his immense pockets. "What can I do for you?"

They looked at one another. With sudden decision Kate said, "We found our way here more or less by accident. We were in Lap-of-the-Gods and before that I'd been to Protempore. They can't stand comparison with Precipice. We'd like to visit with you for a while."

"Mm-hm. Okay . . . probably." Horovitz gestured to the dog. "Nat, go tell the councilmen we got applicants, please."

Natty Bumppo rose, snuffed one last time at the strangers, and padded out. The door had a handle which he could open himself; punctiliously, he also closed it.

Following the animal with his eyes, Sandy said, "Oh, I forgot to tell you our names."

"Kate and Sandy," Horovitz murmured. "I knew to expect you. Polly Ryan said she met you on the railcar."

"She—uh . . . ?"

"You heard of phones, I guess. We have 'em. Appearances to the contrary. Maybe you were reading up on us in that bad guidebook." It was protruding from Kate's side pocket; he leveled an accusing finger at it. "What we don't have is veephone service. The feds have been on at us for years to link into the data-net on the same token basis as the other paid-avoidance communities, but to satisfy their computers you have to have veephone-sized bandpass capacity.

They give all kinds of nice persuasive reasons—they keep reminding us of how Transcience was almost taken over by a criminal syndicate, and how nearly everybody in Ararat was fooled by a phony preacher wanted in seven different states for fraud and confidence-trickery . . . but we prefer to stay out and solve our own problems. They can't oblige us to tie in so long as our taxes amount to more than our PA grants. So, on principle, no veephones. Don't let that mislead you, though, into imagining we're backward. We're just about the size of a late medieval market town, and we offer almost precisely one hundred times as many facilities."

"So you've proved it is cheaper to operate on an ecofast basis!" Sandy leaned forward eagerly.

"You noticed? Very interesting! Most people have preconceived ideas about ecofast building; they have to be factory products, they come in one size and one shape and if you want a bigger one you can only stick two together. In fact, as you say, once you really understand the principle you find you've accidentally eliminated most of your concealed overheads. Been to Trianon, either of you?"

"Visiting friends," Kate said.

"They boast about running at seventy-five percent energy utilization, and they still have to take an annual subsidy from G2S because their pattern is inherently so wasteful. We run at eighty to eighty-five percent. There isn't a community on the planet that's doing better."

Horovitz appended a half-embarrassed smile to the remark, as though to liberate it from any suspicion of conceit.

"And you're responsible for that?" Sandy demanded. "The woman we met—Polly—said you do most of the building."

"Sure, but I can't claim the credit. I didn't figure out the principles, nor how to apply them. That was—"

Kate butted in. "Oh, yes! The railcar-driver said this is the original Disasterville U.S.A.!"

"You heard about that deal?" Horovitz had been loading his pipe with coarse dark tobacco; he almost dropped the pouch and pipe both. "Well, *hell!* So they haven't managed to clamp the lid down tight!"

"Ah . . . What do you mean?"

A shrug and a grunt. "The way I hear it, if you punch for data about the Disasterville study, or about anything to do with Claes College, over the regular continental net, you get some kind of discouragement. Like it's entered as 'of interest only to specialist students,' quote and unquote. Any rate, that's what I heard from Brad. Brad Compton, our librarian."

"But that's awful!" Kate stared at him. "I never did actually punch for those data—my father had a full set of Disasterville monographs, and I read them in my early teens. But . . . Well, isn't it important that one of the projects they dreamed up at Claes turned into a functional community?"

"Oh, I think so. What sheriff wouldn't, with a crime rate of nearly zero?"

"Are you serious?"

"Mm-hm. We never had a murder yet, and it's two years since we had anybody hospitalized after a fight, and as to robbery—well, stealing just ain't a habit around here." A faint grin. "Occasionally it gets imported, but I swear there's no future in it either way."

Kate said slowly, "Don't tell me. Let me guess. Is this place the reason why Claes went under? Did the really bright people stay on here instead of going home?"

Horovitz smiled. "Young lady, you're the first visitor I've met who got that without having to be told. Yup; Precipice skimmed the cream off Claes, and the rump that was left just faded away. As I understand it, that was because only the people who took their own ideas seriously were prepared to face the responsibility entailed. And ridicule, too. After all, at the same time other refugee settlements were at the mercy of crooks and unscrupulous fake evangelists— like we were just talking about—so who was to believe that some crazy mix composed of bits of Ghirardelli and Portmeirion and Valencia and Taliesin and God knows what besides would turn out right when everything else went wrong?"

"I think you must like us," Sandy said suddenly. Horovitz blinked at him. "What?"

"I never saw a façade fall down so fast. The homey-folksy bit, I mean. It didn't suit you anyhow; it's no loss. But on top of being a builder and a sheriff, what are you? I mean, where did you start?"

Horovitz pulled the corners of his mouth down in a lugubrious parody of dismay.

"I plead guilty," he said after a pause. "Sure, I regard myself as local, but I have a doctorate in social interaction from Austin, Texas, and a master's in structural technology from Columbia. Which is not something I customarily admit to visitors, even the bright ones—*particularly* not to the bright ones, because they tend to come here for all possible wrong reasons. We're interested in being functional, not in being dissected by in-and-out gangs of cultural anthropologists."

"How long are you going to wait before becoming famous?"

"Hmm! You *are* a perceptive shivver, aren't you? But a fair question rates a fair answer. We expect half a century will be enough."

"Are we going to survive that long?"

Horovitz shook his head heavily. "We don't know. Does anybody?"

The door swung wide. Natty Bumppo returned, giving Horovitz a nudge with his muzzle as he passed. Behind him came a tall stately black woman in a gaudy shirt and tight pants, arm in arm with a fat white man—heavily tanned—in shorts and sandals like the railcar driver.

Horovitz introduced them as Suzy Dellinger, the mayor, and Brad Compton; they were this year's councilmen for the town. He gave a condensed but accurate version of his conversation with Kate and Sandy. The new arrivals listened intently. Having heard him out, Brad Compton made an extraordinary comment.

"Does Nat approve?"

"Seems to," grunted Horovitz.

"Then I guess we found new tenants for the Thorgrim place. Suzy?" Glancing at the mayor.

"Sure, why not?" She turned to Kate and Sandy. "Welcome to Precipice! Now, from here you go back to the square, take the second alley on your right, and you're on Drunkard's Walk. Follow it to the intersection with Great Circle Course. The house on the near left of that corner is yours for as long as you care to stay."

There was a moment of blank incredulity. Then Kate exclaimed, "Hold it! You're going far too fast! I don't know for certain what Sandy's plans are, but I have to get back to KC in a few days' time. You seem to have decided I'm a permanent settler."

Sandy chimed in. "What's more, on the basis of a dog's opinion! Even if he is modded, I don't see how—"

"Modded?" Horovitz broke in. "No, Nat's not modified. I guess his however-many-great grandfather must have been tinkered with a bit, but he's just the way he grew up. Best of his litter, admittedly."

"You mean there are a lot of dogs like him around Precipice?" Kate demanded.

"A couple of hundred by now," Mayor Dellinger replied. "Descendants of a pack that wandered into town in the summer of 2003. There was a young stud, and two fertile bitches each with four pups, and an old sterile bitch was leading them. She'd been neutered. Doc Squibbs—he's our veterinarian—he's always maintained they must have escaped from some research station and gone looking for a place where they'd be better treated. Which was here. They're great with kids, they can almost literally talk, and if only they lived to a ripe old age there'd be nothing wrong with them at all. Trouble is, they last seven or eight years at most, and that's not fair, is it, Nat?" She reached out to scratch Natty Bumppo behind the ears, and he gave one absent thump with his thick tail. "But we got friends working on that, and we do our best to breed them for longevity."

Another pause. Eventually Sandy said with determination, "Okay, so your dogs can work miracles. But handing us a house, without even asking what we intend to do while we're here—"

Brad Compton gave a hoot of laughter. He broke off in confusion.

"Forgive Brad," Horovitz said. "But I thought we'd been over that. Did you miss my point? I told you, we offer a hundred times as many services as a medieval town the same size. You don't just arrive, squat a house, and live on your federal avoidance grant forever and a day, amen. Now and then people try it. They become unhappy and disillusioned and drift away."

"Well, sure. I mean, I realize you must have all kinds of work to offer us . . . but that's not what I'm driving at. I want to know what the hell supports this community."

The three Precipicians smiled at one another. Mayor Dellinger said, "Shall I tell them?"

"Sure, it's a job for the mayor," Compton answered.

"Okay." She turned to face Kate and Sandy. "We run an operation with no capital, no shareholders and scarcely any plant. Yet we receive a donated income teen times as large as our collective avoidance grants."

"What?"

"That's right." Her tone was sober. "We provide a service which some people—some very rich people indeed—have found so precious that they've done things like covenant to pay us a tithe of their salary for life. Once we were left the income on an estate of sixty million, and though the family tried like hell to overturn the will in the courts . . . I believe you just recognized us, didn't you?"

Shaking, fists clenched, mouth so dry he was almost unable to shape the proper words, Sandy blurted out his guess.

"There's only one thing you could be. But— Oh, my God. Are you really Hearing Aid?"


## CROSS TALK

"After which I immediately wanted to ask how they managed to keep that incredible promise of theirs, but—"

"Wait, wait!" Freeman was half out of his chair, peering closely at his data console as though shortening the range could alter what the instrument display was reporting.

"Is something wrong?"

"I . . . No, nothing's wrong. I merely observed a rather remarkable event." Freeman sank back in his chair, and with an air of guilt produced a handkerchief to mop his face. All of a sudden sweat had burst out in rivers on his forehead.

There was a brief silence. Then:

"Damn, you're right. This is the first time you ever transferred me from regressed to present mode and I didn't have to be steered back to the same subject. Ve-ery interesting! Don't bother telling me this indicates how deeply I was affected; I know, and I still am. What I learned from that first conversation at Precipice left me with a weird tip-of-the-tongue sensation, as though I'd realized the people there had the answer to some desperately urgent problem, only I couldn't work out what problem the answer belonged with. . . . Incidentally, please tell me something. I think I deserve it. After all, I can't prevent you from making me tell you everything, can I?"

Freeman's face was glistening as though he were being roasted on a spit before an immensely hot fire. He mopped away more perspiration before he replied.

"Go ahead and ask."

"If it had become known that I'd called Hearing Aid and talked for an hour about Miranda and myself and Tarnover . . . would I have been expelled via an operating theater?"

Freeman hesitated, folding and refolding his handkerchief prior to returning it to his pocket. At long last he did so, and with reluctance spoke.

"Yes. With an IQ of 85 if you were lucky."

As calmly as before: "What about Hearing Aid?"

"Nothing would have been done to them." The admission was almost inaudible. "You must know why."

"Oh, sure. Sorry—I admit I only asked to see you squirm with embarrassment. But there's such a David-and-Goliath pattern about Precipice versus the U.S. government. Want me to continue?"

"Do you feel up to it?"

"I think so. Whether or not Precipice will work for everybody, it worked for me. And it's high time I faced the reason why my stay there ended in a disaster, when if I hadn't been a fool it need have been no worse than a minor setback."


## THE MESH OF A RIDDLE

"This is the most incredible place. I never dreamed—"

Walking uphill on the aptly named Drunkard's Walk, Kate interrupted him.

"Sandy, that dog. Natty Bumppo."

"He gave you quite a fright, didn't he? I'm sorry."

"No!"

"But you—"

"I know, I know. I was startled. But I wasn't scared. I simply didn't believe it. I thought none of Dad's dogs was left."

"What?" He almost stumbled, turning to stare at her. "What on earth could he have to do with your father?"

"Well, I never heard of anybody else who did such marvelous things with animals. Bagheera was one of Dad's too, you know. Almost the last."

He drew a deep breath. "Kate dear, would you please begin at the beginning?"

Eyes troubled and full of sadness, she said, "I

guess I ought to. I remember asking if you knew about my father, and you said sure, he was Henry Lilleberg the neurophysiologist, and I left it at that. But it was a prime example of what you said only an hour ago Precipice is designed to cure. Slap a label on and forget about it. Say 'neurophysiologist' and you conjure up a stock picture of the sort of person who will dissect out a nervous system, analyze it *in vitro*, publish the findings and go away content, forgetting that the rest of the animal ever existed. That isn't a definition of my father! When I was a little girl he used to bring me amazing pets, which never lasted long because they were already old. But they'd been of service at his labs, and as a result he couldn't bear to throw them down the incinerator chute. He used to say he owed them a bit of fun because he'd cheated them of it when they were young."

"What kind of animals?"

"Oh, little ones at first, when I was five or six—rats, hamsters, gerbils. Later on there were squirrels and gophers, cats and raccoons. Remember I mentioned he had a license to move protected species interstate? And finally, in the last couple of years before he was taken so ill he had to retire, he was working with some real big ones: dogs like Natty Bumppo and mountain lions like Bagheera."

"Did he do any research with aquatic mammals—dolphins, porpoises?"

"I don't believe so. At any rate he couldn't have brought those home for me." A touch of her normal wry humor returned with the words. "We lived in an apt. We didn't have a pool to keep them in. Why do you ask?"

"I was wondering whether he might have been involved with—hell, I don't know which of several names you might recognize. They kept changing designations as they ran into one dead end after another. But it was a project based in Georgia intended to devise animals capable of defeating an invasion. Originally they thought of small creatures as disease-vectors and saboteurs, like they conditioned rats to gnaw compulsively on tire rubber and electrical insulation. Later there was all this hot air generated about surrogate armies, with animals substituted for infantry. Wars would still be fought, with lots of blood and noise, but no soldiers would be killed—not permanently."

"I knew the project under the name of Parsimony. But Dad never worked on it. They kept asking him to join, and he kept declining because they'd never tell him all the details of what he'd have to do. It wasn't until he'd contracted his terminal myelitis that he was able to find out how right he'd been."

"The project was discontinued, wasn't it?"

"Yes, and I know why. They'd been living off Dad's back for years. He was the only man in the country, maybe the world, who was consistently successful in making superintelligent animals breed true."

"Literally the only one?"

"Oh, even he scarcely believed it. He published his data and always swore he wasn't holding anything back, but other researchers found they couldn't get the same results. In the end it became a joke for him. He used to say, 'I just have red fingers.'"

"I see. Like a gardener has green ones."

"Exactly."

"What were his methods?" The question was more rhetorical than literal. But she answered anyway.

"Don't ask me, go punch a code. All the data are on open reels. Seemingly the government must hope another red-fingered genius will chance on them some day."

Eyes fixed on nowhere, he said in a musing tone, "I got disenchanted with biology, but I do recall something about the Lilleberg Hypothesis. An ultrarefined subcategory of natural selection involving hormonal influence not only on the embryo but on the gonads of the parents, which was supposed to determine the crossover points on the chromosomes."

"Mm-hm. He was ridiculed for proposing it. He was slandered by all his colleagues, accused of trying to show that Lysenko was right after all. Which," she added hotly, "was a transparent lie! What he actually did was advance an explanation why in spite of being wrong the Lysenkoists could have fooled themselves. Sandy, why does an establishment always fossilize so quickly? It may be my imagination, but I have this paranoid notion that people in authority today make a policy of seizing on any really original idea and either distorting it or suppressing it. Ted Horovitz was saying something about people being discouraged from digging into the Disasterville studies, for example."

"Do you really have to ask about government?" he countered grayly. "I'd have thought the reason was plain. It's the social counterpart of natural selection. Those groups within society that craved power at the expense of everything else—morality, self-respect, honest friendship—they achieved dominance long ago. The mass of the public no longer has any contact with government; all they know is that if they step out of line they'll be trodden on. And the means exist to make the statement literal. . . . Oh, they must hate Precipice, over there in Washington! A tiny community, and its citizens can thumb their noses at any federal diktat!"

She shuddered visibly. "But the scientists . . . ?" she said.

"Their reaction is a different matter. The explosion of human knowledge has accelerated to the point where even the most brilliant can't cope with it any more. Theories have rigidified into dogma just as they did in the Middle Ages. The leading experts feel obligated to protect their creed against the heretics. Right?"

"That certainly fits in Dad's case," Kate said, nodding and biting her lip. "But—well, he proved his point! Bagheera's evidence, if nothing else."

"He wasn't an isolated success, was he?"

"Hell, no. But the only one Dad was able to save from being sold to the big circus at Quemadura. It was just getting started then, and people were investing a lot of money in it and— Say, look there!"

They were passing a patch of level grass where two young children were lying asleep on a blanket. Beside them was a dog the same type and color as Natty Bumppo but smaller, a bitch. She was gazing levelly at the strangers; one corner of her upper lip was curled to show sharp white teeth, and she was uttering a faint—as it were a questioning—growl.

Now she rose, the hair on her spine erect, and approached them. They stopped dead.

"Hello," Kate said, with a hint of nervousness. "We're new here. But we've just been to call on Ted, and he and Suzy say we can live in the old Thorgrim house."

"Kate, you can't seriously expect a dog to understand a complex—"

He broke off, dumbfounded. For the bitch had promptly wagged her tail. Smiling, Kate held out her hand to be smelt. After a moment he copied her.

The dog pondered a while, then nodded in an entirely human fashion, and turned her head to show that on the collar she wore there was a plaque with a few words stamped on it.

"Brynhilde," Kate read aloud. "And you belong to some people called Josh and Lorna Treves. Well, how do you do, Brynhilde?"

Solemn, the dog offered each of them her right paw, then returned to her guard duty. They walked on.

"Now do you believe me?" Kate murmured.

"Yes, damn it, I have to. But how on earth could a bunch of your father's dogs have found their way here?"

"Like the mayor said, they probably escaped from a research station and went looking for a good home. Several centers had dogs bred by Dad. Say, I wonder how much further it is to Great Circle Course. Can we have come too far? No street names are marked up anywhere."

"I noticed. That's of a piece with everything else. Helps to force you back from the abstract set to the reality. Of course it's something that can only work in a small community, but—well, how many thousands of streets have you passed along without registering anything but the name? I think that's one of the forces driving people to distraction. One needs solid perceptual food same as one needs solid nutriment; without it, you die of bulk-hunger. There's an intersection, see?"

They hurried the last few paces, and—

"Oh, *Sandy!*" Kate's voice was a gusty sigh. "Sandy, can this possibly be right? It's not a house, it's a piece of sculpture! And it's beautiful!"

After a long and astonished silence he said to the air, "Well, thank *you!*"

And in a fit of exuberance swept her off her feet and carried her over the not-exactly-a-threshold.


# THE LOGICALITY OF LIKING

"I wonder what made you like Precipice so much," Freeman muttered.

"I'd have thought it was obvious. The people there have got right what those at Tarnover got completely wrong."

"To me it sounds like the regular plug-in life-style. You arrive, you take on a house that's spare and waiting, you—"

"No, no, *no!*" In a crescendo. "The first thing we found when we walked in was a note from the former occupier, Lars Thorgrim, explaining that he and his family had had to move away because his wife had developed a disease needing regular radiation therapy so they had to live closer to a big hospital. Otherwise they'd never have moved because they'd been so happy in the house, and they hoped that the next people to use it would feel the same. And both their children sent love and kisses. That's not the plug-in life-style, whose basis consists in leaving behind nothing of yourself when you move on."

"But just as when you joined G2S you were immediately whisked away to a welcome party—"

"For pity's *sake!* At places like G2S you need the

excuse of a new arrival to hold a party; it's a business undertaking, designed to let him and his new colleagues snuff around each other's assholes like wary dogs! At Precipice the concept of the party is built into the social structure; those parties were going to be held anyhow, because of a birthday or an anniversary or just because it was a fine warm evening and a batch of homemade wine was shaping well enough to share. I'm disappointed in you. I'd imagined that you would have seen through the government's attempt to deevee Precipice and gone back to the source material."

For the first time Freeman seemed to be visibly on the defensive. He said in a guarded tone, "Well, naturally I—"

"Save the excuses. If you had dug deep, I wouldn't be giving you this as news. Oh, think, man, think! The Disasterville U.S.A. study constitutes literally the only first-rank analysis of how the faults inherent in our society are revealed in a post-catastrophe context. Work done at other refugee settlements was trivial and superficial, full of learned clichés. But after saying straight out that the victims of the Bay Quake couldn't cope because they'd quit trying to fend for themselves—having long ago discovered that the reins of power had been gathered into the hands of a corrupt and jealous in-group—the people from Claes College topped it off with what Washington felt to be the ultimate insult. They said, 'And this is how to put it right!' "

A dry chuckle.

"Worse still, they proceeded to demonstrate it, and worst of all, they stopped the government from interfering."

"How long after your arrival were you told about that?"

"I wasn't told. I figured it out myself that same evening. It was a classic example of the kind of thing that's so obvious you ignore it. In my case specifically, after my last contact with Hearing Aid I'd unconsciously blanked off all further consideration of the problem. Otherwise I'd have spotted the solution at once."

Freeman sighed. "I thought you were going to defend your obsession with Precipice, not excuse your own shortcomings."

"I enjoy it when you needle me. It shows that your control is getting ragged. Let me tatter it a bit more. I warn you, I intend to make you lose your temper eventually, and never mind how many tranquilizers you take per day. Excuse me; a joke in poor taste. But—oh, please be candid. Has it never surprised you that so few solid data emerged from the aftermath of the Bay Quake, the greatest single calamity in the country's history?"

Freeman's answer was harsh. "It was also the most completely documented event in our history!"

"Which implies that a lot of lessons should have been learned, doesn't it? Name a few."

Freeman sat silent. Once again his face gleamed with sweat. He interlocked his fingers as though to prevent them trembling visibly.

"I think I'm making my point. Fine. Consider. Vast hordes of people had to start from scratch after the quake, and the public at large felt obliged to help them. It was a perfect opportunity to allot priorities: to stand back and assess what was and was not worth having among the countless choices offered by our modern ingenuity. Years, in some cases as much as a decade, elapsed before the economy was strong enough to finance the conversion of the original shantytowns into something permanent. Granted that the refugees themselves were disadvantaged: what about the specialists from outside, the federal planners?"

"They consulted with the settlers, as you well know."

"But did they help them to make value judgments? Not on your life. They counted the cost in purely financial terms. If it was cheaper to pay this or that community to go without something, that's what the community wound up lacking. Under the confident misapprehension that they were serving the needs of the nation by acting as indispensable guinea pigs. Where was the follow-up? How much money was allocated to finding out whether a community without veephones, or without automatic instant credit-transfer facilities, or without home encyclopedia service, was in any sense better or worse than the rest of the continent? None—*none!* What halfhearted projects were allowed to show their heads were axed in the next session of Congress. Not profitable. The only place where constructive work was done was Precipice, and that was thanks to amateur volunteers."

"It's easy to prophesy after the event!"

"But Precipice did succeed. The founders knew what they wanted to do, and had valid arguments to support their ideas. The principle of changing one factor and seeing what happens may be fine in the lab. In the larger world, especially when you're dealing with human beings who are badly disturbed following a traumatic experience and have been forcibly returned to basics—hunger, thirst, epidemics—you aren't compelled to be so simplistic. Evidence exists from the historical record that certain social structures are viable and others aren't. The people from Claes recognized that, and did their best to assemble a solid foundation for a new community without bothering to forecast what would evolve from it."

"Evolution . . . or devolution?"

"An attempt to backtrack to that fork in our social development where we apparently took a wrong turning."

"Invoking all kinds of undocumented half-mystical garbage!"

"Such as—?"

"Oh, this ridiculous notion that we're imprinted before birth with the structure of the aboriginal family, the hunter-and-gatherer tribe and the initial version of the village."

"Have you ever tried to silence a baby?"

"What?"

"You heard me. Humans make mouth noises with the intention of provoking a change in the outside world. Nobody denies any longer that even a dumb baby is printed in advance for language. Damn it, enough of our simian cousins have shown they can use a sound-to-symbol relationship! And equally nobody denies that habit patterns involving status, pack leadership— Whoops, hold everything. I just realized I've been manipulated into defending your viewpoint against myself."

Freeman, relaxing, allowed himself a faint smile.

"And if you continue, you'll expose a basic fallacy in your argument, won't you?" he murmured. "Precipice may indeed function, after a fashion. But it does so in isolation. Having worked for a utopia consultancy, you must realize that if they're efficiently shielded from the rest of humanity the craziest societies can work . . . for a while."

"But Precipice is not isolated. Every day between five hundred and two thousand people punch the ten nines and—well, make confession."

"Thereby painting a picture of the state of things outside which can be relied on to make Precipicians shudder and feel thankful. True or false, the impression is no doubt comforting."

Freeman leaned back, conscious of having scored. His voice was almost a purr as he continued, "You spent time actually listening to some of the calls, I presume?"

"Yes, and at her own insistence so did Kate, though since she wasn't planning to stay she wasn't obliged. They're quite literal about their service. From the central, they route calls to private homes where one adult is always on duty. And someone literally sits and listens."

"How about the people who can talk for hours nonstop?"

"There aren't many of them, and the computers almost always spot them before they're well under way."

"For a community so proud of having evaded the data-net, they rely a great deal on computers, don't they?"

"Mm-hm. Must be the only place on Earth where they've made a cottage industry out of the things. It's amazing how useful they are when you don't burden them with irrelevancies, like recording a transaction worth fifty cents."

"I must find out some time where you draw your dividing line: fifty cents, fifty dollars, fifty thousand dollars . . . But go on. What were the calls like?"

"I was astonished at how few cranks there were. I was told that cranks get disheartened when they find they can't provoke an argument. Someone who's convinced all human faults are due to wearing shoes, or who just found evidence to impeach the president scrawled on the wall of a public toilet, wants to be met with open disagreement; there's an element of masochism there which isn't satisfied by punching pillows. But people with genuine problems—they're a different matter."

"Give some examples."

"Okay. It's a platitude you yourself have used to me to say that the commonest mental disorder now is personality shock. But I never realized before how many people are aware they're lapsing into its subclinical penumbra. I recall one poker who confessed he'd tried the White House Trick, and it had worked."

"What sort of trick?"

"Sometimes it's known as going to the Mexican laundry."

"Ah. You route a credit allotment—to avoid either tax or recriminations—into and out of a section of the net where nobody can follow it without special permission."

"That's it. When income-tax time rolls around, you always hear people mentioning it with an envious chuckle, because it's part of modern folklore. That's how politicians and hypercorp execs get away with a tenth of the tax you and I cough up. Well, this shivver I was listening to had vaulted half a million. And he was beside himself with horror. Not terror— he knew he couldn't be caught—but horror. He said it was his first-ever lapse from rectitude, and if his wife hadn't left him for a richer man he'd never have been tempted. Once having done it and found how easy it was, though . . . how could he ever trust anyone again?"

"But he was trusting Hearing Aid, wasn't he?"

"Yes, and that's one of the miracles performed by the service. While I was a minister I was resigned to having the croakers monitor the link to my confessional, even though what was said face-to-face in the actual booth was adequately private. And there was nothing to stop them noticing that a suspect had called on me, ambushing him as he left, and beating a repeat performance out of him. That type of dishonesty is at the root of our worst problem."

"I didn't know you acknowledged a 'worst'—you seem to find new problems daily. But go on."

"With pleasure. I'm sure that if I start to foam at the mouth there's a machine standing by to wipe my chin. . . . Oh, hell! It's hypocritical hair-splitting that makes me boil! Theoretically any one of us has access to more information than ever in history, and any phone booth is a gate to it. But suppose you live next door to a poker who's suddenly elected to the state congress, and six weeks later he's had a hundred-thousand-dollar face-lift for his house. Try to find out how he came by the money; you get nowhere. Or try confirming that the company you work for is going to be sold and you're apt to be tossed on the street with no job, three kids and a mortgage. Other people seem to have the information. What about the shivver in the next office who's suddenly laughing when he used to mope? Has he borrowed to buy the firm's stock, knowing he can sell for double and retire?"

"Are you quoting calls to Hearing Aid?"

"Yes, both are actual cases. I bend the rules because I know that if I don't you'll break me."

"Are you claiming those are typical?"

"Sure they are. Out of all the calls taken, nearly half—I think they say forty-five percent—are from people who are afraid someone else knows data that they don't and is gaining an unfair advantage by it.

For all the claims one hears about the liberating impact of the data-net, the truth is that it's wished on most of us a brand-new reason for paranoia."

"Considering how short a time you spent at Precipice, your identification with it is amazing."

"Not at all. It's a phenomenon known as 'falling in love' and it happens with places as well as people."

"Then your first lover's tiff happened rather quickly, too."

"Needle, needle! Jab away. I'd done something to make amends in advance. A small but genuine consolation, that."

Freeman tensed. "So you were the one responsible!"

"For frustrating the latest official assault on Hearing Aid? Yes indeed. I'm proud of it. Apart from marking the first occasion when I used my talent on behalf of other people without being asked and without caring whether I was rewarded—which was a major breakthrough in itself—the job was a pure masterpiece. Working on it, I realized in my guts how an artist or an author can get high on the creative act. The poker who wrote Precipice's original tapeworm was pretty good, but you could theoretically have killed it without shutting down the net—that is, at the cost of losing thirty or forty billion bits of data. Which I gather they were just about prepared to do when I showed up. But mine . . . Ho, no! That, I cross my heart, cannot be killed without *dismantling* the net."

## THE BREAKDOWN OF
## REPRESENTATIVE GOVERNMENT

SUBJECT HAFLINGER NICHOLAS KENTON
SELECTED
PROPOSE FACTORS TO ACCOUNT FOR SUBJECTS
INFATUATION WITH P A COMMUNITY PRECIPICE CA
(A) FUNCTIONALITY (B) OBJECTIVITY (C) STABILITY
AMPLIFY RESPONSE (A)
(A) IN MOST TOWNS OF SIMILAR SIZE ON THIS

CONTINENT DECISIONS CONCERNING COMMUNAL
SERVICES CAN NO LONGER BE TAKEN BY POPULAR
VOTE OWING TO EXTREME MOBILITY OF POPULATION
AND UNWILLINGNESS OF VOTERS TO PAY FOR
FACILITIES THAT WILL BE ENJOYED ONLY BY THE
SUCCEDENT GROUP E G BOND LEVIES TO FINANCE
SCHOOLS SEWAGE SYSTEMS AND HIGHWAY MAIN-
TENANCE HAVE BEEN REPLACED IN 93% OF CASES BY
PATERNALIST LEVIES ON THE DOMINANT EMPLOYER
***REFERENCE BARKER PAVLOVSKI & QUAINT THE
RESURRECTION OF FEUDAL OBLIGATIONS J ANTHRO-
POL SOC VOL XXXIX PP 2267–2274
   AMPLIFY RESPONSE (B)
   (B) INTENSIVE INTERACTION BETWEEN CITIZENS
DEEVEES INCIDENTAL ATTRIBUTES E G STATUS TYPE OF
JOB RELATIVE WEALTH/POVERTY EMPHASIZES CHAR-
ACTER SOCIABILITY TRUSTWORTHINESS ***REFERENCE
ANON NEW ROLES FOR OLD AN ANALYSIS OF STATUS
CHANGES AMONG A GROUP OF VICTIMS OF THE
GREAT BAY QUAKE MONOGRAPH #14 DISASTERVILLE
USA SERIES
   AMPLIFY RESPONSE (C)
   (C) POPULATION TURNOVER IN PRECIPICE DESPITE
NEAR AVERAGE VACATION TIME MOBILITY IS LOWEST
ON THE CONTINENT AND HAS NEVER EXCEEDED 1%
PER ANNUM ***REFERENCE U S CONTINUOUS
SAMPLE CENSUS
   THANK YOU
   YOU ARE WELCOME

## —AND THE LIKABILITY OF LODGING

The place took possession of them both so rapidly
he could only just believe it. Tongue-tangled, he—
and Kate, who was equally affected—strove to identify
the reasons.

Perhaps most important, there was more going on
here than in other places. There was a sense of time
being filled, used, taken advantage of. At G2S, at
UMKC, it was more a matter of time being divided

up for you; if the ordained segments were too short, you got little done, while if they were too long, you got less done than you could have. Not here. And yet the Precipicians knew how to idle.

Paradox.

There were so many people to meet, not in the way one met them when taking on a new job or joining a new class, but by being passed on, as it were, from one to another. From Josh and Lorna (he, power engineer and sculptor; she, one of Precipice's two medical doctors, organist and notary public) to Doc Squibbs (veterinarian and glass-blower) on to Ferdie Squibbs, his son (electronics maintenance and amateur plant genetics), and his girlfriend Patricia Kallikian (computer programing and anything to do with textiles) on again to . . .

It was giddying. And the most spectacular possible proof of how genuinely economical it was to run on a maximum-utilization basis. Everyone they met seemed to be pursuing at least two occupations, not moonlighting, not scuffling to make ends meet, but because here they had the chance to indulge more than one preference without worrying about the next hike in utilities charges. Accustomed to a routine five percent increase in the cost of electricity, and ten or twelve in any year when a nuclear reactor melted down— because such installations had long ago ceased to be insurable and the cost of failure could only be recouped from the consumer—the strangers were astonished at the cheapness of energy in this self-reliant community.

Wandering about, they discovered how ingeniously the town had been structured, right from the beginning: its main nucleus at Root Mean Square being echoed by subnuclei that acted as a focus for between three and four hundred people, but neither isolated nor inward-looking, and each with some unique attraction designed to draw occasional visitors from other parts of the town. One had a games area, another a swimming pool, another a constantly changing art exhibition, another a children's zoo with scores of tame, cuddly animals, another a view down a vista flanked by unbelievably gorgeous flowering trees . . . and so forth. All, Suzy Dellinger admitted cheerfully, "of malice aforethought"—the founders of the town had tabulated what was known to help a community run pleasantly, then allotted elements of it to suitable sectors of what had then been a settlement of rickety hovels, battered trailer homes and many tents.

For the first year and a half, they were informed, the builders used nothing but scrap. Plus a great deal of imagination, to compensate for a near-total absence of money.

Additionally, the newcomers were immediately involved. Pausing to chat to a big husky man repairing an electrical connector, they were casually requested to help him lever the covering flagstone back into place; on being introduced to one Eustace Fenelli, who ran a popular bar and restaurant, they found themselves carrying a vast pot of minestrone out of the delectably aromatic kitchen—"since you happen to be going that way!" Strolling toward the main square with Lorna Treves, and passing a house from which a white-faced man emerged at a run, overjoyed to find Lorna because—as he said—he'd just called and heard she wasn't home, they wound up standing by with sterile dressings and a bowlful of blood while she delicately removed a huge splinter of glass from the leg of a screaming child.

"I never found this before," Kate whispered later. "This sense that everybody is ready to help everybody else. I'd heard it was possible. But I thought it was obsolete."

He nodded thoughtfully. "On top of that, there's a sense that being helped doesn't demean you. That's what I like most."

Naturally, among the first places they asked to visit was the actual headquarters of Hearing Aid. With a warning that they might not find it particularly impressive, Brad Compton introduced them to the director, Sweetwater. Just Sweetwater. She was a tall, gaunt woman in her sixties, with long-faded traces on her face and arms of what, she commented, had once been elaborate medicine tattoos. She had believed herself to be a reincarnation of a great Shawnee chief, in touch with the spirit of the beyond, and had operated a clairvoyance and prediction business in Oakland.

"But"—with a wry smile—"not one of my spirits warned me about the quake. I had a son, and . . . Oh, it's ancient history. But before I became a medium I'd been a switchboard operator, so I was one of the first people to volunteer to help with what developed into Hearing Aid. You know how it all started? No? Oh! Well, at all the places where the refugees were forced to settle, most of which were a lot less attractive than our own site—though you should have seen it the day we were stopped at gunpoint by the National Guard and told thus far, no further . . . Where was I? Oh, yes: of course everybody, once they'd calmed down, wanted to tell their friends and relatives they'd survived. So the Army spliced in some manual sound-only field telephone trucks, and people were allowed one call apiece not to last more than five minutes, or one other try if the first number didn't answer. I saw people go right back to the end of the line time after time, because their second call had failed and they weren't allowed a third immediately."

As she talked, she was leading Kate and Sandy away from the library—characteristically, the largest single building in Precipice—down a narrow alley they had not traversed.

"It was a terrible time," Sweetwater went on. "But I'm not sorry to have lived through it . . . Then, of course, as soon as it was known that there was a phone service, people started jamming every circuit in and into California because they hadn't heard from their friends or kinfolk, and kept at it all night and all day regardless of how many pleas were made over the TV to get off the phone so they wouldn't hold up the rescue work. They had to cut some cities out of circuit altogether, I remember. Just withdraw the phone service completely."

She shook her head sorrowfully.

"In the end they had to rig facilities for incoming calls because people who got an answer instead of a circuit-overload signal tended not to come back and bother you until tomorrow. Like I say, I volunteered to run a board handling incoming traffic. At first I was kind of sharp with people. You know—brisk, brusque, whatever the hell. 'You will be notified if your son/daughter/mother/father has survived but you're holding up essential rescue work and how'd you like it if someone dear to you were dying *right now* because you're using this circuit?'

"And then I made this peculiar discovery. A lot of the calls were from people not trying to trace friends and relatives at all. Just—I don't know—wanting contact with the disaster, I guess. As though their last consolation was to know that other people were even worse off. So sometimes, especially at night, I let them talk. They were pretty good about it—just a few minutes' catharsis and that was that. Round about this time the people from Claes came in, and they found the same thing among the refugees. People simply needing to talk. Not just the older folk, who'd lost fine homes and prized possessions, but the youngsters. They were worse. I recall one kid—well, nineteen, twenty, she must have been—who ought to have become a famous sculptor. She was so good, they'd fixed her a one-man show at a San Francisco gallery. And she had to cling to a tree and watch as the earth gobbled up everything she'd got ready, plus her home, her studio, the lot. She never carved another thing; she went insane. And there were others. . . . They didn't want counseling, they just wanted to tell people what their lives used to be like. The plans they had for an extension to the house; the way they meant to lay out the garden, only the house headed north and the garden went south; the trip around the world they were going to take next year—lives charted on a course the quake destroyed."

Pausing now before an unremarkable door, she glanced at them.

"Hence—Hearing Aid. Which gave us a common purpose while we reconstructed, and then simply kept on snowballing."

"Is that what made Precipice such a success compared to the other paid-avoidance towns?" Sandy demanded. "Offering a service that other people valued instead of just accepting charity and public money?"

Sweetwater nodded. "Or at any rate one of the things that helped. Common sense in using our few resources was the other. And here's the central."

She ushered them into a surprisingly small room, where some dozen comfortable chairs were occupied by people wearing headphones. There was another dozen vacant. The place was as hushed as a cathedral; only the faintest buzz of sound escaped the headphones. Eyes turned, heads nodded, but otherwise there was no break in the concentration.

The newcomers' attention was instantly riveted by the expression of dismay on the face of one listener, a pretty black woman in her thirties. Sweetwater advanced on her, looking a question, but she shook her head, shut her eyes, set her teeth.

"A bad one there," Sweetwater murmured, returning to the visitors. "But so long as she thinks she can stand it . . ."

"Is the job a great strain?"

"Yes." Sweetwater's tone was like herself: thin and long-drawn-out. "When someone vents a lifetime of hate on you and then makes sure you hear the hideous guggle as he cuts his carotid with a kitchen knife —yes, it's a strain. Once I had to listen while a crazy woman threw spoonfuls of vitriol at her baby, tied in a feeding chair. She wanted to get back at its father. The poor kid's screams!"

"But was there nothing you could do?" Kate blurted.

"Yes. Listen. That's the promise that we make.

We've always kept it. It may not make a lonely hell less hellish, but it makes it a fraction less lonely."

They pondered that a while. Then Kate inquired, "Are these the only people on duty?"

"Oh, no. This central is for people who can't stand their tour at home—interruptions from small children mainly. But most of us prefer to work from home. Granted, the traffic's light right now; you should see our load come Labor Day, the end of the peak vacation season, when people who hoped against hope the summer would improve their lives realize there really will be another winter."

"How soon do you want to call on us?" Sandy asked.

"No hurry. And it doesn't have to be both of you. I gather Kate can't stay."

But it was only the following night that she said suddenly, "I think I will."

"What?"

"Stay. Or rather, go away and come back as quickly as I can. Depending on a permit to move Bagheera."

He started. "Do you really mean it?"

"Oh, yes. You plan to stay, don't you?"

For a while he didn't answer. At last he said, "Were you eavesdropping?"

"No, it's nothing I've heard you or anybody else say. It—well, it's the way you've acted today. All of a sudden you're confident. I can literally scent it. I think maybe you've found the confidence to trust people."

His voice shook a little. "I hope I have. Because if I can't trust them . . . But I think I can, and I think you're right to say I've finally learned how. Bless you, Kate. It was you who taught me. Wise woman!"

"*Is* this a safe place? The one from which you can't be dragged back to Tarnover?"

"They promised me it would be."

"Who did?"

"Ted, and Suzy, and Sweetwater. And Brynhilde."

171

"What?"

"It was like this. . . ."

They had been invited for dinner by Josh and Lorna. Josh loved to cook; now and then he took over at Fenelli's for the hell of it, feeding fifty people in an evening. Tonight he'd settled for ten, but when the company was sitting around in the garden afterward other people wandered up, by ones and twos, and accepted a glass of wine or a mug of beer and eventually there was a full-sized party numbering at least forty.

For a long time he stood by himself in a dark corner. Then Ted Horovitz and Suzy came toward him, intending—he gathered—to join Sweetwater, who was just arriving on her own. Catching sight of him, Ted said, "Sandy, you settling in okay?"

It was a moment of decision. He took that decision. He squared his shoulders and stepped from shadow.

"I'd like a word with you. And I guess it ought to be with Brad, too."

They exchanged glances. Suzy said, "Brad won't be here—he's listening. But Sweetwater's the first alternate councilman."

"Fine."

His palms sweated. his belly was taut, but in his head there was a great cool calm. The four of them found chairs and sat down a little apart from the rest of the party.

"Well, what is it?" Ted rumbled eventually.

Sandy drew a deep breath. He said, "I realized a few hours ago that I know something about Precipice that you don't."

They waited.

"Tell me first, though: am I right in thinking Hearing Aid is defended by a tapeworm?"

After a brief hesitation Sweetwater said with a shrug, "I'd have thought that was self-evident."

"The Fedcomps are getting set to kill it."

That provoked a reaction. All three of his listeners

jolted forward on their chairs; Ted had been about to light his favorite pipe, and it was instantly forgotten.

"But they can't without—" Suzy began.

"I don't want the details," Sandy interrupted. "I'm just assuming that you have the biggest-ever worm loose in the net, and that it automatically sabotages any attempt to monitor a call to the ten nines. If I'd had to tackle the job, back when they first tied the home-phone service into the net, I'd have written the worm as an explosive scrambler, probably about half a million bits long, with a backup virus facility and a last-ditch infinitely replicating tail. It should just about have been possible to hang that sort of tail on a worm by 2005. I don't know whether yours has one or not and it doesn't matter. What does matter is that while I was a systems rash with G2S recently I moused around the net considerably more than my employers required of me, and I ran across something I only today spotted as significant."

They were hanging on his every word now.

"For about eighteen months they've been routinely copying Class-A Star data from G2S and every other hypercorporation with a maximum-national-advantage rating and lifting the copies clear of the net for storage. I thought maybe they were tired of hypercorp execs pulling the White House Trick and other similar gimmicks, so they needed a standard reference to appeal to. It didn't occur to me that this might be the preliminary stages of a worm-killing job. I never guessed that big a worm was free and running. Now I see the implications, and I guess you do too, hm?"

Very pale, Ted said, "Too true! That makes non-sense of the virus facility, let alone the simple scrambler aspect. And in fact our worm doesn't have the kind of tail you mentioned. Later, we were vaguely hoping we could add one . . . but Washington's tolerance of Hearing Aid was wearing thin, and we didn't want to irritate the authorities."

"They must hate us," Sweetwater said. "Really, they must loathe Precipice."

"They're scared of us, that's what it is," Suzy corrected. "But . . . Oh, I find it hard to believe they'd be willing to clear up the sort of mess our worm could cause. I've always understood it works in two stages: if someone tries to monitor a call to Hearing Aid it scrambles the nearest major nexus, and if they did try to kill it, they'd find over thirty billion bits of data garbled randomly but not know where the damage had been done. It might be years before the returns all came in. We never found out whether that virus facility actually works, but the front end—the scrambler—that works fine, and the BDP once proved it to their cost."

Sandy nodded. "But they're prepared to cope with the virus aspect now. Like I said, they've lifted the max-nat-ad stuff out of the net altogether, ready to be slotted in again afterward."

He leaned back, reaching for his glass.

"We're obliged to you, Sandy," Sweetwater said after a brief silence. "I guess we better put on our thinking caps and see what we can—"

He cut her short. "No, I'll do it. What you need is a worm with a completely different structure. The type they call a replicating phage. And the first thing you must give it to eat is your original worm."

"A replicating phage?" Suzy repeated. "I never heard that term before."

"Not surprising. They're kind of dangerous. Plenty of them have been used in restricted situations. Like, come election time, you disguise one and slip it into the membership list of the opposition party, hoping they don't have duplicate records. But there are very few in the continental net, and the only big one is inactive until called for. In case you're interested, it was devised at a place called Electric Skillet, and its function is to shut the net down and prevent it being exploited by a conquering army. They think the job would be complete in thirty seconds."

Ted frowned. "How come you talk about these phages with authority?" he demanded.

"Well . . ." Sandy hesitated, then took the plunge. "Well, I've had mine running behind me for over six years, and it's stood me in good stead. I don't see why one shouldn't do the same for Hearing Aid."

"So what the hell do you use one for?"

Keeping his voice level with immense effort, he told them. They listened. And then Ted did an extraordinary thing.

He whistled shrilly. From where she kept her watch Brynhilde rose and ambled over.

"Is this poker lying?" Ted inquired.

She snuffed at Sandy's crotch—diffidently as though reluctant to take such liberties—shook her head, and went back the way she had come.

"Okay," Suzy said. "What exactly will you need, and how long will it take?"

# DOGGED

"Out of the question," said Dr. Joel Bosch. "He must be lying."

Acutely aware he was sitting in the same office, perhaps even in the same chair, as Nickie Haflinger the day he encountered the late Miranda, Freeman said patiently, "But our techniques eliminate all possibility of deliberate falsehood."

"Clearly that cannot be the case." Bosch's tone was brisk. "I'm very well acquainted with Lilleberg's work. It's true he produced some spectacular anomalous results. His explanations of them, however, amounted to no more than doubletalk. We know now what processes must be applied to produce that kind of effect, and Lilleberg never even pretended to use them. They simply didn't exist when he retired."

"There was considerable controversy over the so-called Lilleberg Hypothesis," Freeman persisted.

"That controversy was long ago resolved!" Bosch snapped. And added with a strained attempt at greater politeness: "For reasons which I'm afraid a . . . a *nonspecialist* like yourself might find difficult to follow. I'm sorry, but there has to be a flaw in your interrogation methods. I suggest you re-evaluate them. Good afternoon."

Defeated, Freeman rose. Suddenly a muscle in his left cheek had started to go tic-tic-tic.

## HIATUS

Outside, the noise of quiet-humming motors as the tribe assembled. Inside, agonized by indecision, she walked back and forth, back and forth, her nails bitten to the quick.

". . . after *that*, of course, I couldn't go on living with him. I mean could I? Flaunting around the neighborhood like that, not caring who knew what he was up to . . ."

The sound of the motors faded. There was a phone in the corner of the room. She made no move toward it, even now.

". . . just sit there! I mean how can you? I mean here I am all alone and it's the third night in a row and last week was the same and in the name of God come, somebody come and put some weight on these empty dusty stairs and . . ."

If he finds out, he'll kill me. I know he will. But once I called them and in a way I guess it saved my sanity. Any rate it got me here without committing suicide. Tonight someone else—and yet I know Jemmy *would* kill me if he guessed.

". . . not so much drinking it as lining it, catch? Jee-sowss if I found him cleaning his teeth with it I wouldn't be surprised and if they marketed a bourbon-flavor toothpaste he'd be the first customer not that he brushes his teeth too often and the stink of them rotting is . . ."

At last, fatalistically, she did approach the phone.

It took her two tries to punch the number; first time, she lost count partway through. The screen lit.

"Hey!" In a desperate whisper, as though Jemmy could hear her from kilometers away. "You got to do something, do it quick! See, my son rides with the Blackass tribe and they just started off for a match with—"

A girl's quiet voice interrupted. "You have contacted Hearing Aid, which exists exclusively to listen. We do not act, intervene or hold conversations. If you wish assistance, apply to one of the regular emergency services."

The stinking stupid twitches! Well, hell, what do I owe them anyway? Let 'em find out what fools they are. If they won't take help when it's offered. . . .

But the tribes must be nearly there by now. Burning and wrecking and looting and killing. And I remember my brother Archie with his eyeball hanging loose on his cheek and him only nineteen.

One last try. Then let 'em go to hell if they prefer.

"Now you *listen* this time! I'm calling you to *warn* you! My son Jemmy is riding with the Blackass tribe out of Quemadura and they got this match with the Mariachis out of San Feliciano and it's about how many houses they can fire in Precipice and the warlord has a mortar, hear me, a real army mortar and a case of shells!"

And concluding in a tone close to sobs: "When he finds out Jemmy's just naturally going to beat me to death. But I couldn't let it happen without I warned you!"

## SLACK SHIFT INTO HIGH GEAR

"Call the sheriff!"

At his yell everyone else on this undemanding shift in the headquarters of Hearing Aid—including Kate, who like himself was being trained under supervision before being permitted to take calls at home—looked daggers. Someone said, "Ssh, I'm listening."

"Two tribes closing on Precipice for a match, and one of them has an army mortar!"

That worked, galvanizing people into action. But a little too late. Kate said, breaking rules and removing her headphones, "A while back I had to kill a call that said something about a tribal match. I wonder if—"

He had begun to turn and look at her when the first explosion smashed the evening quiet.

While the others were still jumping with alarm he completed the turn and said, "You killed a call that tried to warn us?"

To which her answer was drowned out by a sound such as had not been heard before in the history of Precipice, which none who heard it wished to hear again: as though instantly they were trapped inside the largest organ in the world, and its player were striking a full diapason just that teeth-gritting fraction off true pitch. Between a bay and a howl, it was the cry of a hundred and fifty giant dogs answering their leader's call.

*Arrgh-OOO . . . !*

Only the pups were left on guard, and the bitches nursing young litters. The rest of Natty Bumppo's forces tore into the night, following the scent of fear, for that first howl alone had been enough to throw the attackers in confusion. There were shots, and one more mortar shell was fired, but it fell wide.

Thirty minutes, and the dogs drove in the tribers, weeping, bleeding and disarmed, to have their bites bound up before being dumped in the town's various lockable sheds and cellars for want of an actual jail. Two dogs were shot, one fatally, and another was stabbed but survived, while thirty-seven tribers—not prepared to encounter an enemy of this stamp—were placed under arrest. The oldest of them proved to be eighteen.

All this, however, was too late to save the house at Great Circle Course and Drunkard's Walk.

## GRIEVANCE

There were tears glistening on the cheeks of the subject, and the instruments advised returning him to present-time mode. Following their guidance, Freeman waited patiently until the man regained total consciousness.

He said at last, "It's remarkable that you were so affected by the destruction of a house to which you barely had a chance to grow attached. Moreover, even if the first warning call had been heeded, there would still not have been enough time to forestall the attack, and it was the very first shell which struck your home."

"You're soulless. As well as heartless!"

Freeman remained silent.

"Oh-h-h . . . ! Sure, sure, I know. Kate was obeying the regulations; she'd got a grasp of them faster than I had. It is standard practice at Hearing Aid never to accept a call that orders the listener to *do* something, because services exist for that purpose. And even if the woman who called had managed to get the point across about a warning in the first couple of seconds, the reaction would still have been the same. They tell you to try and deevee any call that begins with a hysterical warning, because nine times out of ten it's some religious nut threatening to visit the wrath of God on us. I mean Precipice. And I guess I was aware of that at the time. I know equally well it was pointless to scream and rant at her and I went ahead and did it anyhow, standing there by the burnt-out wreck of the house with the smoke stinging in my eyes and the stench in my nose and a dozen people trying to reason with me. Didn't work. I lost my temper on the grand scale. I think what I did was let go all the potential for rage I'd been bottling up since babyhood. In the end . . ." He had to swallow and resume.

"I did something I probably last did when I was ten. I hit somebody."

"Predictably, it was Kate."

"Yes, of course. And . . ." He started to laugh, incongruously because tears were still bright on his cheeks. "And I found myself a second later sprawling in the dirt, with Brynhilde's paw on my chest and that great-toothed jaw looming close and she was shaking her head and—I swear—going 'tsk-tsk, naughty boy!' I could wish she had been a trifle quicker. Because I've never seen Kate since."

The laughter failed. Misery overspread his face.

"Ah. Losing the house, then, affected you so deeply because it symbolized your relationship with Kate."

"You don't understand a fraction of the truth. Not a millionth of it. The whole scene, the whole framework, was *composed* of loss. Not just the house, even though it was the first place I'd been to where I felt I could grasp all the overtones of the word 'home'— not just Kate, even though with her I'd also started to comprehend for the first time what one can imply by the word 'love.' No, there was more on top of that, something far closer to me. Loss of the control which had enabled me to change identities at will. That blew away on the wind the moment I realized I'd struck the last person in the world I could want to hurt."

"Are you certain she would have kept that casual promise about returning from KC? Obtaining a permit to transport her pet mountain lion would have been incredibly difficult. What grounds did you have for believing that she was sincere?"

"Among other things, the fact that she had kept a promise made to that mountain lion. She's not the sort to forget any promise. And by then I'd figured out why else she'd kept on enrolling for course after unrelated course at the same university. Basically it was to provide her with a sense of pattern. She wanted her world-picture to include a little of everything, viewed from the same spot with the same perspective. She'd have been prepared to continue for another decade if necessary."

"But she met you, and living with you was an education in itself. I see. Well, I can accept the idea. Ten years at Tarnover, at three million per, should indeed have equipped you with data you could pass on."

"I suspect your sense of humor is limited to irony. Do you ever laugh at a joke?"

"Seldom. I've heard virtually all of them before."

"No doubt among the components of human personality you're trying to analyze humor is on the list right next to grief."

"Directly afterward. H follows G."

There was a pause.

"You know, this is the first time I've not been sure whether you're bleating me."

"Work it out for yourself." Freeman rose and stretched. "It will occupy your mind until our next session."


## STRIKE ONE

After hitting Kate . . .

That his world had been repainted in shades of bitterness was no defense. Some of these his new neighbors—his new friends—were old enough to have seen not one house but a whole city fall in ruin.

Anyhow, what apology could he offer in a context where even dogs could distinguish force from violence? The tribers who thought it amusing to lob mortar shells at random into a peaceful community had been rounded up. Some were tooth-marked. But the bites had been precisely controlled. That arm had wielded a gun or knife; therefore those fingers had been obliged to open and let the weapon fall. That pair of legs had tried to carry the owner away; therefore that ankle had been nipped just hard enough to make him stumble. All for good reason.

His reason for hitting Kate was not good. They told him why, in quiet patient tones. Deaf to their arguments, he hurled back false justification mixed with insult, until at last they glanced at one another, shrugged and left him.

It was not cold, that night he spent sitting on a stump and staring at the shell of the house. But in his heart there was an arctic chill of such indescribable shame as he had not felt since he became an adult.

In the end he simply walked away, not caring where.

And came many hours later to the place which had vomited over Precipice the Blackass tribe. It was sweaty dust from all-day walking which made his shoes loathsome to his feet, but it seemed to him like the detritus of human cruelty: the materialized version of bloodlust, its ectoplasm.

"I don't know who I am," he said to an incurious passerby as he entered Quemadura.

"I don't know who the hell you are either," the stranger snapped, pushing past.

He pondered that.


## IGNORANTIA NIHIL EXCUSAT

Ted Horovitz made necessary adjustments to the form-letter program, tapped the print key, and read the result as it emerged from the machine. This, thank goodness, was the last of the thirty-seven.

"Dear Mrs. Young, your son Jabez was arrested here last night while in possession of four deadly weapons of which one, a pistol, had been used within the previous few minutes. The hearing has been set for 10:10 tomorrow. You may wish to employ counsel, in which case the enclosed summary of evidence should be furnished to him or her; otherwise you may rest assured that Jabez will be represented by a competent lawyer appointed by the court. He has declared himself unaware of the fact that under our judicial code conviction for this crime entails a mandatory sentence of not less than one year's supervised rehabilitation during which period the convict is forbidden to leave the town limits. (There is no maximum length for such a sentence.) Please note that one of the oldest of all legal principles states: 'Ignorance of the law excuses nothing.' In other words neither a defense nor an appeal may be founded on the plea, 'I didn't know.' Yours, &c."

Turning hopefully to Brad Compton, who among his various other roles acted as their chief legal counselor, he said, "So that's all until the court assembles, right?"

"Far as I'm concerned," Brad grunted. "But don't relax too soon. I was talking to Sweetwater this morning, and it seems she's found something you have to—"

"Ted!" A shrill cry from outside.

"I could half believe that woman's telepathic," Ted sighed, tapping out his pipe prior to refilling it. "Yes, Sweetwater, come right in!"

She entered, carrying a folded stack of computer printouts, which she dumped on a table at Ted's side. Dropping into a chair, she slapped the pile of paper with her open palm.

"I knew it. I *knew* what Sandy told us the other night at Josh and Lorna's rang a bell in my memory. A long way back—over eleven years—but it was the kind of call you get once in a lifetime. Once I started digging, I got correlation after correlation. Take a look."

Ted, frowning, complied; Brad came around behind his chair to read over his shoulder.

There was a long silence, but for the rustle of the concertinaed sheets.

At last Ted said, not looking up, "Any news of him?"

Sweetwater shook her head. "Nor Kate either."

"Kate left town," Brad said. "Took the railcar about seven thirty. But nobody knows what's become of Sandy."

"All of us, though," Ted muttered, "know what's apt to become of him . . . don't we?"

They both nodded.

"Better call Suzy," Ted said, leaning back with a sigh. "I got a councilman's motion to submit."

"Making Sandy a freeman of Precipice?" Sweetwater suggested. "Making our defenses his defenses?"

"Mm-hm."

"Well, naturally you have my vote. But . . ."

"But what?"

"Have you forgotten? We don't know who he is. He told us what. He didn't think to tell us who."

Ted's jaw dropped. "His code?" he said after a pause.

"I checked immediately. No such. It's been deleted. And doubtless his protective phage went with it."

"That makes the job more difficult," Brad said. "I still think it ought to be done. And when she reads this information you've uncovered, I'm certain Suzy will agree."


## COLLAPSE OF STOUT PARTY

"Interesting. Very interesting. This might save a lot of trouble. Say, Perce!"

"Yes?"

"Know that hole-in-corner place Precipice CA? Looks like their sheriff went a step too far."

"Oh, Gerry. Oh, *Gerry*. If you weren't new around here I guess you'd realize nothing at Precipice can go too far. The pokers from Claes who wrote the deal they have with the government were the smartest con men that ever pulled wool over the eyes of a Washington sheep. But for once I'll bite. It would be great to undermine them. What you got?"

"Well, they arrested these here tribers, and—"

*"And?"*

"Hell, look at the sentences they handed down!"

"Not to leave town for one year minimum, to accept escort by a dog apiece . . . So?"

"Goddammit, escort by a dog?"

"They got kind of weird dogs out there. You didn't check, did you?"

"Well, I guess I—"

"Save it, save it. You didn't check. So, not having checked, what did you expect to get out of this?"

"I though maybe—uh—an injunction? Grounds of cruel-and-unusual? Or even kidnaping. I mean one of the tribers is only thirteen."

"There are four states where they routinely agree applications to be declared competent if the applicant is past his or her thirteenth birthday. California's one. It might be educational for you to find out what the others are. As to cruel-and-unusual, you should also know there's one city where you can still legally be burned alive provided they don't pick a Sunday. They didn't do it much lately, but it's on the books, not repealed. Ask any computer. Oh, get back to work, will you? While you've been gabbing they probably sneaked a brand-new tapeworm past you."

Pause.

"Perce!"

"What is it this time?"

"Remember what you said about a tapeworm?"

"Oh my God. That was a joke. You mean they spat in our eye again?"

"See for yourself, It's kind of—uh—fierce, isn't it?"

"Fierce is only half of it. Well, I guess it better claim its first victim. You found it. You go tell Mr. Hartz to abandon the attack on Hearing Aid."

"What?"

"You heard me. Carry the good news from Y to X! Tamper with this thing, and—and my God! The data-net would be in chaos in one minute flat or maybe sooner! *Hurry!*"


# BIG TOP

Belly sour with hunger, throat dry with dust, he wandered the darkening streets of Quemadura, scarcely aware that he was part of a trend. There were people and vehicles converging. He went with the crowd. Drained, passive, he ignored reality until suddenly he was spoken to.

"Damn it, shivver, you deaf and dumb or something?"

*What?*

He emerged from his chrysalis of overload, blinking, and discovered where he was. He'd seen this place before. But only on three-vee, never in reality. Above all he had never smelt it. The air was foul with the stench of frightened animals and eager people.

Many signs, hurtfully bright, flashed on and off to confirm his discovery. Some said CIRCUS BOCCONI; others stated more discreetly that a Roman-style show would start in 11 minutes. The 11 changed to 10 as he watched.

"What kinda seat you want?" rapped the same grumpy voice. "Ten, twenty, thirty?"

"Uh . . ."

He fumbled in his pocket, finding some bills. As part of the ambience, tickets for this show were issued by a live human being, a scar-faced man missing fingers from his right hand. On seeing cash he scowled; however, the machine at the side of his booth decided it was genuine and parted with a ten-dollar ticket.

Wondering what he was doing here, he followed signs saying $10, $10, $10. Shortly he was in a hall: maybe a converted aircraft hangar. There were bleachers and boxes surrounding an arena and a pit. Machines were hanging up phony-looking decor, banners with misspelled Latin slogans, plastic fasces bundled around dull plastic axes.

Making his way with mechanical politeness to a vacant seat in a high row with a poor view, he shamelessly listened to what the earlier arrivals, the keen 'fishes, were saying.

"Wasting those 'gators on kids, *hell!* I mean I hate my kids as much as anybody, but if you can get real live 'gators—well, *hell!*"

"Hope they got some whites on the menu. Sickantired of these here blacks, allatime wanna make like grandpa, fight a lion singlehanded and clutched but clutched on *the* heaviest dope!"

"Course it's all faked, like they got radio implants

in the animals' brains so they don't get to really hurt anybody 'cause of the insurance being so stiff and—"

A hugely amplified voice rang out. "Five minutes! In just five short minutes the great spectacle begins! Absolutely and positively no one will be admitted after the start of the show! Remember only Circus Bocconi goes out live live *live* in real time up and down the whole West Coast! And we record as well, retransmit to the unlucky portions of the continent!"

Suddenly he was vaguely frightened, and cast around for a chance to leave again. But the customers were coming thick and fast now, and he was unwilling to push against the flow. Besides, there was a camera coasting his way. It rode a jointed metal arm, like a mantis's foreleg, dangling from a miniature electric trolley on a rail under the roof. Its dual eye, faceted, seemed to be focusing on him. He was even more reluctant to attract attention by leaving than he was to stay and watch the show.

He folded his arms close around his body as though to stop himself from shivering.

It would only be an hour, he consoled himself.

The introductory acts he was more or less able to disregard though some nausea gathered in a bubble at the base of his gullet during the second item: imported from Iraq, one genuine snake-eater, an ugly man with a bulging forehead hinting at hydrocephalic idiocy who calmly offered his tongue to a snake, let it strike, then drew in his tongue again, bit off its head, chewed and swallowed, then rose shyly grinning to acknowledge the audience's howls of applause.

Then came a stylized match between gladiators, a nod to the ostensible "Roman" format of the show, which concluded with the retiarius bleeding from a leg wound and the gladiator proper—the man with the sword and shield—strutting around the arena prouder than a turkeycock, having done nothing to speak of.

Dull resentment burgeoned in his mind.

*It's disgusting. Butchered to make a Roman holiday. A cheat from start to finish. Filthy. Horrible.*

187

*This is where parents learn to raise the kids who get their kicks from tribaling a stranger's home. This is where they get taught you should remember how you killed your mother. Cut off your father's balls. Ate the baby to stop mom and dad loving it more than you. Sick. All sick. Crazy sick.*

At Tarnover there had been a kind of subcult for circus. Something to do with channeling aggression into socially acceptable paths. The memory was a dim echo. There was a dreadful confusion inside his head. He was hungry and thirsty and above all miserable.

"And now a short break so our sponsors' messages can reach the world," boomed the master of ceremonies over the monstrously loud PA. "Time for me to let you know about a unique feature of our Roman shows. Al Jackson, who's our champion gladiator, that you saw a minute back . . ."

Pause for a ripple of renewed clapping and shouting.

"Yea-hey! Tough as they come, with family following in his footsteps—y'know his son is warlord of the Blackass tribe?"

Pause. This time not filled. As though the speaker had been waiting for a scream and yell from the tribers, who weren't present.

But he covered the hiatus expertly.

"Al issues a real-time challenge on all these shows —yes, literally a challenge in real time, no fixing, no prearrangement. Want to try your skill against him, take over the net and trident for the final slot? You can, any of you! Just stand up and holler how!"

Without intending, he was on his feet.

"*He* raised the warlord of the Blackass tribe?"

He heard his own voice as though it were coming from light-years' distance.

"Yeah *man!* A son to be proud of, young Bud Jackson!"

"Then I'm going to take Al to little tiny pieces." He was leaving his seat, still listening to himself shout at the top of his lungs. "I'm going to make him weep and beg and plead for mercy. I'm going to teach him all the things his son taught me, and I am going to make him howl, and blubber, and plead and moan. And it's going to go on for a lot longer than this show."

There was a rattle of applause, and the audience sat up and looked eager. Someone patted him on the shoulder as he passed and wished him luck.


## DEFINITION OF TERMS

"A classic instance of the death wish."

"Garbage. I had no least intention of being dead. I'd watched that fat slob. I knew I could dismantle him even though I was weak and excessively angry. Didn't I prove it? He was seven days in the hospital, you know, and he'll never walk straight again."

"Agreed. But on the other hand making yourself conspicuous before a three-vee audience . . . ?"

"Yes. Yes, there was that."


## THE MEDIUM IS THE MESS-UP

Traditionally one had defaced or scrawled on posters and billboards, or sometimes—mainly in rural areas—shot at them because the eyes or nipples of a model formed convenient targets.

Later, when a common gadget around the house was a set of transparent screens (like those later used for the electronic version of fencing) to place over the TV set for mock-tennis and similar games, strangely enough the viewers' ratings for commercials went up. Instead of changing channels when advertising began, people took to switching in search of more of the same.

To the content of which they were paying no attention. What they wanted was to memorize the next movement of the actors and actresses and deform their gestures in hilarious fashion with a magnetic pencil. One had to know the timing of the commercials pretty well to become good at the game; some of the images lasted only half a second.

With horror the advertisers and network officials discovered that in nine cases out of ten the most dedicated watchers could not recall what product was being promoted. For them, it wasn't "that Coke ad" or "that plug for Drāno"—it was "the one where you can make her swipe him in the chops."

Saturation point, and the inception of diminishing returns, was generally dated to the early eighties, when the urban citizen of North America was for the first time hit with an average of over a thousand advertisements *per diem*.

They went right on advertising things, of course. It had become a habit.

## SWORD, MASK AND NET

Chuckling, Shad Fluckner laid aside his magnetic pencil. The commercial break was over and the circus program was due to resume. Employees of Anti-Trauma Inc. were more than just encouraged, they were virtually compelled, to watch the broadcasts from Circus Bocconi in Quemadura. Sponsoring circus was one of the best ways the corporation had found to attract new clients. Precisely those parents who spent most time indulging violence on the vicarious level were those most afraid of what would happen if their children's aggression were to be turned on them. In fact, the more circus the parents watched, the sooner they were inclined to sign the kids up for a course of treatment. The relationship could be shown to be linear plus or minus fourteen percent.

It was no sweat for him. He'd always enjoyed circus anyhow. But if they knew, at Anti-Trauma HQ, what one of their employees had figured out to do to their latest commercial, feathers would well and truly fly. Ho-ho! It was a shame he couldn't share his discovery with anyone; his colleagues would interpret it as disloyal except for those who'd decided it was time to

move to another job, and . . . Well, he had the same
idea in mind himself, and might reach the decision
before the lifetime of the commercial expired. Meanwhile it was great fun to fool with.

Still grinning, he composed himself to watch the
final segment of the show, the bit where Al Jackson
allegedly issued an open challenge to members of the
audience. Rigged for sure, this deal, but occasionally . . .

*Hey.*

*Not so heavily rigged, this one. Not unless they
decided to surple Al and— Goddamn, he's screaming! He really is screaming! This is great stuff for
once. This is really very sick indeed. This is muchis-
simo. Hmm . . . yes!*

Eyes bulbing, he leaned closer to the screen. No
fake, that blood. Nor the howls of agony, either!
Say, who could this poker be who was making mince-
meat of Bocconi's star turn—?

"But it's Lazarus," he said suddenly to the air.
"Beard or no beard, I'd know that shivver anywhere.
And he gave me the slip before and this time—oh,
*this* time . . . !"

## NEXT IN LINE

"And once he was recognized on three-vee it was
only a matter of time," Hartz said, leaning back behind his desk. It was captioned *Deputy Director*.
Thumbing one of many switches, he shut off the rolling replay of the Haflinger tapes.

"Yes, sir," Freeman said. "And the FBI was very
quick to corner him."

"Quicker than you to drain him," Hartz said, and
gave a sleepy smile. In the context of this office, his
home base, he was a different person from the visitor
who had called on Freeman at Tarnover. Perhaps that
was why he had declined an invitation to return.

"I beg your pardon," Freeman said stiffly. "My brief

was to extract all possible data from him. That couldn't be done quickly. Nonetheless, to within a margin of about half a percent, I've achieved it."

"That may be good enough for you. It's not enough for us."

"What?"

"I believe I made myself clear. After your long-drawn-out interrogation of this subject we still do not know what we most want to know."

"That being . . . ?" Freeman's voice grew frostier by the moment.

"The answer, I submit, is self-evident. An intolerable situation exists concerning Precipice vis-à-vis the government. A small dissident group has succeeded in establishing a posture of deterrence in principle no different from that adopted by a crazy terrorist threatening to throw the switch on a nuke. We were ready to eliminate this anomaly. Only Haflinger—Locke— Lazarus—whatever he was calling himself at the time —intervened and sent us back to square one. You have spent weeks interrogating him. In all the mounds of data you've accumulated, in all the kilometers of tape you've totaled, there is no slightest clue to what we want to know."

"How to deevee the phage he wrote to protect Hearing Aid?"

"Ah, brilliant! You worked it out!" Hartz's tone was laden with excess irony. "It is, as I said, intolerable that one small community should interfere with the government's right to monitor subversion, disaffection and treason. We have to know how to discontinue that tapeworm!"

"You're crying for the moon," Freeman said after a pause. "Haflinger doesn't know how to do that himself. I'd stake my reputation on it."

"And that's your final word?"

"Yes."

"I see. Hmm. Regrettable!" Hartz tipped his chair back as far as it would go, twisted it through a few degrees, gazed with concentration into the far corner of the room. "Well, what about the other contacts he had? What about Kate Lilleberg, for instance? What have you found out about her recent actions?"

"She would appear to have reverted to her former plans," Freeman sighed. "She's back in KC, she's filed no application to move her pet mountain lion, and in fact I can think of only one positive decision she has made since her return."

"That being, I gather, to alter one of her majors for the coming academic year. She now plans to take data processing, doesn't she?"

"Ah . . . Yes, I believe she does."

"A strange coincidence. A very weird coincidence indeed. Don't you think?"

"A connection is possible—in fact it's likely. Calling it coincidence . . . no."

"Good. I'm glad that for once you and I agree on something." Hartz returned his chair to the upright position and leaned intently toward Freeman. "Tell me, then: have you formed any opinion concerning the Lilleberg girl? I appreciate you never met her. But you've met people intimately involved with her, such as her mother, her lover and sundry friends."

"Apparently a person with considerable common sense," Freeman said after a pause for reflection. "I can't deny that I'm impressed with what she did to help Haflinger. It's no small achievement to elude . . ."

His words faded as though he had suddenly begun to hear what he was saying ahead of time.

"Go on," Hartz purred.

"I was going to add: such an intensive hunt as has been kept up over six years now. Since Haflinger absconded, I mean. She seemed to—well, to grasp the scale of it at once."

"And didn't disbelieve what he told her, either. Did she?"

"She didn't behave as though she did. No."

"Hmm . . . Well, I'm pleased to inform you that you'll have adequate opportunity to confirm or deevee your opinion." Hartz hit another switch; the wall screen in the office lit, showing a vastly enlarged face.

"Computer evaluation here at BDP suggests that

your no doubt sophisticated techniques might benefit from reinforcement by—what to call it?—an alternative approach, let's say, which may strike you as old-fashioned yet which has something to be said in its favor. Because we intend to destroy that tapeworm Haflinger gave to Hearing Aid!" With a sudden glare. "And before the end of this year, what's more! I have the president's personal instructions to that effect."

Freeman's mouth worked. No sound emerged. He was gazing at the screen.

"Despite any impression I may have given to the contrary," Hartz continued, "we here in Washington are most cognizant of your skill, patience and thoroughness. Certainly we don't know anyone who could have done a better job. That's exactly why we're sending you a new subject."

"But . . ." Freeman raised a shaky finger to point. "But that's Kate Lilleberg!"

"Yes indeed. That is Kate Lilleberg. And we expect her presence at Tarnover to afford the extra leverage you need in order to pry the last most precious secret out of Nickie Haflinger. Now you must excuse me. I can't spare you any more of my time. Good afternoon."

# BOOK 3

SPLICING THE BRAIN RACE

## MAN PROPOSES

"Now the way *I* see it—"
"Who the hell do you think you are?"


## THE LONG AND THE SHORT OF IT

This is a basic place, a farm. Listen to it.
*Land. House. Barn. Sun. Rain. Snow. Field. Fence.
Pond. Corn. Wheat. Hay. Plow. Sow. Reap. Horse.
Pig. Cow.*
This is an abstract place, a concert hall. Listen to it.
*Conductor. Orchestra. Audience. Overture. Concerto. Symphony. Podium. Harmony. Instrument.
Oratorio. Variations. Arrangement. Violin. Clarinet.
Piccolo. Tympani. Pianoforte. Auditorium.*

But consider also:
*Harp. Horn. Drum. Song. Pipe.*
And similarly:
*Alfalfa. Rutabaga. Fertilizer. Combine harvester.*

Assign the following (no credit) to one or other
of the categories implied by the foregoing parameters:*
*Bit. Record. Memory. Switch. Program. Transistor.
Tape. Data. Electricity. On-line. Down-time. Printout.
Read. Process. Cybernetics.*


## A CASE OF ARRESTED DEVELOPMENT

For the first time since the arrival on her thres-

---

* Do not on any account give the same answer tomorrow as
you give today.

hold of the—late?—Sandy Locke, Kate's annunciator sounded when she wasn't expecting anybody.

These days, you simply did *not* go call on somebody without advance warning. It wasn't worth it. For one thing, people were spending less time in their homes, statistics said, than ever before in history—despite the arrival of the world in full color and mock solidity thanks to three-vee in the corner of the living room. And for another, perhaps more important, calling without notice was liable to get you webbed in a net of unbreakable plastic, possibly even gassed, at any home above the poverty level.

So you used the veephone first.

In the middle of her largest room, whose walls she was redecorating with enormous photo-enlargements of microscopic circuit elements—eventually, touched in with metallic paint, they would be quite an efficient private computer—Kate stopped dead and pondered.

*Well, no harm in looking at whoever it is.*

Sighing, she switched on the camera and found herself staring at a man she didn't know: young, fair, untidy, in casual clothes.

"You're Kate!" he said brightly.

"And you are—?"

"Name of Sid. Sid Fessier. Been spending summer vac in the paid-avoidance zones. Ran into a poker name of Sandy, said to greet you when I bounced off KC, and when it turned out I'd picked a hotel just one block distant . . . Guess I should have called ahead, but hell—one block on a fine day like today!"

"Well, great. Come on up."

He whistled as he climbed the stairs: a reel or jig. And when she opened the door, hit her with a webber that tied her into an instant package.

"Bagheera!" she screamed, falling sidelong as the strands of plastic tangled around her legs.

*Pop.*

Still gathering himself for a pounce which could have carried him the full length of the hallway, straight to the intruder's head, the mountain lion flinched, moaned, made as though to scrabble at an irritation on his chest—and collapsed.

He was good, this man, and very fast. Even as he returned the gun to his pocket he was slapping a patch of adhesive plastic over Kate's mouth to silence her.

"Anesthetic dart," he murmured. "No need to worry about him. He'll be taken care of. Right as rain in two or three hours. But I had to give him the maximum dose, you know. Not my favorite pastime, messing with a beast like him."

Having eased the door softly shut, he now produced a communicator and spoke to it. "Okay, come and pick her up. But best be quiet. This looks like a neighborhood where folk still take an interest in other people's business."

"You got the lion?"

"Think I'd be talking to you if I hadn't?"

Tucking the communicator away again, he added over her furious futile grunts and snorts, "Save your breath, slittie. I don't know what you've done, but it's serious. I have a warrant for your arrest and detention without bail signed by the deputy director of the Federal Bureau of Data Processing, who's kind of high on the Washington totem pole. Anyhow, I'm not the shivver to argue with. Just an errand boy, me."

## DIFFERENTIATED

Things had changed. Not merely on the surface, although his situation was radically altered. Instead of being switched on and off by drugs and cortical stimulation, he had been allowed to sleep naturally last night: moreover, in a real room, hotel-stark but comfortable and well equipped, with actual windows through which he had been able to confirm that he really was at Tarnover. During his interrogation he had been kept in a sort of compartment, a man-sized pigeonhole, where machines maintained his muscle tone for want of walking.

Aside from that, though, something subtler, more significant had occurred.

What?

The door of his room opened with a click of locks. A man appeared—commonplace, clad in white, armed. He had expected that if he was taken anywhere away from the room it would be under escort. Rising, he obeyed an order to go into the corridor and turn left.

It was a long walk, and there were many turns. Also there was a descending flight of steps, thirteen of them. Eventually there was a lost corner. Rounding it, he found himself in a passage of which one side was composed of one-way armor glass.

Gazing through it into a dimly lighted room beyond was Freeman.

He accorded the newcomer a nod, then tapped the glass with one soft fingertip.

Beyond, a very thin girl lay naked and unconscious on a padded table while a nurse shaved her head down to the scalp.

There was a long silence. Then, at last:

"Mm-hm. I expected that. But, knowing you as well as I do, I'm prepared to believe it wasn't your idea."

After which there was another silence, broken this time by Freeman. When he spoke, his voice was full of weariness.

"Take him back to his quarters. Let him think it over for a while."

## YES, MR. KELLY! WAS IT ABOUT ANYTHING?

"It should never be forgotten that during all the time we were studying bats, bats had a unique opportunity to study us."

# I AM

What he had said to Freeman was quite true. Ever since, with the conclusion of the intensive phase of his interrogation, he had been able to reason clearly again, he had been expecting to be told that Kate also had been dragged here for "examination."

Not that that made any difference, any more than reciting "nine-eighty-one-see-em-second-squared" makes one better able to survive a fall off a cliff.

He sat in the room assigned to him, which doubtless was monitored the clock around, as though on a stage before a vast audience alert to criticize any departure from the role he was meant to be playing.

The one factor operating in his favor was this: that after years of playing roles, he was finally playing himself instead.

*All the data they have, he told himself, relate to others than myself: Reverend Lazarus, Sandy Locke —yes, even Nickie Haflinger. Whoever I am now, and I'm none too sure of my identity at this stage, I definitely am not Nickie Haflinger!*

He started to list the ways in which he wasn't the person he was named after, and found the latest was the most important.

*I can love.*

A chill tremored down his spine as he considered that. There had been little love given or received in Nickie's early life. His father? Resentful of the burden his son imposed, intolerant of the demands of parenthood. His mother? Tried, for a while at least, but lacked an honest basis of affection to support her; hence her collapse into alcoholic psychosis. His temporary surrogate parents? To them one rent-a-boy was like another, so many dollars per week high by so many problems wide.

His friends during his teens, while he was here at Tarnover?

But love was not part of the curriculum. It was

THE SHOCKWAVE RIDER

parts. It was split up. It was "intense emotional in-volvement" and "excessive interdependence" and "typical inflated adolescent libido" . . .

Now, on the other hand, when this new strange person he was evolving into thought of Kate, he clenched his fists and gritted his teeth and shut his eyes and dissolved into pure raw hate, unresisting.

All his life he had had to control his deep reactions: as a pre-teen kid, because if you didn't you could be the one sanded on the way home tonight; as a teener, because every moment of the day and night students here were liable for reassessment to make sure they were worthy of staying, and the first five years he had wanted to stay more than anything else in the world and the second five he had wanted to use Tarnover instead of being used by it; thereafter because the data-net now ramified into so many areas of private life that his slightest error could bring hunters closing in for the kill.

It followed that yielding to emotion, whether pos-itive or negative, had always seemed dangerous. It was bad to let himself like another person too much; if a child, he or she would run tomorrow with a different gang, mercurial, and whoop and holler after you to your hour of blood and tears; if an adult, he or she would depart for some other job and leave behind merely a memory and a memento. Equally it was bad to let yourself fear or detest somebody too much; it led into areas where you couldn't predict your own behavior or that of others. "Here be tygers!"

But the capacity for emotion was in his mind, though he'd been unaware of the fact. He recalled with a trace of irony how he had looked over the detensing machine in G2S's transient accommodation block and pitied those with the ability to form strong attachments.

*I was pitying myself, I guess. Well, pity was the most that I deserved.*

Now he was being forced to recognize just how intensely he could feel, and there was a sound logical reason for encouraging the process.

202

The data Freeman and those behind him had in store were derived from a coldly calculating person— call him Mister X Minus E. Substitute throughout Mister X Plus E.

*And what you're going to wind up with, you sons of bitches, is what you fear above all. A unique solution in irrationals!*

A little rain started to smear the west-facing window of his room. He rose and walked over to stare out at the clouds, tinted with red because the sun was setting and the rain was approaching from the east.

*I am in approximately the position of someone attempting to filch enough plutonium from a nuclear research plant to build a bomb. I must sneak the stuff out without either causing a noticeable stock-loss, or triggering the perimeter detectors, or incurring radiation burns. Quite a three-pipe problem, Watson. It may take as long as a week, or even ten days.*

## MIRROR, MIRROR

You are in circular orbit around a planet. You are being overtaken by another object, also in circular orbit, moving several km./sec. faster. You accelerate to try and catch up.

See you later, accelerator.

*Much* later.

## HARTZ AND FLAWS

In the interrogation room the three-vee screen had been replaced by a stretch mirror. Not wanting to seem to look too hard or long at the naked body of the girl stretched out in the steel chair, Hartz glanced at his reflection instead. Catching sight of a smear of perspiration on his forehead, he pulled out a large handkerchief, and inadvertently dislodged his visitor's authorization card, which he was not quick enough to catch before it fluttered to the floor.

Freeman courteously picked it up and handed it back.

Muttering thanks, Hartz replaced it, harrumphed loudly into his handkerchief and then said, "Your reports have been meager, to say the least."

"I would naturally have informed you at once had there been any significant developments."

"Oh, there have been! That's why I'm here!" Hartz snapped, and decided there was no point after all in pretending not to look at the girl. Scrawny as she was, bald, childishly bare-bodied, she scarcely resembled a human being: more, a laboratory animal, some oversize strain of mutant hairless rat.

"What developments?" Freeman stiffened almost imperceptibly, and the tone of his voice hinted at harshness, but only hinted.

"You don't know, hm?" was Hartz's scathing retort. "But you met her mother, so you should! At least you must realize how much weight she swings thanks to her post with G2S!"

"Her mother," Freeman returned with strained politeness, "has been extensively profiled. There's no untoward emotional involvement between the pair of them."

"Her profile," Hartz repeated heavily. "I see. What can you tell me about her from her profile?"

"That Ina Grierson is not unhappy at her daughter's departure from KC. This releases her to accept the kind of post she has been looking for elsewhere."

"My God. Haven't you gone beyond this profile thing? Didn't you check out the real world lately?"

"I've done precisely as I was instructed!" Freeman flared. "And what is more, instructed by you!"

"I expect people to use their wits when I give them orders, not leave a continental mess for others to clear away!"

For a long moment the men locked eyes. At last Freeman said placatingly, "What appears to be the trouble?"

"Appears? Oh, not appears. This is only too real."

Hartz mopped his face again. "This girl has been here a week now—"

"Five days."

"It's a full week since her arrest. Don't interrupt." Hartz thrust his handkerchief back in his pocket. "If we didn't have a strong ex-Tarnover faction to vote our way on the UMKC board of administration, we'd— Oh, hell, I shouldn't have to tell you this. You should know it already."

"If there was something you wanted me to know, you could perhaps have taken steps to pipe the data to me," Freeman said in a tight voice. "Since you didn't, tell me now."

Hartz's face reddened, but he bit back the angry reply which clearly had been trembling on his lips. Achieving calm with an effort, he said, "Outside the P-A zones, hardly anybody goes twenty-four hours without using his or her code for credit purposes. Consequently the location of anybody on the continent can be determined near as dammit at any time. Kate Lilleberg is an adult, sure, but she's also *in statu pupillari* and has never filed a don't-talk order in respect of her mother, her only near relative. So ever since she was whipped out of KC there have been fifty or sixty people with an interest in tracing her, most of whom are on the faculty at UMKC but one of whom, the most troublesome, is a head-of-dept at G2S. How much more do I have to spell out before you realize what a hornets' nest you've wished on me?"

"I've done what?" Freeman said slowly.

"Didn't it cross your mind that if a week passed without her using her code, that would arouse suspicions?"

"What didn't cross my mind," Freeman retorted, "was that you'd expect me to make myself responsible for all the fiddling details! Since you insist, I'll take time out and construct some convincing fiction: have her code reported in, for example, from a town in the P-A zones where it can easily take a week for a

205

credit entry to reach the net. The rest, however, I'm afraid I must leave to—"

"Forget it. We already tried that. The moment we realized you hadn't seen to it. Have you forgotten the pose Haflinger adopted at G2S?"

Freeman looked blank. "How is that relevant?"

"Heaven send me patience. He took a job as a systems rash, didn't he? That position gave him damned near as much access to the net as I can get, cheating on G2S's max-nat-ad rating. In fact he moused around so much it started to interfere with his regular work, so he wrote a program into the G2S computers to take care of the routine stuff by itself. You didn't stress that in your interrogation report, did you?"

Freeman's mouth worked. No sound emerged.

"And the program is still functional," Hartz blasted, "and Ina Grierson has got to it! And worst of all, it's so simple she knows damned well the entries we filed behind her daughter's code are faked!"

"What? How?"

"How the hell do you think? What did Haflinger want to find out, using stolen G2S codes? Whether his own 4GH was still valid, *right?* And how could he have done that without being able to strip away an ex-post-facto cover label from a federal-authorized implant? Data concerning 4GH codes are not meant to be accessible to the public. They're routinely disguised, aren't they? Well, what Haflinger did was to peel them naked automatically, and in a way our top experts never thought of!"

Clenching his fists, he concluded, "Now maybe you see what a fix you dumped me in!"

His face like a stone image, Freeman said, "Oh, I think the credit belongs to Haflinger, not me. And I'm sure he'll be delighted with this news."

"What the hell do you mean?"

"Among the other data you neglected to supply to me was the fact that you came here to make wild accusations. On the reasonable assumption that you only intended to witness Kate's routine interrogation, I didn't cancel my usual instructions to have Haflinger brought here to watch in the hope it might erode his self-control. Your suggestion, I beg to remind you."

Checking his watch, he added, "So for the past four, four and a half minutes Haflinger has been behind that stretch one-way mirror, seeing and hearing everything in this room. As I say, he must be very pleased."

## EXCERPT FROM A NEWS BULLETIN

". . . a blow dealt to the hopes of those who were confidently forecasting this academic year would be relatively free of student unrest. Convinced that one of their number, missing since a week ago, has been kidnaped by government agents, a mob of fifteen hundred students today tribaled more than half of the thirty-nine police fireposts on campus at UMKC. As yet no count of casualties came to hand, but . . ."

## ATAVISM

Facing Rico Posta, Ina felt her cheeks grow pale. But she maintained her voice at normal pitch and volume.

"Rico, whatever you and the rest of the board may say, Kate *is* my daughter. You punch for a double-check on those phony reports about her using her code at Interim."

"Who says they're phony?"

"Our own computers say so!"

"Uh-uh. A program written by one Sandy Locke says so, and he turned out to be a twitch and—"

"While he was saving us a couple of million a year you didn't think he was a twitch. Otherwise you wouldn't have been among the first to say he should be permed."

"Well, I . . ."

She leaned earnestly forward.

"Rico, something muddy's going on. You know it,

though you haven't admitted it to yourself. Did you try asking for data about Sandy recently?"

"As a matter of fact—yes."

"And there aren't any, are there? Not even a report of his death!"

"I guess he could have left the country."

"Passport?"

There was a silence that crackled like the harbinger of an electrical storm.

Ina said at last, "Ever read a book called *1984*?"

"Sure, in a college literature class." Rico pursed his lips and gazed into nowhere. "I get what you mean. You think he's been—uh—declared an unperson."

"Right. And I think they've done the same to Kate."

"I . . ." He had to swallow. "I guess I wouldn't put it past them, knowing what one does about that gang in Washington. Say, you know something? I get nightmares now and then. About how I punch my code into a board and the signal comes back: deeveed!"

Ina said, "Me too. And I can't believe we're the only ones."


## STARTING TO GROW AGAIN

Since they quit shaving his scalp daily it had begun to itch. So far he had resisted the temptation to scratch, but he was compelled to rub now and then. To the onlookers, whom he knew to exist though he was not aware of their identity, he imagined that he might perhaps give the impression of being puzzled by the information he was taking in. He was watching a three-vee news broadcast. He'd spent much of his time catching up with the world since he was transferred to these more comfortable quarters.

In fact he was not in the least disoriented by what he learned. There were different items to report—another realignment of alliances in Latin America, a fresh outburst of unauthorized *jehad* in the Yemen, a new product about which the FDA was expressing doubts, something called an A-C Group Granulyser used in upgrading vegetable protein to compete with meat . . .

But the habit patterns, inevitably, had survived. To the air, with a wry grin, he murmured, "How long, O Lord? How long?"

In his private estimation: not long now.

And, as though on cue, the lock of the door clicked. He glanced around, expecting one of the usual armed men in white come to take him elsewhere.

To his surprise, however, the visitor was Freeman. And alone.

He carefully closed the door before speaking; when he did so, it was in a perfectly neutral tone.

"You probably noticed that I authorized the delivery of some refreshments to your quarters last night. I need a stiff drink. Make it whisky on the rocks."

"I take it you're not here?"

"What? Oh!" Freeman gave a hideous grin; his facial skin stretched so tight over his bones that it threatened to tear. "Quite correct. The monitors are being fed a wholly convincing set of lies."

"Then—congratulations."

"What do you mean?"

"This took a lot of courage on your part. Most people lack the guts to disobey an immoral order."

Slowly, over several seconds, Freeman's grin transformed into a smile.

"Goddamn," he said. "Haflinger or whatever you'd rather call yourself. I fought like hell to stay objective, and I didn't make it. Turns out I kind of like you. I can't help it."

Angrily he kicked around a chair and slumped into it.

A few moments later, over full glasses:

"Tell me something. What reflex got punched by whom to trigger this reaction?"

Freeman bridled. "No need to gibe at me. You

can't take credit for everything that's happened inside my head."

"At least you say credit, not blame . . . I suspect you found out you hate the people who give you your orders."

"Ah . . . Yes. I got loaded with my final straw when they decided to bring Kate here. You were right about it not being my idea. So I did as I was told, neither more nor less."

"So Hartz blasted you for not being smarter than he is. Galling, isn't it?"

"Worse. Much worse." Cradling his glass in bony fingers, Freeman leaned forward, staring at nothing. "All argument aside, I do believe that we need wisdom. Need it desperately. I have a conception of how it would be manifest. Hartz doesn't have it. I think you do. And as to Kate . . ." The words trailed away.

"Kate Lilleberg is wise. No question of it."

"I'm obliged to agree." With a trace of defiance. "And because of it—well, you've seen."

"What else would you expect? I don't mean that sarcastically, by the way. Just as my recruitment to Tarnover was predictable once they learned of my existence, so her arrest was predictable when I led them to her."

After a fractional hesitation Freeman said, "I get the idea you stopped classing me as one of *them.*"

"You absconded, didn't you?"

"Hah! I guess I did." He emptied his glass and waved aside the offer of a refill. "No, I'll fix it. I know where . . . But it isn't right, it can't be right! What the hell did she do to deserve indefinite detention without trial, being interrogated until her soul is as naked as her body? We went off the track somewhere. It shouldn't have turned out this way."

"You think I may have notions about a different way?"

"Sure." This response was crisp and instant. "And I want to hear them. I've lost my bearings. Right now I don't know where in the world I am. You may find it hard to believe, but—well, I've always had an article

of faith in my personal universe to the effect that max-
imizing information flow is objectively good. I mean
being frank, and open, and candid, telling the truth as
you see it regardless of the consequences." A harsh
laugh. "A shrink I know keeps insisting it's overcompensation for the way I was taught to hide my body
as a kid. I was raised to undress in the dark, sneak
in and out the bathroom when nobody was looking,
run like hell when I flushed the can for fear someone
would notice me and think about what I'd done in
there . . . Ah, maybe the poker's partly right. Anyhow, I grew up to be a top-rank interrogator, dedicated to extracting information from people without
torture and with the least possible amount of suffering. Phrase it that way and it sounds defensible,
doesn't it?"

"Of course. But it's a different matter when the data
you uncover are earmarked for concealment all over
again, this time becoming the private property of those
in power."

"That's it." Freeman resumed his chair, fresh ice
cubes tinkling in his refilled glass. "I took on the assignment to interrogate you like any other assignment.
The list of charges against you was long enough, and
there was one in particular that touched me on a sore
spot. Feeding false data into the net, naturally. On top
of which I'd heard about you. I moved here only three
years ago—from Weychopee, incidentally, the place
you know as 'Electric Skillet'—and even then there
was vague gossip among the students about some
poker who once faded into the air and never got
caught. You've become a sort of legend, did you
know?"

"Anybody copying my example?"

Freeman shook his head. "They made it tougher to
bow out. And maybe no one since your day has turned
up with the same type of talent."

"If so, doubtless he or she would have been drawn
to your notice. You're a person of considerable standing, aren't you, Dr. Freeman? Or is it Mr. Freeman? I

seem to have your measure pretty accurately. I'll stab for 'mister.' "

"Correct. My degrees are scholarates, not mere doctorates. I've always been very proud of that. Like surgeons over in Britain, taking offense at being called Dr. So-and-so. . . . But it's irrelevant, it's superfluous, it's silly! Know what hit me hardest when I listened to your account of Precipice?"

"Tell me."

"The dense texture of people's lives. Filled out instead of being fined down. I'm trained in three disciplines, but I haven't broadened out as a person from that base. I've fined down, focusing all I know along one narrow line."

"That's what's wrong with Tarnover, isn't it?"

"I—I *half* see what you mean. Amplify, please."

"Well, you once defended Tarnover with the argument that it's designed to provide an optimal environment for people so well adjusted to the rapid change of modern society that they can be trusted to plan for others as well as for themselves. Or words to that effect. But it's not happening, is it? Why? Because it's still under the overriding control of people who, craving power, achieved it by the same old methods they used in—hell, for all I know, in predynastic Egypt. For them there's only one way to outstrip somebody who's overtaking you. Go faster. But this is the space age, remember. And the other day I hit on a metaphor that neatly sums my point."

He quoted the case of two bodies each in circular orbit.

Freeman looked faintly surprised. "But everybody knows—" he began, and then checked. "Oh. No, not everybody. I wish I'd thought of that. I'd have liked to ask Hartz."

"I'm sure. But think it through. *Not* everybody knows. In this age of unprecedented information flow, people are haunted by the belief they're actually ignorant. The stock excuse is that this is because there's literally too much to be known."

Freeman said defensively, "It's true." And sipped his whisky.

"Granted. But isn't there another factor that does far more damage? Don't we daily grow more aware that data exist which we're not allowed to get at?"

"You said something about that before." Freeman's forehead creased with concentration. "A brand-new reason for paranoia, wasn't that it? But if I'm to accept that you're right, then . . . Damnation, it sounds as though you're determined to deevee every single course of action we've taken in the past half century."

"Yes."

"But that's out of the question!" Freeman straightened in dismay.

"No, that's an illusion. A function of a wrongly chosen viewpoint. Take it by steps. Try the holist approach, which you used to decry. Think of the world as a unit, and the developed—the *over*-developed—nations as analogous to Tarnover, or better yet to Trianon. And think of the most successful of the less-rich countries as akin to those P-A communities which began under such unpromising circumstances yet which are turning out to be more tolerable places to live than most other cities on the continent. In short, what I'm talking about is Project Parsimony writ large: the discontinuation of an experiment that cost far too much to set up and hasn't paid off."

Freeman pondered for a long while. At last he said, "If I were to agree that you're right, or even partly right, what would you expect me to do?"

"Well—ah . . . Well, you could start by letting me and Kate go."

This silence was full of struggle. Eventually, with abrupt decision, Freeman drained his glass and rose, feeling in the side pocket of his jacket. From it he produced a flat gray plastic case, the size of his palm.

"It's not a regular portable calculator," he said in a brittle voice. "It's a veephone. Screen's under the lid. Flex and jack inside. There are phone points there, there and there." Pointing to three corners of the room. "But don't do anything until you get a code to do it with."

## AT THE DISSOLUTION

*What was I saying about overcompensation?*

There had been a lot of whisky, of course, and he was unused to drinking.

*But am I drunk? I don't feel I am. More, it's that without being partly stonkered I couldn't endure the torrent of dreadful truth that's storming through my brain. What Hartz said to me. What Bosch almost said, only he managed to check himself. But I know damn well what he substituted with "nonspecialist." Why should I spend the rest of my life knuckling under to liars like Bosch? Claiming the dogs they have at Precipice can't exist! And blockheads like Hartz are even worse. Expecting the people they lord it over to think of things they aren't smart enough to think of themselves, then denying that the fault is theirs!*

Carefully Freeman locked his apartment, setting the don't-disturb signs: one on the door, one on each of the veephones.

*Now if I can just find my way to the index of re-served codes activated when they surpled 4GH . . . From Tarnover if from anywhere it should be possible to pull one out and upgrade it to status U-for-unquestionable. That's the best trick of all. If Haflinger had latched on to it he need never have been caught.*

Owlishly, but with full command of his not inconsiderable faculties—more important, not obliged to make do with the limited and potentially fallible input of a pocket veephone such as the one with which doubtless Haflinger would shortly be performing his own personal brand of miracle—he sat down to his data console. He wrote, then rewrote, then rewrote, a trial program on tape that could be tidily erased. As he worked he found himself more and more haunted by a tantalizing idea.

*I could leech three codes as easily as two. . . .*

Eventually the program was status go, but before feeding it he said to the air, "Why not?" And checked how many codes were currently on reserve. The answer was of the order of a hundred thousand. Only about five depts would have dug into the store since it was ordained, so . . .

*Why the hell not? Here I am pushing forty, and what have I done with my life? I have talents, intelligence, ambition. Going to waste! I hoped I'd be useful to society. I expected to spend my time dragging criminals and traitors into the light of day, exposing them to the contumely of honest citizens. Instead the biggest criminals of all escape scot-free and people like Kate who never harmed anybody . . . Oh, shit! I stopped being an investigator years ago. What I am now is an inquisitor. And I've lost all faith in the justice of my church.*

He gave a sudden harsh laugh, made one final tiny amendment to his tape, and offered it up to the input.

## THE INFLUENCE OF AFFLUENCE

"For the convenience of the lazy plebeians, the monthly distributions of corn were converted into a daily allowance of bread . . . and when the popular clamor accused the dearness and scarcity of wine . . . rigid sobriety was insensibly relaxed; and although the generous design of Aurelian does not appear to have been executed in its full extent, the use of wine was allowed on very easy and liberal terms . . . and the meanest Roman could purchase, with a small copper coin, the daily enjoyment of a scene of pomp and luxury which might excite the envy of the kings of Asia. . . . But the most lively and splendid amusement of the idle multitude depended on the frequent exhibition of public games and spectacles . . . the happiness of Rome appeared to hang on the event of a race."

Always scribble, scribble, scribble! Eh, Mr. Gibbon?

## LET NOT THY WRONG HEAD KNOW
## WHAT THY RIGHT HEAD DOETH

Having completed his preparations, he disconnected
the phone that had proved so invaluable, folded it,
concealed it tidily in the inside pocket of his issue
jacket. Then he hung that over a chair back, completed undressing normally, and went to bed at approximately his regular time.

What followed was a miniature—a microcosm—of
his life, condensed into a span of no more than thirty-
five minutes.

At an unidentifiable time of night one of the silent
anonymous white-garbed escorts roused him and instructed him to dress quickly and come along, unper-
turbed by this departure from routine because for him
routine might be expected to consist in unpredictabil-
ity. It was, had been for centuries, a cheap and simple means of deranging persons under interrogation.

He led the way to a room with two doors, otherwise
featureless apart from a bench. That was as far as his
orders told him to go; with a curt command to sit
down and wait, he departed.

There was a short period of silence. Finally the
other door opened and a dumpy woman entered,
yawning. She carried clothing in a plastic sack and a
clipboard with a form on it. Grumpily she requested
him to sign it; he did so, using the name she was expecting, which was not his own. Satisfied, yawning
more widely than ever, she went out.

He changed into the garments she had brought: a
white jersey shirt, blue-gray pants, blue jacket—well-
fitting, unremarkable, unmemorable. Bundling up
what he had worn in the sack, he went out the same
way she had gone, and was in a corridor with several
doors leading off it. After passing three of them, two
to right and one to left, he arrived at a waste-reclama-
tion chute and rid himself of his burden. Two doors

farther along was an office, not locked. It was equipped with, among other things, a computer terminal. He tapped one key on its input board.

Remotely locked, a drawer slid open in an adjacent file stack. Among the contents of the drawer were temporary ID cards of the type issued to visitors on official business.

Meanwhile the printout station of the computer terminal was humming and a rapid paper tongue was emerging from it.

From the same drawer as the ID cards he extracted a neopolaroid color camera, which he set to self-portrait delay and placed on a handy table. Sitting down to face the camera, he waited the requisite few seconds, retrieved the film, placed his picture on the card and sealed it over with a device which, as the computers had promised, was also kept in the drawer. Finally, he typed in his borrowed name and the rank of major in the U.S. Army Medical Corps.

By then the computer had printed out what it was required to furnish: a requisition, in duplicate, for the custody of Kate Grierson Lilleberg. Having been prepared with a light-writer, which unlike old-fashioned mechanical printers was not limited to any one type style—or indeed to any one alphabet, since every single character was inscribed with a laser beam at minimum power—only examination under a microscope could have revealed that it was not a U.S. Army Form RQH–4479, the standard form of authority to transfer a prisoner from civil to military custody.

Suitably armed now, he replaced everything he had disturbed, tapped the computer board one more time to activate the final part of the program he had left in store, and left the room. Dutifully, the machines remote-locked the cabinet again, and the door of the office, and then undertook such other tasks as deleting their record of either having been unlocked during the night, and making a note of the "fact" that a temporary ID card had been accidentally spoiled so the stock in hand was one fewer than could be accounted for by recent visitors.

The door at the extreme end of the corridor gave into the open air, at the head of a flight of stairs leading to a dark concrete parking bay where an electric ambulance was standing. Its driver, who wore army uniform with Pfc's badges, gave an uncertain salute, saying, "Major . . . ?"

"At ease," the newcomer said briskly, displaying his ID card and duplicate forms. "Sorry to have kept you. Any trouble with the girl?"

The driver said with a shrug, "She's out, sir. Like a busted light-tube oh-you-tee."

"That's how it should be. They gave you your route card?"

"Sure, they brought it when they delivered the girl. Oh, and this as well. Feels like her code card, I guess." The soldier proffered a small flat package.

Peeling off the cover proved him half right. Not one code card, but two.

"Thanks. Not that she'll have much use for it where she's going."

"I guess not." With a sour grin.

"You already changed your batteries, did you? Fine —let's get under way."

Dark roads thrummed into the past to the accompaniment of a rattling of numbers, not spoken. He had memorized both codes before starting his veephone-mediated sabotage, but there was a lot more to this escape than simply two personal codes. He wanted everything down pat before the ambulance first had to stop for electricity, and the range of this model was only about two hundred miles.

Best if the driver didn't have to get hurt. Though having been fool enough to volunteer for army service, of course, and worse still, having been fool enough to accept orders unquestioningly from a machine . . .

But everybody did that. Everybody, all the time. Otherwise none of this would have been possible.

Similarly, none of it would have had to happen.

Splicing the Brain Race

# FOR PURPOSES OF DISORIENTATION

At present and with luck from now on and forever
regardless of what code I wear I am being Nicholas
Kenton Haflinger. And whoever doesn't like it will
have to lump it.

# PRESIDING AT AWAKE

"What the—? Who—? Why, Sandy!"

"Quiet. Listen carefully. You're in an army ambulance. We're about two hundred miles east of Tarnover supposedly on the way to Washington. The driver
believes I'm a Medical Corps major escorting you.
There was no convincing story I could invent to justify clothing fit for you to cross a public street in. All
you have is that issue cotton gown. What's more they
shaved your head. Do you remember anything about
this, or did they keep you all the time in regressed
mode?"

She swallowed hard. "I've had what seem like
dreams since they—they kidnaped me. I don't know
what's true and what isn't."

"We'll sort that out later. We're laying over to
change batteries. I sent the driver for coffee. He'll be
back any moment. I'll find some other excuse to make
him hang around, because I've seen an automat where
I can buy you a dress, shoes and a wig. At the next
stop be ready to put them on and vanish."

"What—what are we going to do? Even if it comes
off?"

Cynically he curled his lip. "The same as I've been
doing all my adult life. Run the net. Only this time in
more than one sense. And believe you me, they aren't
going to like it."

Shutting the ambulance's rear door again, he said
loudly to the returning driver, "Damn monitors up
front! Showed the sedative control had quit. But she's

219

lying like a log. Say, did you spot a men's room? I guess before we get back on the road I ought to take a leak."

Over the hum of the many steam and electric vehicles crowding the service area the driver answered, "Right next to the automat, sir. And—uh—if we're not pulling out at once, I see they got Delphi boards and I'd kinda like to check out a nervous ticket."

"Sure, go ahead. But keep it down to—let's say five minutes, hm?"

## TEMBLOR

"What do you mean, he can't be reached? Listen again and make sure you know who I'm asking for. Paul—T-for-Tommy—Freeman! Want I should spell it?

"His new code? What about his—? Are you certain?

"But they don't have any goddamn right to snatch him out from— Oh, shit. Sometimes I wonder who's in charge around this country, us or the machines. Give me the new code, then.

"I don't *care* what it says in back of its head listing. Just read it over to me. If you can, that is!

"Now you listen to me, you obstructive dimwit. When I give an order I expect it to be obeyed, and I won't be talked back to by a self-appointed shithouse lawyer. You're addressing the Deputy Director of the Federal Bureau of Data Processing Services, and— That's more like it. Come on.

"It begins with *what* group? No, don't bother to repeat it. I heard you. Oh my God. Oh my God."

## SPELLED "WEEKEND" BUT PRONOUNCED "WEAKENED"

A highway line drawn from Tarnover to Washington: a line to connect tomorrow with yesterday, via today. . . .

The most mobile population in all of history, the only one so totally addicted to going for the sake of going that it had deeveed excessive cost, energy crises, the disappearance of oil, every kind of obstacle in order to keep up the habit, was as ever on the move, even though half the continent was overlaid by end-of-fall weather, strong winds, low temperatures, rain turning to sleet. It was notoriously the sort of season that urged people to stop looking for and start finding.

He thought about that a lot during the journey.

Why move?

To choose a place right for sinking roots.

Go faster in order to drop back to a lower orbit? Doesn't work. Drop back to a lower orbit; you go faster!

Even Freeman had had to have that pointed out to him. He knew obscurely he wouldn't have to explain it to Kate. And she couldn't be the only person who understood the truth by instinct.

Washington: yesterday. The exercise of personal power; the privileges of office; the individualization of the consensus into a single spokesman's mouth, echo of an age when communities did indeed concur because they weren't assailed with a hundred irreconcilable versions of events. (These days the typical elected representative is returned with fewer than forty percent of the votes cast; not infrequently he's detested by four-fifths of those he purports to speak for, because the population of the state or district has turned over. They'll surple him at the next opportunity, chafe until it arrives. Meanwhile his old supporters have scattered to upset another applecart. Voting registers are maintained by computers nowadays; all it takes to enter you on the roll at your new address is one, count it one, veephone call.)

Tarnover: tomorrow, sure. But hopefully the wrong tomorrow. Because it's planned and controlled by people who were born the day before yesterday.

How do you cope with tomorrow when (a) it may not be like the real tomorrow but (b) it's arrived when you weren't ready for it?

One approach is offered by the old all-purpose beatitude: "blessed are they who expect the worst . . ." Hence reactions like Anti-Trauma Inc. Nothing worse can happen in later life than what was done to you as a child.

(Wrong tomorrow.)

Another is inherent in the concept of the plug-in life-style: no matter where you go, there are people like the ones you left behind, furniture and clothes and food like the ones you left behind, the same drinks available across any bar: "Say, settle a bet for us, willya? Is this the Paris Hilton or the Istanbul Hilton?"

(Wrong tomorrow. It offers the delusive hope that tomorrow will be pretty much like today, but it got here and it isn't.)

Yet another lies in preparing for it: using public Delphi boards, for example, to monitor what people are ready to adapt to, yearn to adapt to, and won't adapt to at any price.

(Wrong tomorrow. They decided to let traditional market forces flywheel the weight of decision. The favorite who started at odds-on broke his leg at the first fence and the race is far from over.)

Yet another lies in the paid-avoidance areas: you trade in your right to the latest-and-greatest against an allowance of unearned credit, enough to keep body and soul together.

(Wrong tomorrow. It's going to overtake you anyway, and city-smashing quakes are part of it.)

While still another consists in getting good and clutched by some heavy brand of dope, so things that happen can't really hurt.

(Wrong tomorrow. Ash longer, *vita brevis*.)

And so forth.

Religion?

Change cities, by order. Last place it was a Catholic framework; here it's Ecumenical Pentecostal and the minister is kind of into the Tao.

Chemicals?

Almost everybody is high like troops on the way to battle. Shaking! You hear tension sing in the air you breathe. The only way you want awareness shifted is back to normal.

Trust in authority?

But it's your right as a free and equal individual to be as authoritative as anybody else.

Model yourself on a celebrity?

But you were celebrated last week, you had a record-breaking Delphi ticket or your kid was on three-vee defying 'gators or you notched up one full year in the same house and the reporter called in from the local station. For ten whole minutes you've been famous too.

Collapse into overload?

That's already happened, nearly as often as you've been to bed with a head cold.

And patiently, from every single one of these possible pathways, they've turned you back to where you were with a smile of encouragement and a pat on the shoulder and a bright illuminated certificate that reads NO EXIT.


Therefore the world keeps turning, the ads keep changing, there are always programs to watch when you switch on the three-vee, there's always food in the supermarket and power at the socket and water at the sink. Well, not quite always. But near as dammit.

And there's nearly always a friend to answer the phone.

And there's nearly always credit behind your code.

And there's nearly always some other place you can go.

And when the night sky happens to be clear, there are invariably more stars in it, moving faster, than were put there at the Creation. So that's okay.

Pretty well.

More or less.
HELP!

For these and sundry other reasons, at their next battery stop he gave the driver the slip and Kate her dress and shoes and wig and melted into the mass of people boarding a shuttle bus bound for the nearest veetol port. For the driver, who was sure to be puzzled, he left a note saying:

*Thanks, soldier. You were very helpful. If you want to know how helpful, punch this code into the nearest phone.*

The code, naturally, being his own new acquisition.

## PRECEPT DINNED INTO TRAFFIC PATROL OFFICERS DURING TRAINING

Someone is apt to swoop on you from a great height if you ticket a vehicle with a heavy federal code behind the wheel.

## MOUSING AROUND UNDER THE FEET OF ELEPHANTS

"Where are we going?" Kate whispered.

"I finally located my place to stand."

"Precipice?" she suggested, half hopefully, half anxiously. "Surely that's where they'll head for straight away."

"Mm-hm. Sorry, I don't mean place. I mean *places*. I should have figured this out long ago. No one place could ever be big enough. I have to be in a hundred of them, all at the same time, and a thousand if I can manage it. It's bound to take a while to put my insight into practice, but—oh, maybe in a couple of months we shall be able to sit back and enjoy the fireworks."

"I always did like fireworks," she said with the ghost of a smile, and took his hand.

## FOUR–WAY INTERSECTION
## WITH STOP SIGNS

These days it was easy to lose track of what features belonged with what names. Therefore there were captions under each of the faces on the four-station secure link, names and offices. Hartz gazed at the split-screen array before him, reading from left to right.

From Tarnover, its chancellor: Admiral Bertrand Snyder, ascetic, gray-haired, short-spoken, who had been famous under the sobriquet of "Singleminded Snyder" during the Hawaiian Insurrection of 2002 . . . but that was before he entered the Civil Service and a cloud of secrecy.

From the Southern White House, the president's special adviser on security, plump and bespectacled Dr. Guglielmo Dorsi, no longer known even to his intimates (though it had not proved possible to eradicate the nickname entirely from his dossiers) as Billy the Shiv.

And from another floor of this same building, his own superior, the Full Director of the Bureau, Mr. Aylwin Sullivan, tall, beak-nosed, shock-haired, and deliberately shabby. It had been the style for those working with computers when he launched out on his rocket-like career. Nonetheless it was odd to look at his open-neck shirt, pocketful of old pens, five-o'week shadow, black-rimmed nails.

As though the past had stepped into the present.

All three of the faces on the screen frowned at Hartz: Snyder with annoyance, Dorsi with suspicion, Sullivan with impatience. They let pecking order decide who should speak. Highest in the hierarchy Sullivan said, "Are you insane? Only a few days ago you insisted we deevee all the 4GH codes assigned to FBI, CIA, Secret Service—and now here you are claiming that the U-group codes must be junked too! You couldn't cause more trouble if you were a paid subversive."

225

Dorsi said, "Let me remind you of this, too. Upon my asking what to use when we replaced the 4GH, you personally advised me that there was no known means of leeching any code from the reserve and assigning it to U-group status without that fact being revealed in your own bureau's computers. No record of such action can be found, can it? I can just see the president's face if I were to go to him with such a crazy story."

"But when I said that I didn't know—" Hartz began. Snyder cut him short.

"What's more, you've made a direct attack on my integrity and administrative efficiency. You've said in so many words that the person you claim to have carried out this act of sabotage is a graduate of Weychopee who moved to Tarnover at my special request and who was cleared by me in person for essential work here. I wholly agree with Mr. Sullivan. You must have taken leave of your senses."

"Therefore," Sullivan said, "I'm requiring you to take leave of absence as well. Preferably indefinite. Are we through with this conference? Good. I have other business to attend to."

## FOR PURPOSES OF OBFUSCATION

I know damn well I am Paul Thomas Freeman, aged thirty-nine, a government employee with scholars' degrees in cybernetics, psychology and political science plus a master's in data processing. Similarly I know that if as a kid I hadn't been recruited much as Haflinger was, I'd probably have wound up as a petty criminal, into smuggling or dope or maybe running an illegal Delphi pool. Maybe I might not have been as smart as I imagine. Maybe I'd be dead.

And I also know I've been brilliantly maneuvered into a corner where I sacrificed everything I've gained in life on a spur-of-the-moment impulse, threw away my career, let myself in—quite possibly—for a treason trial . . . and with no better excuse than that I like

Haflinger better than Hartz and the buggers at his
back. A corner? More like a deep dark hole!

So why the hell do I feel so goddamn *happy?*


## FULCRUM

When he finished explaining how he had contrived
their escape, Kate said incredulously, "Was that all?"

"Not quite. I also made a call to the ten nines."

"Ah. I should have guessed."


## A MATTER OF HYSTERICAL RECORD

When the short-lived Allende government was
elected to power in Chile and needed a means of
balancing that unfortunate country's precarious economy, Allende appealed to the British cybernetics
expert Stafford Beer.

Who announced that as few as ten significant quantities, reported from a handful of key locations where
adequate communications facilities existed, would en-
able the state of the economy to be reviewed and
adjusted on a day-to-day basis.

Judging by what happened subsequently, his claim
infuriated nearly as many people as did the news that
there **are** only four elements in the human genetic
code.


## LIKE THEY SAY, IT'S
## BOUNCE OR BREAK

At Ann Arbor, Michigan, research psychologist
Dr. Zoë Sideropoulos had house guests for a week.
She was an expert in hypnosis and had written a well-
known study of the regression effect which, in suitable
cases, makes possible the recovery of memories ordinarily lost to conscious awareness without such crude
physical aids as electrodes planted in the subject's
brain.

During the week she made exceptionally intensive use of her home computer terminal. Or rather, that was what the machines believed.

When he was able to take a break from using Dr. Sideropoulos's terminal—a new and extremely efficient model—Kate brought him omelets and the nearest surviving commercial equivalent of "real beer."

"Eat before it's cold," she commanded. "Then talk. In detail and with footnotes."

"I'm glad you said that. We're going to have a lot of time to fill. I need to scramble some circuitry at Canaveral, or wherever, rather more completely than you scrambled these eggs, and I know for sure I'm going to have to make the computers do things they're specifically forbidden to. But not to worry. When they built their defenses they weren't reckoning on somebody like me."

He set about demolishing the omelet; it lasted for a dozen hungry bites.

"But I *do* worry," Kate muttered. "Are you *certain* you can trust Paul Freeman?"

He laid aside his empty plate. "Remember how at Lap-of-the-Gods you upbraided me because I wouldn't believe anyone else was on my side?"

"*Touchée.* But I want my answer."

"Yes. There's an honest man. And finally he's figured out what constitutes evil in the modern world."

"So what's your definition?"

"One that I already know you agree with, because we talked about Anti-Trauma Inc. If there is such a phenomenon as absolute evil, it consists in treating another human being as a thing."

In a dry voice she said, "I won't argue."

At Boulder, Colorado, Professor Joachim Yent of the School of Economics and Business Administration had house guests for a few days. During that time, it was duly recorded that he made exceptionally frequent use of his home computer terminal.

"Kate, when you take a liking to somebody, do you speed up or slow down?"

"Do I what—? Oh, got it. Slow down, I guess. I mean to get where we can talk to each other I quit skipping for a while."

"And *vice versa?*"

"Most times, no. In fact you're the only person I ever met who could work it the other way—uh . . . Sandy? What is your name, damn it? I just realized I still don't know."

"You decide. Stick with Sandy if you like, or switch to what I started out with: Nicholas, Nickie, Nick. I don't care. I'm myself, not a label."

She puckered her lips to blow him a kiss. "I don't care what you're called, either. I only know I'm glad we slowed down to the same speed."

At Madison, Wisconsin, Dean Prudence McCourtenay of the Faculty of Laws had house guests for a long weekend. It was similarly recorded that during their visit she made more than averagely frequent use of her domestic computer terminal.

It was becoming very cold. Winter had definitely begun.

"Yes, slowing down to the same speed is what everybody needs to do. With a lot of incidental energy to be dissipated. In fact a good many brakes are apt to melt. But the alternative is a head-on flat-out smash."

"Why?"

"Because everybody isn't like you yet."

"Sounds like a monotonous world!"

"I mean in the sense of being equally able to cope."

"But . . ." She bit her lip. "It's a fact of existence that some can and some can't. Punishing those who can't is cruel, but holding back those who can for the sake of the rest is—"

He broke in. "Our present society is cruel both ways. It does punish those who can't cope. We bought our veephones and our data-net and our asteroid ore and the rest of it by spending people who wound up dead or in mental hospitals." His face darkened briefly. "*And* it holds back those who can cope. I'm an example of that."

"I find it terribly hard to believe, seeing what you can do now you're working at full stretch!"

"But I *have* been held back, damn it. I didn't know how much I could achieve until I saw you, shaven and limp like a lab specimen due to be carved up and thrown away with no more memorial than entry in a table of statistics. The sight forced me into—I guess you'd say mental overdrive."

"What was it like?"

"As inexplicable as orgasm."

In Shreveport, Louisiana, Dr. Chase Richmond Dellinger, a public-health analyst under contract to the city, had house guests during whose stay he had unusually frequent recourse to his home computer terminal. In the south it was still pleasantly warm, of course, but there was a lot of rain this year.

"So I absolutely had to find a way out—not just for you, not just for me, but for everybody. In an eyeblink I had discovered a new urge within myself, and it was as fundamental as hunger, or fear, or sex. I recall one argument I had with Paul Freeman . . ."

"Yes?"

"The idea came up that it took the advent of the H-bomb to bring about in human beings the response you see in other animals when confronted with bigger claws or teeth."

"Or a dominant figure in his private cosmos. Like Bagheera rolling over kitten-style to greet me when I get back from school. I do hope they're looking after him properly."

"We've been promised that."

"Yes, but . . . Never mind. I didn't mean to change the subject."

"On principle I differed with him, but he was quite justified in saying that for all we know maybe that is the case. Well, if it's true that our threshold of survival-prone behavior is so high it takes the prospect of total extermination to activate modes of placation and compromise, may there not be other processes, equally life-preserving, which can similarly be triggered off only at a far higher level of stimulus than you find among our four-legged cousins?"

On his ranch in northern Texas, political historian Rush Compton and his wife Nerice, some years his junior and in occasional practice as a market-research counselor, entertained a couple of house guests. Considerable use was made of their home computer terminal. The weather was fresh and clear, with intermittent gusts of sharp northerly wind.

"Wait a moment. That threshold may be dangerously high. Think of population."

"Yes indeed. I started with population. Not having a fixed breeding season was among the reasons why mankind achieved dominance; it kept our numbers topped up at an explosive rate. Past a certain stage restrictive processes set in: male libido is reduced or diverted into nonfertile channels, female ovulation is irregularized and sometimes fails completely. But long before we reach that point we find the company of our fellow creatures so unbearable we resort to war, or a tribal match. Kill one another or ourselves."

"So our evolutionary advantage has turned unnoticed into a handicap."

"Kate, I love you."

"I know. I'm glad."

At his secluded home in Massachusetts, Judge Virgil Horovitz, retired, and his housekeeper Alice Bronson —he was widowed—entertained house guests and used his computer terminal for the first time since his retirement. A gale had stripped most of the trees around his house of their gorgeous red-gold foliage; at night, frost made the fallen leaves crackle and rustle underfoot.

"But what the hell can we do with an insight like yours? We've had insights before, from social theorists and historians and politicians and preachers, and we're in a mess in spite of all. The idea of turning the entire planet into a madhouse in the hope of triggering off some species-saving reflex—no, it's out of the question. Suppose at some early stage of your scheme we hit a level where a billion people go collectively insane?"

"That's the best we can look forward to, and I do mean *the best*, if the people at Tarnover are allowed their way."

"I think you're serious!"

"Oh, maybe it wouldn't be a whole billion. But it could be half the population of North America. And a hundred and some million is enough, isn't it?"

"How would it happen?"

"Theoretically at least, one of the forces operating on us consists in the capacity, which we don't share with other animals, to elect whether or not we shall give way to an ingrained impulse. Our social history is the tale of how we learned to substitute conscious ethical behavior for simple instinct, right? On the other hand, it remains true that few of us are willing to admit how much influence our wild heritage exercises on our behavior. Not directly, because we're not still wild, but indirectly, because society itself is a consequence of our innate predispositions."

With a rueful chuckle, he added, "You know, one of the things I most regret about what's happened is that I could have enjoyed my arguments with Paul Freeman. There was so much common ground between us. . . . But I didn't dare. At all costs I *had* to shake his view of the world. Otherwise he'd never have toppled when Hartz pushed him."

"Stop digressing, will you?"

"Sorry. Where were we? Oh, I was about to say that at Tarnover they're mistakenly trying to postpone the moment where our reflexes take over. They ought to know that's wrong. Freeman himself cited the best treatment for personality shock, which doesn't use drugs or any other formal therapy, just liberates the victim to do something he's always wanted and never achieved. In spite of evidence like that, though, they go on trying to collect the people most sensitive to our real needs so that they can isolate them from the world. Whereas what they ought to be doing is turning them loose in full knowledge of their own talent, so that when we reach the inevitable overload point our reflexes will work for instead of against our best interests."

"I recall a point made in one of the Disasterville monographs. I think it was number 6. Stripped of the material belongings which had located them in society, a lot of refugees who formerly held responsible, status-high positions broke down into whining useless parasites. Leadership passed to those with more flexible minds—not only kids who hadn't ossified yet, but adults who previously had been called unpractical, dreamers, even failures. The one thing they had in common seemed to be a free-ranging imagination, regardless of whether it was due to their youth or whether it had lasted into maturity and fettered them with too great a range of possibilities for them to settle to any single course of action."

"How well I know that feeling. And wouldn't an injection of imagination be good for our society right now? I say we've had an overdose of harsh reality. A bit of fantasy would act as an antidote."

Near Cincinnati, Ohio, Helga Thorgrim Townes, dramatist, and her husband Nigel Townes, architect, had house guests and were debbed for an exceptional amount of time rented on the data-net. Slight snow was falling in the region, but as yet had not settled to any marked extent.

"I'm not sure that if I hadn't met people from Tarnover I would believe you. If I can judge by them, though . . ."

"Be assured they're typical. They've been systematically steered away from understanding of the single most important truth about mankind. It's as though you were to comb the continent for the kindest, most generous, most considerate individuals you could find, and then spend years persuading them that because such attitudes are rare, they must be abnormal and should be cured."

"What most important truth?"

"You tell me. You've known it all your life. You live by its compass."

"Anything to do with my reason for getting interested in you in the first place? I noticed how hard you were trying to conform to a stock pattern. It seemed like a dreadful waste."

"That's it. One charge I made against Freeman which I won't retract: I accused him of dealing not in human beings but in approximations to a pre-ordained model of a human being. I really am glad he decided to give it up. Bad habit!"

"Then I know what you're talking about. It's the uncertainty principle."

"Of course. The opposite of evil. Everything implied by that shopworn term 'free will.' Ever run across the phrase 'the new conformity'?"

"Yes, and it's terrifying. In an age when we have more choice than ever before, more mobility, more information, more opportunity to fulfill ourselves, how is it that people can prefer to be identical? The plug-in life-style makes me puke."

"But the concept has been sold with such persistence, the majority of people feel afraid not to agree that it's the best way of keeping track in a chaotic world. As it were: 'Everybody else says it is —who am I to argue?'"

"I am I."

*"Tat tvam asi."*

During the six weeks that the process took, approximately thirteen percent of households owning domestic computer terminals made above-average use of the machines in excess of the normal variation plus-or-minus ten percent. This was up by less than one percent over last year's figures and could be ascribed to the start of the academic year.

## SHADOWS BEFORE

"Hey, those odds . . . they doubled kinda fast, didn't they?"

"What do you mean you can't raise him? He's a five-star priority—his phone can't be out. Try again."

"Christ, look at this lot, will you? Can't the twitches keep their minds made up two days together?"

"Funny to get this on a weekend, but . . . Oh, I'm not going to complain about the chance to pick our new location from a list this long. Makes a change, doesn't it, from all the time going where we're told and no option?"

"But—but Mr. Sullivan! You did authorize it! Or at any rate it has your code affixed!"

## HOMER

"It feels so strange," Kate said as the cab turned the corner of her home street. Her eyes darted from one familar detail to another.

"I'm not surprised. I've been back to places, of course, but never to resume the same role as when I was there before . . . nor shall I this time, of course. Any objections?"

"Reservations, maybe." With a distracted gesture. "After having been so many different people in such a short time that I can't remember all my names: Carmen, Violet, Chrissie . . ."

"I liked you specially when you were Lilith."

She pulled a face at him. "I'm not joking! Knowing that here if anywhere I'm bound to be recognized, even though we made sure the croakers pulled their watch—I guess I wasn't quite ready for it."

"Nor was I. I'd have liked to run longer and do more. But they're no fools, the people who monitor the Fedcomps. Already I'm pretty sure they have an inkling of what's about to crash on them. Before they react, we have to capitalize our last resources. You're still a *cause célèbre* around KC, and judging by how she looked and sounded Ina is boiling with eagerness to put a good heavy G2S code between us and disaster."

"I'm sure you're right. Your logic is flawless. Even so—"

"You don't have to live by logic. You're wise. And that can transcend logic. No matter how logical your choice may seem in retrospect."

"I was going to say: even so it'll feel strange to go in and not have Bagheera come to rub against my ankles."

The apt had been searched by experts. That aside, it was unchanged, though dusty. Kate picked up the paintbrush she had been using when "Fessier" called and grimaced at its clogged bristles.

"Anything missing?" he inquired, and she made a fast check.

"Nothing much. Some letters, my address-and-code book . . . Things I can live without. Most are still furnishing my head. But"—she wrinkled her nose—"the power was off for some time, wasn't it, before you had it restored?"

"Sure, from the day after you were 'naped."

"In that case, the moment I open the refrigerator the apt will be uninhabitable. I distinctly recall I'd laid in two dozen extra eggs. Come on, we have a lot of garbage cans to fill. There's going to be a party here tonight."

"A party?"

"Naturally. You never heard of Doubting Thomas? Besides, students are a gabby lot. What you've done is going to be on all strands of the net by this time tomorrow. I want it on the mouth-to-mouth circuit too."

"But you know damn well I've written in a program that will call a press conference—"

"At noon the day after the balloon goes up," she cut in. "Nick, Sandy, whatever the hell, *darling*, the avalanche you plan to start may have swept us into limbo long beforehand. If you're going to hurt them as much as you think, you and I can't safely plan so far ahead."

He thought about that for a long moment. When he answered his voice shook a little.

"I know. I just haven't faced the idea. Right, leave the clearing-up to me. Get on that phone and contact everybody you can. And you might as well enroll Ina's help, get her to bring some friends from G2S."

"I already thought of that," she said with composure, and punched her mother's code.


# THE HATCHING OF THE WORM

On her way to visit friends for dinner, Dr. Zoë Sideropoulos paused before her home computer terminal long enough to activate a link to the continental net and strike a cluster of three digits on the board. Then she went out to her car.

Returning from an evening seminar, Professor Joachim Yent remembered what day it was and punched three digits into the board of his computer terminal.

Dean Prudence McCourtenay was in bed with a cold; she was a martyr to them every winter. But she had five veephones in her seven-room house, one being at her bedside.

Dr. Chase R. Dellinger took five from unexpected work at his lab—something suspect about a batch of newly imported mushroom spawn, perhaps contaminated with a mutant strain—and on his way back paused at a computer remote and tapped three digits into the net.

Nerice Compton misdialed a phone call and swore convincingly; she and Rush had friends in for drinks tonight.

Judge Virgil Horovitz had had a heart attack. At his age, that was not wholly unexpected. Besides, it had happened twice before. On returning from the hospital, his housekeeper remembered to activate the computer terminal and press three digital keys.

At a party with friends, Helga and Nigel Townes demonstrated some amusing tricks one could play with a computer remote. One aborted after three digits. The rest worked perfectly.

In any case, a complete emergency backup program was available which would have done the job by itself. However, many times in the history of Hearing Aid it had been proven that certain key data were better stored externally to the net.

By about 2300 EST the worm needed only fertilization to start laying its unprecedented eggs.


## PARTY LINE

"I'll be damned! *Paul!* Well, it's great to see you. Come on in."

Blinking shyly, Freeman complied. Kate's apartment was alive with guests, mostly young and in brilliant clothes, but with a mix of more soberly clad people from G2S and the UMKC faculty. A portable coley unit had been set up and a trio of dancers were cautiously sticking to the chords of a simple traditional blues prior to launching a collective sequence of variations; as yet, they were still feeling out the unit's tone-color bias.

"How did you know we were here? And what are you doing in KC, anyway? I understood you went to Precipice."

"In a metaphorical sense." Freeman gave a grin that made him look oddly boyish, as though he had shed twenty years with his formal working garb. "But it's an awfully big place when you learn to recognize it. . . . No, in fact I figured out weeks ago that you were sure to be back sooner or later. I asked myself what the least likely place would be for me to find you, and—uh—took away the number I first thought of."

"It's alarming to think someone found my carefully randomized path so predictable. Ah, here comes Kate."

Freeman stiffened as though to prepare for a blow, but she greeted him cordially, asked what he wanted to drink, and departed again to bring him beer.

"Isn't that her mother?" Freeman muttered, having scanned the visible area of the apartment. "Over there in red and green?"

"Yes. You met her, didn't you? And the man she's talking to."

"Rico Posta, isn't that his name?"

"Right."

"Hmm . . . What precisely is going on?"

"We had kind of a big temblor for a while, because of course once the news broke that Kate was back and she actually was kidnaped by a government agent as the students have been claiming, they were set to go tribal the campus. We put that idea into freeze, after a lot of argument, by hinting at all sorts of dire recriminations. And that's what we're discussing at the moment. Come and join us."

"Such as—"

"Well, we'll start by deeveeing Tarnover."

Freeman stopped dead in midstride, and a pretty girl banged into him and spilled half a drink and there was a period of apologies. Then: *"What?"*

"It's an obvious first step. A full Congressional inquiry should follow publication in the media of the Tarnover and Crediton Hill budgets. The others are in the pipeline, with Weychopee last because it's hardest to crack open. And as well as financial revelations, naturally, there will be pictures of Miranda and her successors, and the fatality rates among the experimental children, and so on."

"That looks like Paul Freeman!" Ina exclaimed, rising. She sounded alarmed.

"Yes indeed. And a bit dazed. I just began to tell him what we're up to."

Kate arrived with the promised beer, delivered it, sat down on the arm of the chair Ina was using. Rico Posta stood at her side.

"Dazed," Freeman repeated after a pause. "Yes, I am. What's the purpose of attacking Tarnover first?"

"To trigger a landslide of emotionalism. I guess you, coming fresh from an environment dedicated to rationality, doubt it's a good policy. But it's exactly what we need, and records from Tarnover are a short means to make it happen. Lots of things make people angry, but political graft and the notion of deliberately maltreating children are among the most powerful. One taps the conscious, the other the subconscious."

"Oh, both hit the subconscious," Ina said. "Rico has the same nightmare I do, about finding someone got to my credit records and deeveed everything I worked for all my life. And I don't stand a prayer of finding out who's responsible." She turned to face her daughter squarely. "What's more . . . Kate, I never dared tell you this before, but when I was pregnant with you I was so terrified you might not—uh—come out right, I—"

"You overloaded a few years later, and after that you were obsessively worried about me, and when I grew up you still worried because I'm a nonconformist. And I'm plain too. So what? I'm bright and I bounce. I'm a credit to any mother. Ask Nick," she added with a mischievous grin.

Freeman glanced around. "Nick? You recovered from your prejudice against the name, then—Old Nick, Saint Nicholas and the rest?"

"As well as being the patron saint of thieves, Saint Nicholas is credited with reviving three murdered children. It's a fair human-type compromise."

"You've changed," Freeman said soberly. "In a lot of ways. And . . . and the result is kind of impressive."

"I owe much of it to you. If I hadn't been derailed from the course I'd followed all my life— You know, that's what's wrong with us on the public level. We fret about how to keep going the same old way when we should be casting around for another way that's better. Our society is hurtling in free fall toward heaven knows where, and as a result we've developed collective osteochalcolysis of the personality."

"The way to go faster is to slow down," Kate said with conviction.

Freeman's brow furrowed. "Yes, perhaps. But how do we choose this better direction?"

"We don't have to. It's programed."

"How can that possibly be true?"

Rico Posta spoke up in a strained tone. "I didn't believe it either, not at first. Now I have to. I've seen the evidence." He took an angry swig of his drink. "Hell, here I am allegedly vice-president in charge of long-term corporate planning, and *I* didn't know that G2S's social-extrapolation programs automatically mouse into a bunch of federal studies from Crediton Hill! Isn't that crazy? It was set up by my last-but-two predecessor, that system, and he left under a cloud and omitted to advise the poker who took over. Nick got to it with no trouble, and he's taken me on a guided tour of a section of the net I didn't know existed."

Pointing with a shaking hand, he concluded furiously: "On that goddamn veephone right over there! I feel sick, just *sick*. If a veep for G2S can't find out what's happening under his nose, what chance do ordinary people have?"

"I wish I'd been here," Freeman said after a pause. "What do these Crediton Hill studies indicate?"

"Oh . . ." Posta took a deep breath. "More or less this: the cost of staying out front—economically, in terms of prestige, and so forth—has been to invoke the counterpart of the athlete's 'second wind,' which burns up muscle tissue. You can't keep that up forever. And what we've been burning is people who could have been useful, talented members of society if the pressure had been less intense. As it was, they turned to crime or suicide or went insane."

Freeman said slowly, "I remember thinking that I could easily have taken to peddling dope. But I can't see the world the way you do, can I? I owe to the people who recruited me for Weychopee the fact that I didn't wind up in jail or an early grave."

"Is our society on the right lines when one of its most gifted people can find no better career than crime unless literally millions per year of public money are lavished on him?"

Nick waited for an answer to that question. None came.

Around them the party was in full swing. The coley dancers had the measure of the unit. Their numbers had trebled without causing more than an occasional screech, and their chord pattern had evolved into a full AABA chorus of thirty-two bars, still in the key of the original blues though one of the more adventurous girls was trying to modulate into the minor. Unfortunately someone else was trying to impose triple time. The effect was . . . interesting.

Watching the dance, Freeman said helplessly, "Oh, what difference does it make whether I agree or not? I gave you your U-group codes. I knew damn well that was like handing you an H-bomb, and I went right ahead. I only wish I could believe in what you're doing. You sound like an economist—worse, like a nihilist, planning to bring the temple pillars down around our ears."

"The name for what we're doing wasn't coined by any kind of radical."

"It has a name?"

"Sure it does," Kate said firmly. "Agonizing re-appraisal."

Nick nodded. "During all my time at Tarnover it was drummed into me that I must search for wisdom.

It's the beginning of wisdom when you admit you've gone astray."

The coley dancers dissolved into discords and laughter. As they scattered in search of fresh drinks they complimented one another on the length of time they had managed to keep dancing. An impatient exhibitionistic youth promptly jumped up and conjured a specialty number from the invisible beams. After the complexities of the nine-part dance it seemed thin and shallow in spite of being technically brilliant.

"Sweedack," Freeman said eventually, his face glistening with sweat. "I guess now we hold tight and wait for the tsunami."

## THE RACE BETWEEN GUNS
## AND ARMOR

On the tree of evolution, last season's flowers die, and often the most beautiful are sterile.

While Triceratops sported his triple horns, while Diplodocus waved his graceful tail, something without a name was stealing their tomorrow.

## AN ALARMING ITEM TO FIND ON YOUR
## OVERNIGHT MAIL-STORE REEL

*Origin:* Tarnover Bioexperimental Laboratory
*Reference:* K3/E2/100715 P
*Subject:* In-vitro genetic modification (project #38)
*Nature:* Controlled crossover in gamete union
*Surgeons:* Dr. Jason B. Saville, Dr. Maud Crowther
*Biologist i/c:* Dr. Phoebe R. Whymper
*Mother:* Anon. volunt. GOL ($800 p.w., 1 yr.)
*Father:* Staff volunt. WVG ($1,000, flat pmt.)
*Embryo:* Female
*Gestation:* — 11 days
*Survival time:* appx. 67 hr.
*Description:* Typical class G0 and G9 faults, viz.

243

cyclopean eye, cleft palate, open fontanelle, digestive
system incomplete, anal-vaginal fusion, pelvic deformities
and all toes absent. Cf. project #6.

*Conclusion:* Programed inducement of crossover only
partially successful employing template solution #17K.

*Recommendation:* Repeat but attempt layering of
template on crystalline substrate (in hand) or use of gel
version (in hand).

*Disposition of remains:* Authorized (initialed JBS).


## AN ALARMING ITEM TO FIND ON YOUR CREDIT-RATING STATEMENT

Inspection of computerized records has revealed that
over half the credit standing to your name derives from
nonlegal undertakings, details of which have been for-
warded to the Attorney General of the United States. In
anticipation of criminal proceedings your permissible
credit is limited to the Federal Supportive Norm, viz.
$28.50 per day.

The Commission on Poverty has held this insufficient to
provide an adequate diet; however, upgrading to the
proposed norm of $67.50 per day still awaits presiden-
tial approval.

This is a cybernetic datum for the public service.


## AN ALARMING ITEM TO FIND ON YOUR DESK COME MONDAY MORNING

*To all employees of Marmaduke Smith Metal Products Inc.*

The decision taken to commission the building and
launching of an orbital factory for your company by
Ground-to-Space Industries Inc. (contract noncancelable)
was reached as the result of a warning from the chief
accountant Mr. J. J. Himmelweiss that the corporation
faces certain bankruptcy.

At the same meeting of the Board which confirmed the
placing of the G2S contract all officers were voted an

additional 100 percent of their respective holdings of stock to dispose of at temporarily inflated prices prior to the company's voluntary liquidation which is scheduled for the end of next month.

Thsi is an unauthorized cybernetic announcement.

## AN ALARMING ITEM TO FIND ON A COSMETICS PACKAGE

This product contains a known allergen and a known carcinogen. The manufacturers have expended over $650,000 in out-of-court settlements to avoid legal suits by former users. This is a cybernetic datum imprinted on the wrapper without the manufacturers' knowledge or consent.

## AN ALARMING ITEM TO FIND ON A PACK OF "HONEST-TO-GOODNESS"® BEEF STEW

Despite being advertised as domestic, this stew contains 15 to 35 percent imported meat originating in areas where typhus, brucellosis and trichinosomiasis are endemic. Authority to label the contents as domestic produce was obtained following the expenditure of appx. $215,000 in bribes to customs and public-health inspectors. This is a cybernetic datum derived from records not intended for publication.

## AN ALARMING ITEM TO FIND ON A MONTHLY AUTO-DEBIT NOTICE

*Advice to clients of Anti-Trauma Inc.*

A status check of the first one hundred juveniles treated according to this corporation's methods, all of whom are now at least three years past termination of their courses of therapy, reveals that:

66 are receiving prescribed psychotropic drugs;

THE SHOCKWAVE RIDER

62 are classed educationally subaverage;
59 have recently reported nightmares and hallucinations;
43 have been arrested at least once;
37 have run away from home at least once;
19 are in jail or subject to full-time supervision orders;
15 have been convicted of crimes of violence;
15 have been convicted of theft;
13 have been convicted of arson;
8 have been committed to mental hospitals at least once;
6 are dead;
5 have wounded parents, close relatives or guardians;
2 have murdered siblings;
1 awaits trial for molesting a girl aged three.

Totals do not sum to 100 because most are entered under more than one head. This is a cybernetic announcement in the public interest.

## AN ALARMING ITEM TO FIND ON YOUR OVERDUE–TAX DEMAND

*For the information of the person required to pay this tax*
Analysis of last year's federal budget shows that:
\*\*\*17% of your tax dollar went on  boondoggles
\*\*\*13% ................... propaganda, bribes and kickbacks
\*\*\*11% ................... federal contracts with companies
which are (a) fronting for criminal activities and/or
(b) partly or wholly owned by persons subject to indictment for federal offenses and/or (c) hazardous to health and the environment. Fuller details may be obtained by punching the code number at top left of this form into any veephone. They take about 57 minutes to present.

This is a cybernetic datum appended without Treasury Department authorization.

## AN ALARMING ITEM TO HEAR OVER THE VEEPHONE

"No, Mr. Sullivan, we can't stop it! There's never been a worm with that tough a head or that long a tail! It's building itself, don't you understand? Already it's passed a billion bits and it's still growing. It's the exact inverse of a phage—whatever it takes in, it adds to itself instead of wiping . . . Yes, sir! I'm quite aware that a worm of that type is theoretically impossible! But the fact stands, he's done it, and now it's so goddamn comprehensive that it can't be killed. Not short of demolishing the net!"

## THE OUTCOME OF THE BRAIN RACE (COMPUTED)

The first shall be last and the last shall be first.

## THE WHOLE CONTINENT ON THE BRINK OF ONE PRECIPICE

The press conference automatically called by Nick's program was to be held in the largest auditorium on the UMKC campus. The students had been delighted to commandeer it. Discreetly, the university authorities declined a request from the state governor to intervene. Among the persons credited with work on Miranda and those like her were two incumbent faculty members, and they were—sensibly—spending today behind locked doors and steel shutters. The students were very unhappy about those deformed babies.

Moreover, for the first time in well over a generation, the mass of public opinion was in agreement with the students. Gratifying. If it didn't heal the split, at least it moved the split to a healthier location.

The hall was packed—it was crammed. If modern technology hadn't shrunk three-vee cameras and sound-recording equipment to a size that the engineers of fifty years ago would have called impossible, the puzzled but dutiful reporters who had arrived to cover a story they were certain must be sensational . . . whatever the hell it was, would have been unable to put anything on their tapes. As it was, they were obliged to use poles, electric floaters and their longest-range mikes and lenses because they couldn't get anywhere near the rostrum, and there was a squabble over priority in respect of lines of sight which delayed the start of the conference until well past the scheduled time of noon.

At long last, however, Kate was able to appear on stage, to be greeted by a standing ovation that threatened never to end. It took her a long time to pat down the noise. When she finally did so, the putter-of-cats-among-pigeons made his appearance, and the audience settled to an expectant hush.

"My name is Nicholas Haflinger." In a loud clear voice, capable of filling the auditorium without the aid of microphones. "You're wondering why I've called you here. The reason is simple. To answer all your questions. I mean—*all*. This is the greatest news of our time. As of today, whatever you want to know, provided it's in the data-net, you can now know. In other words, *there are no more secrets*."

That claim was so sweeping that his listeners sat briefly stunned. Long seconds slid away before there came a diffident call from a woman reporter near the front, one of the lucky ones who had arrived early.

"Rose Jordan, W3BC! What about this story that was on the beams, the bait that pulled us in? This thing where you said G2S will sue officials of the Bureau of Data Processing for kidnaping one of its employees, and also some girlfriend of his?"

"That was me, and the story's absolutely true," Kate said. "But you didn't have to come here for the details. Ask any veephone."

"Yesterday you'd have had to come here," Nick amplified. "If there's one thing BDP has brought to a fine art, it's preventing the public from digging unpleasant truths from behind the scenes in government . . . right?"

A rattle of agreement: from the students on principle, but from several reporters too, who looked so glum one might presume they'd encountered that kind of trouble.

"Well, that's over. From now on: ask and you shall know."

"Hey!" In an incredulous tone from a man beside Rose Jordan. "All kind of weird stuff has been coming off the beams since yesterday, like they've been paying women to bear kids that are sure to be deformed. You mean this is supposed to be true?"

"What makes you doubt it?"

"Well—uh . . ." The man licked his lips. "I called my office half an hour back and my chief said it's been authoritatively deeveed. By Aylwin Sullivan personally. Something about a saboteur."

"That must be me." Cocking one eyebrow. "Any word of this sabotage being stopped?"

"Not that I heard."

"Good. At least they didn't make that ridiculous promise. Because it can't be stopped. I guess you all know about tapeworms . . . ? Good. Well, what I turned loose in the net yesterday was the father and mother—I'll come back to that in a moment—the father and mother of all tapeworms.

"It consists in a comprehensive and irrevocable order to release at any printout station any and all data in store whose publication may conduce to the enhanced well-being, whether physical, psychological or social, of the population of North America.

"Specifically, whether or not anybody has required a printout of it, information concerning gross infringements of Canadian, Mexican and/or United

States legal enactments respecting—in order of priority —public health, the protection of the environment, bribery and corruption, fair business and the payment of national taxes, shall be disseminated automatically to all the media. For this purpose 'gross' is defined by setting a threshold: no such infringement shall be published unless at least one person made from it an illegal profit of at least ten thousand dollars."

He had straightened as he spoke. Now he was arrow-rigid, and his voice boomed in huge resounding periods like the tolling of a death bell.

"This is indeed the father and mother of a tapeworm. It's of a type known as parthenogenetic. If you're acquainted with contemporary data-processing jargon, you'll have noticed how much use it makes of terminology derived from the study of living animals. And with reason. Not for nothing is a tapeworm called a tapeworm. It can be made to breed. Most can only do so if they're fertilized; that's to say, if they're interfered with from outside. For example the worm that prevents the Fedcomps from monitoring calls to Hearing Aid, and the similar but larger one that was released at Weychopee—Electric Skillet— to shut down the net in the event of enemy occupation: those are designed to lie dormant until tampered with. That's true of all phage-type worms.

"My newest—my masterpiece—breeds by itself. For a head it wears a maximum-national-advantage rating, a priority code that I stole from G2S. It was allocated to the corporation because like other hypercorps it's been treated for years as though it were above the law. Imagine how embarrassing it would be to make known all the bribes, all the graft, all the untaxed kickbacks, which don't appear in G2S's annual report to the stockholders. . . .

"Right behind that, my worm wears a U-group code, which does the same for individuals. The owner of a U-group code will never find himself in court. *Never*. No matter if he rapes the mayor's daughter at midday on Main Street. You don't believe me? Go punch a veephone. Ask for a plain-language printout of the status label worn by a U-group code. As of about an hour and a half ago it will print out for anybody . . . and it's enlightening."

Two or three people rose in the body of the hall as though bent on confirming Nick's assertion. He paused to let the disturbance subside.

"In back of that again, there's the key which opens the secure data banks at all secret psychological research establishments, including Tarnover and Crediton Hill. Behind that is one which opens the Treasury files on tax-avoidance suits unpursued by presidential order. Behind that is the one which opens similar files belonging to the Attorney General. Behind that is the one which opens the files of the Food and Drug Authority. And so on. By now I don't know exactly what there is in the worm. More bits are being added automatically as it works its way to places I never dared guess existed. The last I found out about before I came along to talk to you was a key for the CIA's sexual-blackmail file. There's some raunchy material in there, and I predict it will be popular home viewing this winter.

"A couple of final points before someone asks me. First, is this an unforgivable invasion of privacy? Invasion of privacy it is; unforgivable . . . Well, do you believe that justice shall not only be done but shall be seen to be done? The privacy my worm is designed to invade is that privacy under whose cover justice is not done and injustice is not seen. It doesn't care whether the poker who leeched his tax-free payoff spent it on seducing little girls; it cares only that he was rewarded for committing a crime and wasn't brought to book. It doesn't care if the shivver who bought that congressman was straight or gay; it cares only that a public servant took a bribe. It doesn't care if the judge who misdirected the jury was concerned to keep her lover's identity secret; it cares only that a person was jailed who should have been released.

"And—no, it *can't* be killed. It's indefinitely self-perpetuating so long as the net exists. Even if one segment of it is inactivated, a counterpart of the missing portion will remain in store at some other station and the worm will automatically subdivide and send a duplicate head to collect the spare groups and restore them to their proper place. Incidentally, though, it won't expand to indefinite size and clog the net for other use. It has built-in limits."

He gave a faint smile.

"Though I say so myself, it's a neat bit of work."

All of a sudden a man no older than his thirties, but pot-bellied, who had been in a seat near the back of the hall, came yelling down the aisle.

"Traitor!" he howled. "Goddamned stinking traitor!"

With his right hand he was tugging at something under his jacket; it appeared to have caught. It came free. It was a pistol. He tried to aim it.

But a quick-witted student in a seat on the aisle stuck out his leg. The fat man went sprawling with a yell, and next moment a booted foot tramped on his right wrist and he was disarmed.

From the platform Nick said, "Ah. That's the first. It won't be the last."


## AND THE TRUTH SHALL MAKE YOU YOU

Q *This place Tarnover you keep talking about. I never heard of it.*

A *It's a government establishment, one of several. All are under the direction of the spiritual successors of the people who deployed nuclear weapons in overkill quantity. Or maybe I should cite the people who thought nothing of taking a fee to condition little boys out of playing with themselves.*

Q *What?*

A *You don't believe there were such people? Punch for data concerning the income of the Behavioral Science*

Department of the Lawrence campus of the University of
Kansas back around 1969, 1970. I swear it's true.

Q Same again, but this time Weychopee.

A Ah, yes. Working for G2S I moused deep into their
banks. That's Electric Skillet, the continental defense
center. By defense they mean they override the controls
on all incoming chunks of asteroid ore and send them
crashing down on the eastern hemisphere like a rain of
thousand-ton hailstones. I haven't yet checked out how
many of the people who bought asteroid drivers from
G2S realized that facility was built in.

Q But that's insane!

A Sure it is. The blast wave from the impact would level
every structure on this continent taller than fifteen meters.
They don't care. They want to turn Ragnarök into rain-
of-rocks. Excuse me. Yes?

Q The bottom dropped out of stock in Anti-Trauma. Your
doing?

A Mostly theirs. Their failure rate has never fallen below
sixty-five percent, but they've kept it such a close secret
that last year they doubled their clientele. Never again,
I hope.

Q Some weird things happened to Delphi odds lately.

A I'm glad you brought that up. Data from Crediton Hill
are in the net by now. Check them out. A lot of you
probably have deeveed tickets you can claim against.
The legislation authorizing Delphi betting obliged the
organizers to make refunds if it could be shown that the
pool was manipulated, and there's no reference to the
organizers themselves being exempt.

Q But I thought the whole point of Delphi was to tell
the government what changes the public was ready for.
You mean it's been turned around?

A Go find a veephone and ask for the incidence of
federal intervention per annum for the last five years.

Q How the hell were you able to build a tapeworm this
complicated?

A It's a talent, like a musician's, or a poet's. I can play
a computer read-in literally for hours at a time and never
hit a wrong note.

Q Christ almighty. Well, this flood of data you let loose

253

THE SHOCKWAVE RIDER

may be okay for people like you. Me, I'm scared shitless.
A I'm sorry you're scared of being free.
Q What?
A The truth shall make you free.
Q You say that as though you believe it.
A Well, hell! If I didn't . . . ! Anybody here get nightmares because you know data exist you can't get at and
other people can? Anybody suffering with chronic anxiety, insomnia, digestive trouble, general stress response
syndrome? Mm-hm. Turn any wet stone and you find
victims. And as to the underlying cause . . . Any of you
play at fencing? Yes? Then you know how frustrating it
is to find that your opponent has claimed a point slam
in the middle of your best potential triangle. All your
cherished schemes go crash because he outsmarted you.
Well, that's a game. When it's a matter of real life it's
not fun any more, is it? And up to now the data net has
been consciously manipulated to prevent us finding out
what we most need to know.
Q Come again?
A We know, we feel in our guts, that decisions are constantly being made which are going to wreck our ambi-
tions, our dreams, our personal relationships. But the
people making those decisions are keeping them secret,
because if they don't they'll lose the leverage they have
over their subordinates. It's a marvel we're not all gib-
bering with terror. A good few of us do wind up gibber-
ing, don't they? Others manage to keep afloat by denying—repressing—awareness of the risk that it's all going
to go smash. Others still drive themselves into null pas-
sivity, what's been called "the new conformity," so that
even if they are suddenly unplugged from one side of
the continent and relocated on the other they'll be able
to carry on without noticing the change. Which is sick.
Is the purpose of creating the largest information-trans-
mission system in history to present mankind with a
brand-new reason for paranoia?
Q And you think what you've done is going to put all
this to rights.
A Do I sound that arrogant? I hope not! No, what I've
done at best means there's a chance of it coming right

*that didn't exist before. A chance is better than no chance. The rest . . . Well, it's up to all of us, not just to me.*

## SIEGE PERILOUS

It was quiet at Kate's home: outside, where volunteer students patrolled the streets for three blocks in all directions, proud that here of all places had been chosen to unleash the avalanche of truth; inside also, where Freeman was working at a remote data console donated by G2S on Rico Posta's authority, coupled via regular phone lines to the corporation's own immense computer facilities.

The veephone was quiet too. There had been so many calls, they had recruited a filtration service.

Bringing coffee, Kate said, "Paul, how's it going?"

"Ask Nick. He can keep more things in his head at one time than I can."

Working with an ordinary desk calculator and a scratch pad, Nick said, "Fairly well. There already were a couple of resource-allocation programs in store, and one of them is very damned good. Very flexible. The update facility is particularly elegant."

"Better than this, then," Freeman muttered. "I just found a loophole you could fly an orbital factory through. But I got to one thing that ought to wring some withers."

"Tell me!" Nick glanced up alertly.

"Proof that all poverty on this continent is artificial except what stems from physical illness, mental incapacity or private choice. Like homesteading a patch of the Canadian northwoods . . . or going into a monastery. That's about—oh—a quarter of one percent, max."

Kate stared at him. "You make it sound as though we'd be better off, not worse, after some kind of continental disaster. And that's absurd!"

"Not entirely." Nick went on tapping his calculator as he spoke. "One case that comes to mind. During and after World War II they cut food rations in

Britain to what most of us would think of as starvation level. Two ounces of margarine a week, an egg a month if you were lucky, things like that. But back then they had more sense than they do now. They hired top-rank dietitians to plot their priorities. They raised the tallest, handsomest, healthiest generation in their history. When rickets reappeared again after rationing ended, it made national headlines. We think of abundance and good health as going hand in hand. It doesn't follow. That way lies heart failure, too."

The phone sounded. Kate gave a start. But Nick had come to a point where he could break off and ponder what he had written. Reaching out absently, he turned the camera so he could be seen by the caller.

And exclaimed, "Ted Horovitz!"

The others tensed, everything else forgotten.

The sheriff of Precipice exhaled gustily and wiped his face.

"Lord, after fighting my way past your filtration service I was afraid I might be too late! Listen carefully. This is a breach of Hearing Aid rules but I think it's justified. Ever hear of a shivver named Hartz? Claims to be the former Deputy Director of BDP."

Freeman leaned into camera field. "I didn't know about the 'former' bit," he said. "But the rest is solid."

"Then get the hell away from where you are. Clear the house—the surrounding streets too, for preference. He says a hit job has been authorized against you. Category V, he called it."

Freeman whistled. "That means 'execute regardless of casualties'—and they generally use a bomb for those!"

"It figures. We got a tip about someone smuggling a bomb into Precipice, too. Sent Natty Bumppo and the rest of the dogs on perimeter patrol—Oh, I'll tell you when you get here."

"You're able to transport three?" Nick rapped.

Freeman cut him short. "Not me. I stay close to G2S. I need their facilities. Don't argue!" He smiled;

he was more relaxed now, able to do so without looking like a death's head. "I've done some bad things with my life. If I finish this job I can make up for them all at one go."

Horovitz glanced at his watch. "Right. I've arranged for you to be met in about ten minutes. Jake Treves was intending to stop by your place, of course, but I contacted him and warned him there'd be a change of rendezvous. Make a suggestion and I'll pass the word for him to be there."

## NIGHT ERRAND

"You look kind of down," the driver said.

"Hell, with the continent crumbling around us . . . !" The passenger in the rear seat of the quiet electric car fumbled with the lock of the briefcase across his knees. "Everything's gone into a spin. First I get the order to do the job, then they say hold it, we may send in the National Guard instead, then they say back to plan one after all. Jesus, the damage that's been done while they were dithering! Okay, this will be close enough."

The driver said in astonishment, "But we're still five blocks away!"

"They got all them students on guard. Could be armed."

"Yeah, but . . . Look, I drove this kind of mission before. If you're planning to hit them from here you—"

"Save it. I got what you wouldn't believe." The passenger clicked open his case and began to assemble something slim and tapered and matt-black. "Pull over. I got to launch it from a dead stop."

Obeying, the driver glanced in his mirror. His eyes widened.

"That little-bitty thing brings down a house?"

"Told you you wouldn't believe it," the passenger answered curtly. He lowered his window and leaned out.

"So what in the—?"

"None of your business!"

Then, relenting with a sigh: "Ah, what difference does it make? Classified—top secret—doesn't matter since that bugger turned his worm loose. Tomorrow anybody can get at plans for this gadget. It's called a kappa-bird. Ever hear the name?"

The driver frowned. "Believe I did. You got two other cars around the area, right?"

"Mm-hm. Giving a one-meter fix on the roof of the target."

"But—hell, a whole *house?*"

"Instant firestorm. Hotter than the surface of the sun." The passenger gave a wry chuckle. "Still want to be closer when she blows?"

The driver shook his head emphatically.

"Nor me. Okay, there she goes. Swing around, head south, don't hurry."

Later there was a bright reflection on the low gray cloud sealing in the city.

## WELL DOCUMENTED

Dutifully, at each state border control post, Dr. Jake Treves presented a succession of documents to the inspectors: his own ID, his certificate of professional status, his permit as a research biologist to transport protected species interstate, and his manifest for this particular journey.

Upon which the dialogue developed in predictable patterns.

"You really got a mountain lion in this truck?"

"Mm-hm. Safely sedated, of course."

"Say! I never saw a live mountain lion. Can I . . . ?"

"Sure."

Invited to slide back the door over a peephole, the inspectors saw an elderly though still sleek male specimen of *Felis concolor,* drowsy but alert enough to curl his lip in annoyance.

Also they smelt a strong feline stench. From an

aerosol can. Very useful to induce big cats to breed in captivity.

"Faugh! Sure hope for your sake you got air conditioning in your cab!"

And for getting up the nose of nosyparkers.

## COUNCIL OF PERFECTION

For a while Bagheera had padded around Ted Horovitz's moss-green office, searching for Natty Bumppo, whose trace-scent was everywhere, but all the adult dogs were still on perimeter patrol. Now he way lying contentedly at Kate's side while she gently scratched him behind the ears. Occasionally he emitted a purr of satisfaction at having been reunited with her.

The problem of what to do when he discovered he was among more than a hundred dogs built to his own scale would have to wait.

Looking around the company of local people—Josh and Lorna Treves, Suzy Dellinger, Sweetwater, Brad Compton—Ted said briskly, "Now I know Nick and Kate got a lot of questions for us. Before we get into that area, any of you got questions for them? Keep 'em short, please. Yes, Sweetwater?"

"Nick, how long before they see through your doubletalk about a parthenogenetic worm?"

Nick spread his hands. "I've no idea. People like Aylwin Sullivan and his top aides probably suspect the truth already. What I'm banking on, though, is . . . Well, there are two factors. First, I really did write one worm that's too tough for them to tackle. Second, from their point of view, whatever this new gimmick may be it's doing precisely what a parthenogenetic worm would do if such a thing could be written. Now there's a recherché theorem in n-value mean-path analysis which suggests that at some stage in the evolution of a data-net it must become possible to extract from that net functional programs that were never fed into it."

"Hey, hey!" Brad Compton clapped his plump

259

hands. "Neat, oh *very* neat! That's what they call the virgin-birth theorem, isn't it? And you've given them a nice subtle signpost to it!" He chuckled and clapped again.

"That's the essence. Not original. I stole the idea. The western powers, back in World War II, pioneered the trick. They set their scientists to building devices which looked as though they absolutely must do *something,* put them in battered metal cases, took them out on a firing range and shot them up with captured enemy ammunition. Then they arranged for the things to be found by the Nazis. One such bit of nonsense could tie up a dozen top research personnel for weeks before they dared decide it wasn't a brand-new secret weapon."

A ripple of amusement ran around the group.

"In any case," Nick added, "it won't make much odds how soon they decide they've been misled. They'd still have to shut down the net to stop what's happening, wouldn't they?"

"No doubt of that," Mayor Dellinger said crisply. "At latest count we have ninety-four sets of those Treasury files they changed the lock on, and over sixty of the FBI files, and—well, nothing that I know of has been copied to fewer than forty separate locations. And while the Fedcomps are tracing them we can be sure that people we don't know about will be making copies in their turn."

"People we'd better not know about," Lorna Treves muttered. Her husband gave a vigorous nod.

"Yes, it's a fraught situation. Granted, it's what we always said we were preparing for, but . . . Oh well; the fact that it took us by surprise is just another example of Toffler's Law, I guess: the future arrives too soon and in the wrong order. Nick, how long before they conclude Kate's home was empty when they bombed it?"

"Again I can't guess. I didn't find time on the way here to stop off at a phone and inquire."

That provoked another unison smile.

"In any case," Ted put in, "I've been taking precautions. Right now, after the media showing of their press conference, Nick and Kate have about the most recognizable faces on the continent. So they're going to be recognized. In one location after another and sometimes simultaneously. Oh, we can keep them hopping for several days."

"Days," Josh Treves echoed. "Well, I guess it's all been computed."

Brad nodded. "And, remember, we're dipping the biggest CIMA pool in history."

There was a pause. Kate stirred when she realized no one else was about to speak.

"Can I put a question, please?"

Ted waved her an invitation.

"It seems kind of silly, but . . . Oh, hell! I really want to know. And I think Nick does too."

"Whatever it is," Nick said dryly, "I agree. I'm still operating ninety percent on guesswork."

"You want the story of Precipice?" Ted grunted. "Okay, I'll tell it. But the rest of us better get back to work. Among other things the crisis is overextending the resources of Hearing Aid, and if we don't cope . . ."

"Brad can stay too," Sweetwater said, rising. "He just came off shift, and I won't have him back after the last call he handled."

"Rough?" Nick said sympathetically. The plump librarian swallowed hard and nodded.

"See you later," Suzy Dellinger said, and led the way out.

Leaning back with his hands on his ample paunch and gazing at the shimmering green ceiling, Brad said, "Y'know, we wouldn't be telling you this if you'd done as Polly Ryan suggested the day you arrived."

"What do you mean?" Kate demanded.

"Come ask for a sight of our first edition of the 'Disasterville U.S.A.' series. How many of the monographs did your father have?"

"Why, the full set of twenty!"

"Which, of course, looked to him, as to everybody,

261

like a nice round number. Our edition, though, contains a twenty-first. The one that no publisher would handle, no printer would set in type—the one that finally in desperation we printed ourselves and had ready for distribution, only one night a bomb went off in the shed where we'd stored our first ten thousand copies and they burned to ash. Obviously we were fighting a losing battle. So . . ." He sighed.

Kate leaned forward tensely. "What was the twenty-first about?"

"It accounted with names, dates, places, photostats of canceled checks—all the necessary evidence—for half a million of the four million dollars of public money which by then had gone astray and never reached the refugees who were supposed to benefit."

"You're not telling the whole story," Ted said in a brittle voice. "Kate, when you were first here you asked whether Claes College broke up because most of its members stayed at Precipice—remember?"

She nodded, her face strained.

"The answer's yes. After the night when that shed was bombed, they didn't have a choice. Brad and I helped to bury them."

There was a long empty silence. Eventually Kate said, "This last monograph—did it have a title?"

"Yes. Prophetically enough, it was to be called *Discovering the Power Base.*"

The next silence stretched so long, the air felt as though it were being drawn out until it threatened to snap. At last Nick uttered a gusting sigh.

"Hell, I never looked at it that way. I must be blind."

"I won't argue," the sheriff said, his expression very grave. "But you were not alone. Yet in retrospect . . . Figure it this way. You equip the population of a whole continent with unprecedented techniques: access to information, transportation, so much credit nobody need ever be poor again—assuming, that is, that it's properly shared. Just about at the same time, you admit there's no point in fighting any more major wars because there's too much to lose and not enough to win. In Porter's famous phrase, it's time for the brain race.

"But you're in government. Your continuance in power has always depended on the ultimate sanction: 'if you don't obey we'll kill you.' Maybe you weren't consciously aware of that basic truth. Maybe it only became clear to you, against your will, when you were obliged to try and work out why things were no longer ticking along as smoothly as they used to. As a result, naturally, of the shift in emphasis from weaponry to individual brilliance as the key national resource.

"But brilliant individuals are cantankerous, unpredictable, fond of having their own way. It seems out of the question to use them as mere tools, mere objects. Almost, you find yourself driven to the conclusion that you're obsolete. Power of your kind isn't going to be viable in the modern world.

"And then it dawns on you. There's another organization exercising immense power which has always been dependent on individuals far more troublesome than those you're being defeated by. In some cases they're outright psychopathic."

"And this organization is equally determined to maintain its place in the sun," Brad supplemented. "It's equally willing to apply the final sanction to those who disobey."

Kate's jaw dropped.

"I think we got through," Ted murmured.

"Yes—yes, I'm afraid so." Kate folded her hands into fists. "But I can't bring myself to believe it. Nick . . . ?"

"Since your apt was blown up," Nick said stonily, "I've been prepared to believe anything about them. It was a miracle we had enough warning to clear the streets. Or did we . . . ? Ted, I've been meaning to ask. Was anybody injured?"

The sheriff gave a sour nod. "I'm afraid some of the students didn't take the warning literally. Ten were hurt. Two of them have died."

Kate buried her face in her palms, her shoulders shaking.

"Go ahead, Nick," Ted invited. "Spell it out as you see it. You yourself said yesterday: the truth shall make us free. That holds good no matter how abominable the truth."

"There was exactly one power base available to sustain the old style of government," Nick grunted. "Organized crime."

Ted rose and set to pacing back and forth, back and forth. He said, "Of course that's not exactly news. It must be fifty or sixty years since the traditional fortunes that used to put this party, then the other, into office either ran dry or came under the control of people who weren't willing to play along. That left a vacuum. Into it criminals looking for ways to convert their huge financial resources into real power flooded like water through a breached dam. They'd always been intimately involved at city and state level; now was their chance to ascend the ladder's final rung. It's true that the syndicate's first attempt at the presidency was pretty much of a bust. They didn't realize how bright a spotlight could be shone on 1600 Pennsylvania. Moreover, they used tricks that were already well known, like laundering their bribe-money through Mexico and the Virgins. But they learned fast."

"They did indeed," Brad said. "The moral of monograph 21 lies not in the half-million dollars we were able to trace, but in the rest of the money which we couldn't. We know where it went—into political war chests—but we stood no chance of finding the evidence."

"In the context of the world nuclear disarmament treaty," Ted muttered, "we were hoping for something better."

"I bet you were." Nick was scowling. "Oh, I should have figured this out long ago."

"You weren't so favorably placed," Brad countered dryly. "Sharing a tent with ten refugees, without a change of clothing, decent food or even safe water to drink, it was easy to spot the resemblance between the federal agent and the *mafioso*. The fact that they were invariably on the friendliest terms merely underlined what we'd already realized."

"I should have got there by another route," Nick said. "I should have wondered why behavioral science received such colossal government subsidies during the eighties and nineties."

"An important point," Ted said with a nod. "Consistent with the rest of the pattern. The behaviorists reduced the principle of the carrot and the stick to the same kind of 'scientific' basis as the Nazis used for their so-called racial science. It's not surprising they became the darlings of the establishment. Governments rely on threat and trauma to survive. The easiest populace to rule is weak, poor, superstitious, preferably terrified of what tomorrow may bring, and constantly being reminded that the man in the street must step into the gutter when his superiors deign to pass him by. Behaviorist techniques offered a means to maintain this situation despite the unprecedented wealth, literacy and ostensible liberty of twenty-first-century North America."

"If you recognize in Ted's description a resemblance to Sicily," Brad murmured, "that's not purely coincidental."

Kate by now had recovered her self-control and was leaning forward with elbows on knees, listening intently.

"The data-net must have posed a terrible threat to them," she suggested.

"True, but one they were able to guard against," Ted answered. "Until now, I mean. They took every precaution. They built the Delphi system on the base provided by the existing gambling syndicates. They claim it was modeled on the stock market, but there was really very little difference, since by then gambling money was one of the two or three biggest sources of speculative investment. They took to leaving tribes alone when they went on the warpath, and the result was that the most ambitious kids, the ones with both rage and intelligence, wound up dead or crippled. That came naturally. Since time immemorial they'd been carefully isolating gang wars from involvement with the general public. Also they turned over the massive computer capacity designed to get men safely to and from the Moon to tracking a population moving to a new place at the rate of twenty percent a year. And so on. I don't need to recite the whole list."

"But if they were so careful how did you—?" Kate checked and bit her lip. "Oh. Stupid of me. Hearing Aid."

"Mm-hm." Ted dropped back into his chair. "Our computer capacity at Precipice has been adequate to dissect out patterns from the calls made to Hearing Aid for about—oh—sixteen or seventeen years. Now and then, moreover, we've had a single call that opened up a whole new area of investigation for us. Yours while you were at Tarnover, for example." He nodded at Nick. "We've quietly followed up one lead after another, accumulating things like the keys needed to open Federal-secure data banks, convinced that ultimately a crisis must occur that would leave the public dazed and panicky. At which time they would want to be told where they were in the world. To further our design we created the—the underground railroad which we passed you along: friends, colleagues, associates, supporters, sympathizers, in literally hundreds of different professions."

"Paul Freeman put it neatly," Nick said. "According to him, Precipice is a very big place once you learn to recognize it."

Ted chuckled. "Oh, yes! If you count in all those people whom we've created freemen, entitled to be defended by our defenses, our population totals five or six times what you find in a census return."

"We had models to copy," Brad said. "The old hippie movement, for one. The eighteenth-century community of science. An organization called Open Door which flourished in the middle of the last century. And so forth."

"Your foresight was fantastic," Kate said warmly.

"Pretty fair," Ted acknowledged. "Above average, that's for certain. But we never foresaw that the crisis would arrive in the shape of one young man!"

"Not one," Nick said. "Several. Tarnover deserter, life-style counselor, preacher, fencing hustler—"

"Person," Kate said firmly, and laid her hand over his. "And by the way, Ted!"

"Yes?"

"Thank you for saving Bagheera."

"Wasn't too hard. Did you talk to Jake Treves on the way here, find out why he was able to help out?"

She shook her head. "He put us straight into the concealed compartment. We didn't show our heads the whole time."

"Safer that way, I guess. Well, Jake is one of the people working on the problem of how to get our dogs to live to a ripe old age. It's part of a wide program to find out how stress is linked to aging. When you get the chance you'll enjoy talking to Jake, you know. Your father's hypothesis—"

He was interrupted. Distant in the night there was a sharp bark, followed by another and another.

Brad cocked his head. "Sounds as though Nat caught the bomber we're expecting."

Ted rose to his feet. "If so," he grunted, "I wouldn't care to be in his shoes."


## AMONG THE FACTORS THAT CLIMAXED IN A BREAKDOWN OF GOVERNMENT

*1: Thank you for your inquiry concerning the whereabouts of Secret Service Operative Miskin A. Breadloaf. He is under intensive medical care at Precipice CA recovering from injuries sustained while resisting arrest by Sheriff Theodore Horovitz. He was in possession of six self-seeking catapult bombs, U.S. Army Code QB3, issued to him at 1010 PST yesterday from stocks held in the National Guard Armory at San Feliciano CA in pursuance* of *Confidential Presidential Directive* #919 001 HVW, which states in full:

"I'm sick of Hearing Aid. Get the buggers who run it and never mind who else you hurt."

2: As a result of the failure of Mr. Breadloaf's mission a strike has been authorized against Precipice CA at 0130 PST tomorrow by aircraft based at Lowndes Field near San Diego. Since this is to be carried out with junior nukes (USAF Code 19L-12) Mr. Breadloaf is not expected to survive.

(NB: part 2 of the foregoing message is a cybernetic datum published in direct contravention of DoD Regulation #229RR3X3, as being conducive to the physical, psychological and/or social well-being of the population.)

## EXTREMELY CROSS SECTION

"Wipe that grin off your face! You knew the company was going broke and I can prove it!"

"Precipice? Where's that?"

"My sister went blind, near me? Blind! And she never used any eye makeup except your brand!"

"Bomb an American city? Oh, it must be a mistake."

"It was my money, and I sweated blood to earn it, and it went to feather your stinking nest!"

"Precipice? Seems to me I heard that name before."

"Christ, what you did to the poor little slittie! She hasn't had a good night's sleep in months, she always wakes up screaming and howling, and I was fool enough to bring her back for more. I could never look her in the face again if I didn't ruin yours."

"What was that about Precipice?"

"Damn right I voted for him. But if I'd known then what I know now I wouldn't have cast a vote. I'd have cast a brick."

"A strike? With nukes? My God, I know Hearing Aid isn't exactly popular, but—!"

"Jim, I don't believe you know my lawyer Charles Sweyn. He has something to give you. Charlie? Fine.

You'll notice the summons mentions damages of fifty million."

"I thought we were talking about some town called Precipice."

"I read what it said on that tax form and I swear to God I'll pay you in buckshot if you show your filthy nose around my place!"

"Really? I always wondered where their base was."

"Precipice?"

"Hearing Aid?"

"Nukes?"

"My God! Do you think they know about this? Where's a phone? *Quick!*"

## TOUCH AND GO

Past one A.M. at the headquarters of Hearing Aid. Ordinarily a dead time of night because most of the continent had orbited into sleep and only a handful of the most lonely, the most dismal, the most despairing were still anxious to talk to an anonymous listener.

Tonight was different. The room was crackling with restrained tension. The goal to which since its foundation Precipice had been dedicated was upon them, and they had never expected it to be so soon.

Solemn expressions were on the faces of the dozen people present. Only half of them were engaged in listening duty; other calls were being relayed to private homes. The remainder were monitoring the progress of their super-tapeworm.

To them generally Nick said, turning away from his board, "News from Paul Freeman. He got that body-and-soul program on the move, the one he hoped to adapt from the existing federal resources-allocation program. He said it was tough."

"That was the postwar one?" Sweetwater inquired.

"Right." Nick stretched his long arms. "Consequently it was drafted to ensure that only people the government approved of would be allotted food, medicine, clothing and power."

"You mean," Kate supplied, "it was built to make

269

certain that the people fool enough to drag us into a major war would wind up on top again afterwards."

"So they could screw us up the next time, right. But Paul managed to peel away that factor by substituting a half-like basis for entitlement to credit, and left the rest intact to run the net with even more authority than it had when it was an arm for Weychopee. He was there when it was written. Spotted its weaknesses right away."

"So what does it do now?" Brad Compton demanded.

"Not a few good things. If people vote for Proposition #1, no greedy shivver will get his wall-to-wall three-vee so long as anybody's homeless. He won't get his round-the-planet airship cruise so long as people are dying from any disease we know how to cure."

"Smooth enough for starters," Sweetwater said. "But has there been any progress on your side, Nick —rationalizing the tax structure? That's what I want to know about. When I think how angry I got paying off the croakers in Oakland because of their local ordinance against mediums . . . !"

"Oh, yes. Proposition #2 is cooking as nicely as #1," Nick said, and tapped a quick code into his board. "It went back to have a couple of loopholes deleted, and if there's no further snag . . . Ah, good. Coming up in about two minutes."

Suzy Dellinger said absently, "You know, I always wondered what democracy might smell like. Finally I detect it in the air."

"Curious that it should arrive in the form of electronic government," Sweetwater murmured.

Brad Compton glanced at her. "Not really, when you think about the history of liberty. It's the story of how principle has gradually been elevated above the whim of tyrants. When the law was defined as more powerful than the king, that was one great breakthrough. Now we've come to another milestone. We're giving power to more people than have ever before enjoyed it, and—"

"And it makes me feel," Nick interrupted, "the way they must have felt when they started the first nuclear chain reaction. Will there still be a world in the morning?"

There was a short pause, silent but for the hum of the electrical equipment, as they contemplated the continental pre-empt scheduled for the day after tomorrow. From 0700 local until 1900 every veephone on the continent would display, over and over, two propositions, accompanied by a spoken version for the benefit of the illiterate. Most would be in English, but some would be in Spanish, some in Amerind languages, some in Chinese . . . the proportions being based on the latest continental census. After each repetition would follow a pause, during which any adult could punch into the phone his or her code, followed by a "yes" or a "no."

And according to the verdict, the computers of the continent would respond.

Proposition #1 concerned the elimination of all but voluntary poverty. Proposition #2—

"Here it comes," Nick said, scanning the columns of figures and code groups appearing on his screen. "Seems to be pretty well finalized. Categorizes occupations on three axes. One: necessary special training, or uncommon talent in lieu—that's to cover people with exceptional creative gifts like musicians or artists. Two: drawbacks like unpredictable hours and dirty working conditions. Three: social indispensability."

Brad slapped his thigh. "What a monument to Claes College!"

"Mm-hm. There'll be a footnote on every single printout explaining that if we'd paid attention to what the Claes group discovered by working among the Bay Quake refugees this could have been settled a generation back. . . . Hmm! Yes, I think this balances out very nicely. For instance, a doctor will score high on special training and social importance too, but he can only get into the top pay bracket if he accepts responsibility for helping emergency cases, instead of keeping fixed office hours. That puts him high on all three scales. And a garbage collector, though rating low on special training, will do well on scales two and three. All public servants like police and firemen will automatically score high on scale three and most on scale two as well, and—oh, yes. I like the look of it. Particularly since a lot of parasites who were at the top in the old days will now pay tax at ninety percent because they score zero on all three axes."

"Zero?" someone demanded in disbelief.

"Why not? People in advertising, for example."

The questioner's eyebrows rose. "Never thought of that before. But it figures."

"Think they'll stand for it?" Kate said nervously, patting Bagheera who lay at her side. Since meeting Natty Bumppo he had refused to be left out of sight of her, although he and the dog had exhibited mutual tolerance, as favorable a reaction as might have been hoped for.

"Their choice is to close down the net," Nick said, and snapped his fingers. "Thereby breaking their own necks. Suzy, you look worried."

The mayor nodded. "Even if they don't deliberately blow the net when they find they can't interfere with our pre-empt, to make some kind of grand suicidal gesture . . . there's another and more disturbing question."

"What?"

"Are people scared into their right minds yet?"

The following silence was broken by the soft buzz of an incoming call. Kate switched it to her board and put on her phones.

Seconds later she uttered a loud gasp, and all heads turned to her.

Peeling off her phones again, she spun her chair, her cheeks as pale as paper and her eyes wide with fear.

"It can't be true! It simply can't be true! My God,

it's already twenty past one—the plane must have taken off!"

"What? What?" A chorus of anxious voices.

"That caller claimed to be a cousin of Miskin Breadloaf. The would-be bomber you arrested, Ted. She says Precipice is going to be attacked with nukes at 0130!"

"Ten minutes? We can't possibly evacuate the town in ten minutes!" Suzy whispered, clenching her fists and staring at the wall clock as though willing it to show some earlier time.

"We'll have to try!" Ted snapped, jumping to his feet and heading for the door. "I'll get Nat to rouse everybody and—" He checked. Nick had suddenly launched into a burst of furious activity, punching his board with fingers that flew faster than a pianist's.

"Nick! Don't waste time—move! We need everybody's help!"

"Shut up!" Nick grated between clenched teeth. "Go on, wake the town, get everybody away that you can . . . *but leave me alone!*"

"Nick!" Kate said, taking an uncertain pace toward him.

"You too! Run like hell—because this may not work!"

"If you're going to stay then I—"

"Go, damn it!" Nick hissed. *"Go!"*

"But what are you trying to do?"

*"Shut—up—and—go!"*

Suddenly Kate found herself out in the chilly dark, and at her side Bagheera was trembling, the hairs on his nape raised and rough under her fingers. There was incredible noise: the dogs barking, Ted shouting through a bullhorn, everybody who could find any means of banging or rattling or clanging using it to create a racket no one could have slept through.

"Leave town! Run like hell! Don't take anything, just run!"

From nowhere a dog appeared in front of her. Kate

stopped in alarm, wondering whether she could hold Bagheera back if he was frightened and confused enough to pounce.

The dog wagged its great tail. She abruptly recognized Natty Bumppo.

Head low, neck in a concave bend, in a wholly uncharacteristic puppy-like posture, he approached Bagheera, giving a few more ingratiating strokes with his tail. Bagheera's nape hairs relaxed; he allowed Nat to snuff his muzzle, though his claws were half-unsheathed.

What was the meaning of this pantomime? Should Nat not be on duty, waking people with his barking?

And then Bagheera reached a conclusion. He stretched his neck and rubbed his cheek against Natty Bumppo's nose. His claws disappeared.

"Kate!" someone shouted from behind her. She started. Sweetwater's voice.

"Kate, are you all right?" The tall Indian woman came running to her side. "Why aren't you—? Oh, of course. You daren't let loose Bagheera!"

Kate took a deep breath. "I thought I couldn't. Nat just set me right."

"What?" Sweetwater stared incomprehension.

"If human beings had half the insight of this dog . . . !" Kate gave a near-hysterical laugh, releasing her grip on Bagheera's collar. Instantly Natty Bumppo turned around and went bounding into the darkness with Bagheera matching him stride for stride.

"Kate, what the hell are you talking about?" Sweetwater insisted.

"Didn't you see? Nat just made Bagheera a freeman of Precipice!"

"Oh, for—! Kate, come with me! We only have seven minutes left!"


There was no chance to organize the flight; the Precipicians simply scattered, taking the shortest route to the edge of town and continuing into the surrounding farmland. Gasping, her feet cut by sharp grass and stones, Kate was overtaken by a bitch loping easily with a screaming child astride her back; she thought it might have been Brynhilde. Then a branch whipped across her face and she almost fell, but a strong arm caught and steadied her, hurried her another dozen paces, then hurled her to the ground in what shelter was offered by a shallow dip.

"No point in trying to go on," Ted's gruff voice said out of darkness. "Better to be closer behind a good solid bank of earth than further away and on your feet in the open."

Two more people tumbled over the rim of the hollow. One she didn't know; the other was the restaurant keeper, Eustace Fenelli.

"What *is* all the panic?" he demanded with a trace of petulance.

Rapidly Ted explained, and concluded after a glance at his watch, "The strike is scheduled for 0130, in about a minute and a half."

For a moment Eustace said nothing. Then, with magnificent simplicity, making the single word into a whole encyclopedia of objurgation: *"Shit!"*

To her astonishment Kate had to giggle.

"I'm glad someone finds it funny!" Eustace grunted. "Who——? Oh, Kate! Hello. Is Nick here too?"

"He wouldn't come," she said in the steadiest voice she could achieve.

"He what?"

"He stayed behind."

"But——! You mean nobody could find and tell him?"

"No. He . . . Oh, *Ted!"*

She turned blindly and fell against the sheriff's shoulder, her body racked with dreadful sobs.

Faint in the distance they could now hear the teeth-aching whine of electric lifters, the superpowerful type fitted to low-level short-range strike planes. It grew louder.

Louder.

Louder.

## THE LINE OF MOST RESISTANCE

*To the President of the United States*

URGENT AND MOST SECRET

Sir:

Copied to you herewith is a signal received at Lowndes Field at 0014 hours today, purporting to emanate from yourself as commander in chief and ordering a nuclear strike at coordinates that manifestly are within the continental United States.

In view of the fact that it was superficially convincing, being properly enciphered in a one-time cipher scheduled for use today, it came close to causing a disaster, specifically the death of approx. 3000 civilians in the town of Precipice CA. I regret to have to advise you that the mission was actually initiated, and only by a miracle was it aborted in time (on receipt of DoD signal #376 774 P, which warned all naval, military and air force bases that saboteurs might have gained access to the data net).

I have taken steps to discipline the officer who authorized inception of the mission, and upon my own responsibility have issued a signal summarizing the matter to all West Coast bases. I respectfully suggest that the some be done on a national basis, and at once.

> I remain, Sir,
> (signed)
> Wilbur H. Neugebauer, General

## AFTER TOUCH AND GO, GO

They saw the plane as it swooped. They saw it clearly by the eerie blue glow around its repulsors, gulping vast quantities of air into electrical fields so

276

fierce that were a man to put his arm incautiously within their shining ring he would withdraw a stump after mere seconds.

They heard it, too: a howl as of a banshee.

But as it crossed the town . . . it let fall nothing.

After an hour of waiting, teeth chattering, fists clenched, scarcely daring to raise their heads in case the threatened attack should after all take place, the inhabitants of Precipice rediscovered hope.

And through the dark they stumbled and staggered homeward to an orchestra of wailing children.

Somehow—Kate never knew quite how—she found that she was walking with Bagheera at her side again, while next to Ted and a couple of paces ahead was Natty Bumppo.

Bagheera was purring.

It was as though he felt flattered at being declared an honorary dog.

Cautiously Ted opened the door of the Hearing Aid headquarters, while Kate and Sweetwater craned to look past him. Behind, half a dozen other people— Suzy, Eustace, Josh and Lorna, Brad, those who had begun to guess the explanation for their salvation— waited in impatience.

There was Nick, hands on arms, slumped forward fainting over his board.

Kate thrust past Ted and ran to his side, calling his name.

He stirred, licking his lips, and sat upright, putting his right hand to his temple. He seemed giddy. But on seeing Kate he forced a smile, and continued it to the others who by now were flooding into the room.

"It worked," he said in a thin, husky voice. "I never dared believe it would. I was so scared, so terrified. . . . But I was just in time."

Ted halted before him, gazing around the room.

"What did you do?"

Nick gave a faint chuckle and pointed to his screen. On it a signal from someone called General Neugebauer to the president was cycling over and over in clear text, there being too much of it to display all at once.

"It was a close call," he added. "Damned close. The duty officer at Lowndes must be used to doing as he's told and no questions please. . . . When I realized the plane was already on its way I nearly collapsed."

Sweetwater, pushing her way through the crowd, stared at the screen.

"Hey," she said after a moment's thought. "*Was* there a Department of Defense signal number whatever?"

"Of course not." Nick rose, stretched, stifled a colossal yawn. "But it seemed like the quickest solution to invent it."

"Quickest!" Sweetwater withdrew half a pace, eyes large with awe, and started to count off on her fingers. "Near as I can figure it, you had to write the signal in proper jargon, find a reference number for it, encode it in the proper cipher for today, feed it to Lowndes over the proper circuit—"

"Mark it for automatic decipherment instead of being left over to the morning like most nighttime signals traffic," Ted butted in. "Right, Nick?"

"Mh-hm," he agreed around another and fiercer yawn. "But that wasn't what took the time. I had to track down General Neugebauer's home code, which is ex-directory at all levels below Class Two Star priority. *And* he wasn't happy at being woken up, either."

"And you did it in less than ten minutes?" Kate said faintly.

Nick gave a shy grin. "Oh, looking back on it, I feel I had all the time in the world."

Drawing herself up to her full height, Suzy Dellinger advanced on him.

"It doesn't often happen," she said with a trace of awkwardness, "that a mayor of this town has to undertake the sort of formal ceremony you find in other places. We tend to do it without the trimmings. This is that sort of occasion. I don't have to ask permission of my fellow citizens. Anybody who disagreed wouldn't be a Precipician. Nicholas Kenton Haflinger, in my official capacity, I'm proud to convey the thanks of us all."

She made to shake hands with him. And was forestalled.

Natty Bumppo had as usual taken station next to his owner. Unexpectedly he rose, shouldered Suzy aside, planted his vast front paws on Nick's chest, and slapped him across both cheeks with his broad red tongue.

Then he resumed his stance beside Ted.

"I—uh . . ." Nick had to swallow before he could go on. "I guess that must be what you call an accolade."

Suddenly everyone was laughing, except him. And except Kate, whose arms were around him and whose face was wet with tears.

"Nothing like this happened before, did it?" she whispered.

"Not that I know of," he answered softly.

"And you did the right thing, the only thing . . ." She caught him around the neck and drew his ear close to her mouth to utter words no one else was meant to hear.

*"Wise man!"*

Upon which he kissed her, thoroughly and for a long time.

THE CONTENT OF THE PROPOSITIONS

#1: That this is a rich planet. Therefore poverty and hunger are unworthy of it, and since we can abolish them, we must.

#2: That we are a civilized species. Therefore none shall henceforth gain illicit advantage by reason of the fact that we together know more than one of us can know.

## THE OUTCOME OF THE PLEBISCITE

Well—how did you vote?